John Milton

Selections from the prose works of John Milton with critical

remarks and elucidations

John Milton

Selections from the prose works of John Milton with critical remarks and elucidations

ISBN/EAN: 9783337113117

Printed in Europe, USA, Canada, Australia, Japan

Cover: Foto ©Andreas Hilbeck / pixelio.de

More available books at **www.hansebooks.com**

SELECTIONS

FROM THE

PROSE WORKS OF JOHN MILTON.

SELECTIONS

FROM THE

PROSE WORKS OF JOHN MILTON

WITH

CRITICAL REMARKS AND ELUCIDATIONS.

EDITED BY THE

REV. JAMES J. G. GRAHAM, M.A., Oxon,

VICAR OF MUCH COWARNE, HEREFORDSHIRE.

"Cujus e stylo, nimirum horridulo et incompto, aurum et margaritas effodere possimus."—MILTON's *Prolusiones Oratoriæ.*

" I have been looking into some of Milton's prose works lately, of which, I am ashamed to say, I was and am grossly ignorant. It must be a most expressive warning to men of genius, to read, as they often may in his Tracts, one sentence *written as if an angel had held the pen*, and the next, as it seems to me, more like Cobbett's style than any other I know of."—*Letter of the Rev. John Keble to Sir J. T. Coleridge.*

IN ONE VOLUME.

LONDON:

HURST AND BLACKETT, PUBLISHERS,

13, GREAT MARLBOROUGH STREET.

1870.

LONDON : PRINTED BY MACDONALD AND TUGWELL, BLENHEIM HOUSE

TO HER,

THE PERFECT WIFE,

" MY SUM OF EARTHLY BLISS,"

TO WHOM I LONG HAVE OWED SUCH BLISS

AS MILTON ONLY KNEW FOR ONE BRIEF YEAR,

I DEDICATE

IN GRATITUDE THIS LABOUR OF LOVE.

CONTENTS.

NOTE.

BELIEVING, as the Editor does, in the Divine right of Bishops—that Episcopacy is a Divine institution, "platformed in the Bible," and deducible from Apostolical times, he would gladly ignore, as much as possible in the following Extracts, Milton's hatred of Prelacy, which is easily accounted for. His sledge-hammer blows fall harmlessly, and beside the mark, on those well versed in History, and the original Greek of the New Testament. His arguments are inconclusive and oftentimes suicidal, and directed against individuals of the Order, such as Bishop Mountain and Archbishop Laud, rather than against the Order itself. Bishops are not infallible, but Episcopacy is not to be abandoned because we do not approve of some particular act of some individual Bishop. Those of his day had but lately shaken off that "worst of superstitions, and the heaviest of all God's judgments—Popery;" and there is an evident confusion in Milton's mind of Papistical and Reformed Bishops. He was his own Bishop and Pope, and went wrong because he considered his own opinion orthodox and everybody else's heterodox. Ipse dixit—nay, ipsissimus—not only the αὐτὸς ἔφη of the Pythagorean school, but αὐτότατος. I John Milton have said it. The Reader is once for all apprised that any passage savouring of disrespect and dislike to Episcopacy has been inserted for special reasons, since to eliminate such altogether from our Selections would be like acting 'Hamlet' with the part of *Hamlet* left out. He is further requested to observe that the quotations from Milton are marked by two inverted commas, from all other authors by one. Footnotes are abandoned, as it is thought that such information as is usually given in them might with advantage be incorporated in the text.

The profits of the First Edition will be devoted to the Restoration of Much Cowarne Parish Church.

THE EDITOR'S PREFACE.

IN the mottoes which appear on our title-page we
have at once the reason and the plan of this labour of love in which we are about to engage. Here
we find such a man as Keble, highly educated and
well read in our older and better writers, a double
First-Classman of Oxford, confessing his ignorance of
the prose works of our great national poet, and in the
same breath declaring that, when he did turn his attention to them, he there often discovered sentences
of such transcendent excellence that they appeared
'written as if an angel had held the pen.' We believe that angels do guide the pen of those who, however encompassed with human infirmity, stand forth,
in the dark and evil days of trouble, and rebuke, and
blasphemy, the champions of God's eternal truth.
Such a one was Milton ;—and surely it is well worth
while to rescue from oblivion, and " not willingly let
die," any such magnificent passage which has fallen
from the pen of so great a man, though it may lie
buried beneath a mass of rubbish. To search after

B

these in a reverential and loving spirit, and to hold them forth to the admiring gaze of others, rejecting all that seems written in the style of Cobbett, by whose side we can hardly conceive an angel to have sat, save to weep, is the plan of the following work; and the reason which has induced us to undertake it is the notorious prevailing ignorance, even amongst literary men, of the prose works of John Milton.

The fact is indisputable, that, while everybody is familiar with his poetry, nobody, except here and there an individual, reads or appreciates his prose. We appeal to the experience of any one who may chance to have taken this volume into his hands. It is more than probable that he will have to confess with Keble, 'I am ashamed to say I was, and am, grossly ignorant of Milton's prose works.' The volumes are found in few small libraries, and where they are found, they lie unopened by the owners, and are consigned 'to the dust and silence of the upper shelf.' No one is louder in deploring this fact than Lord Macaulay, in his celebrated Essay on Milton. 'It is to be regretted,' he says, 'that the prose writings of Milton should, in our time, be so little read. As compositions, they deserve the attention of every man who wishes to become acquainted with the full power of the English language. They abound with passages compared with which the finest declamations of Burke sink into insignificance. They are a

perfect field of cloth of gold. The style is stiff with
gorgeous embroidery. Not even in the earlier books
of the Paradise Lost has the great poet ever risen
higher than in those parts of his controversial works
in which his feelings, excited by conflict, find a vent
in bursts of devotional and lyric rapture. It is, to
borrow his own majestic language, " a sevenfold
chorus of hallelujahs and harping symphonies." ' He
then goes on to say—' We had intended to look
more closely at these performances, to analyse the
peculiarities of the diction, to dwell at some length
on the sublime wisdom of the Areopagitica, and the
nervous rhetoric of the Iconoclast, and to point out
some of those magnificent passages which occur in the
Treatise of Reformation and the Animadversions on
the Remonstrant.' Yet Macaulay took care never to
do this; he never resumed the subject, and, therefore, we are compelled to regard this expression of
his intention as a mere rhetorical flourish. We
heartily wish he had fulfilled his half-implied promise,
especially as ourselves have failed to discover the nervous rhetoric of the Iconoclast, though we fully ap-
preciate the sublime wisdom of the Areopagitica—
have failed to detect the magnificent passages of the
Animadversions on the Remonstrant, though we are
enchanted with those which occur in the Treatise of
Reformation.

Here, then, we fancy that we have found an untrodden field. But let it not be thought that we are presuming to do what Macaulay left undone; we only wish we possessed a tithe of his powerful critical skill and acumen. Still, we flatter ourselves that we shall be doing good service to the cause of literature, if we direct attention to these long-forgotten creations of our great national poet, so full of interest and instruction, and select from the prose works of John Milton all that is really valuable and worth preserving. He himself has told us that "a wise man, like a good refiner, can gather gold from the drossiest volume." And believing this, and that the grains of gold are there, the work before us will be to "find out the precious gem of truth, as amongst the numberless pebbles of the shore;" to separate the gold from the dross; the sentences 'written as if an angel held the pen,' from the sentences written 'in Cobbett's style;' the sentences "of a venturous edge, uttered in the height of zeal (and who knows whether they might not be the dictates of a Divine Spirit?)" from those uttered, we are constrained to confess, in malice and bitterness, and all uncharitableness; and thus to save our readers the cost of purchasing, and the trouble of wading through, the five volumes of Bohn's edition, or the two quartos of Dr. Birch's edition, or the three large folios of Toland's edition.

For much, very much of Milton's prose is scarcely

worth reading. His political opinions are republican, visionary, and Utopian ; and his religious opinions are for the most part equally erroneous, onesided, and overstrained. No wonder they made so little impression on his contemporaries. They despised them; we abhor them. No one would rise from their perusal a better man, a better citizen, or a better Christian. When stript of the truly magnificent language in which he knows so well to clothe them, and seen in their naked deformity, the politician, however liberal, and the Christian, however puritancial, would infallibly shrink from their adoption.

Perhaps it may seem strange that the Editor, who calls himself a staunch Conservative and moderate High Churchman, should desire to direct public attention to the writings of a red-hot republican; especially in these unsettled times when the foundations of the earth seem out of course, and all time-honoured and long-tried, and therefore sacred, institutions seem in peril, and the revolutionary days of Milton may again recur, as history is known to repeat itself. But in defence we may say that it is lawful to be taught even by an enemy—that a close study of Milton's works will prove him to have been less revolutionary, and less puritanical, than he is commonly supposed to have been—that most men of his way of thinking are better than their opinions, and themselves would pause before they carried them out to their legitimate consequences—that the lucubrations of a mind which could conceive Paradise Lost or the Areopagitica must always have a certain value, whether or not we agree with some particular conclusions ; and for other reasons which appear in the course of these prefatory remarks, we do not shrink from avowing our deep admiration and fervent love for this great and good man.

The sound common-sense of Englishmen may, we trust, avert the apprehended danger arising from the levelling and revolutionary principles so rife amongst us—such common-sense, for instance, as Dr. Johnson evinces in the following anecdote, given in Boswell's Life of Johnson, vol. i., p. 305. ' One day, at the house of Catharine Macaulay Graham, the celebrated author of the History of England, History of America, and other works chiefly philosophical, and, by the way, a great-aunt of the Editor, the Doctor put on a very grave countenance, and said to her, ' Madam, I am now become a convert to your way of thinking. I am convinced that all mankind are upon an equal footing; and to give you an unquestionable proof than I am in earnest, here is a very sensible, civil, well-behaved fellow-citizen, your footman ; I desire that he may be allowed to sit down and dine with us.' I thus, sir, showed her the absurdity of the levelling doctrine. She has never liked me since. Sir, your levellers wish to level *down* as far as themselves ; but they cannot bear levelling *up* to themselves. They would all have some people under them; why not, then, have some people above them?'

But Milton, republican as he was from the force of circumstances, and the unhappy times in which his lot was cast, was, as we have said, far superior to his views, and was always sincere and honest. His mind was essentially a religious mind. The subjects he chose, in prose or verse, were themselves sacred, or had a sacred tendency. And we are not surprised at this, when we remember that he contemplated taking Holy Orders. Thither he bent all his studies; and as in mature life he produced the Paradise Lost, so in earliest youth he had been " smit with the love of sacred song," paraphrasing Psalms at fifteen, and at twenty-one producing his inimitable Ode on the Nativity. In the strength and pride of manhood, he forsook his first love, and abandoning his high calling, launched on the troubled waters of political and party strife. Here religion was still the lodestar that through all kept his life and spirit pure. And twenty years after, when he abandoned prose, and once more with renewed ardour " wandered where the muses haunt," "escaped the Stygian pool" of politics and controversy, " though long detained in that obscure sojourn," his lyre will respond to none but sacred themes.

'Η βάρβιτος δὲ χορδαῖς
Ἔρωτα μοῦνον ἠχεῖ.

'But my perverse, rebellious lyre
Breathes nought but love and soft desire.'

No holier songs than the Paradise Lost and Regained ever fell from the enraptured lips of sacred
heaven-inspired bard; and what greatly enhances the
spotless purity of these productions is the time at
which they were composed, when 'obscene tumult
raged all around him, the effect of the prevalence of
Puritanism under the Commonwealth.' It was now
the Restoration, and the reaction of vice and im-
morality had set in. In the midst of all, and undis-
turbed by all, this great, and pure, and good man,
'tried at once by pain, danger, poverty, obloquy, and
blindness, meditated a song so sublime, and so holy,
that it would not have misbecome the lips of those
ethereal Virtues whom he saw with that inner eye
which no calamity could darken, flinging down on the
jasper pavement their crowns of amaranth and gold.'
But all his life through Milton was ever the same
holy and saintly man, uncorrupted and uncorruptible,
like his own seraph Abdiel, "faithful found, among
the faithless faithful only he." How can we help
admiring and loving him? We care not for his political and public character—we know that he had
strange notions concerning divorce and polygamy;
we have heard of his unkind daughters and unkinder

first wife ; we remember that the taint of Arianism is
found in his later works, but still we can pardon all
his faults, and revere and love the genius and the
virtues of the man, the poet, and the Christian. We
confess to liking him best when he has on his singing
robes, but his prose has a charm for us which we find
nowhere else. Every word of his poetry, and many
passages of his prose, have a magical influence on our
minds, and act almost like an incantation. Macaulay
makes this remark with reference to his poetry ; we
maintain that it is equally true with regard to several
passages which occur in his prose writings. We will
quote the beautiful words of the great Essayist :
'There would seem, at first sight, to be no more in
his words than in other words. But they are words
of enchantment. No sooner are they pronounced
than the past is present, and the distant near. New
forms of beauty start at once into existence, and all
the burial-places of the memory give up their dead.
Change the structure of the sentence, substitute one
synonyme for another, and the whole effect is destroyed. The spell loses its power, and he who
would then hope to conjure with it would find himself as much mistaken as Cassim in the Arabian tale,
when he stood crying, ' Open Wheat,' ' Open Barley,'
to the door which obeyed no sound but ' Open Se-
same.' Yes, there is a charm in many of those remarkable passages which we propose hereafter to

recite, for which we know not how to account.
'Their merit lies less in their obvious meaning than
in their occult power.' They have a sort of fascina-
tion for us which we cannot describe. They ring in
our ears much in the same way as Sir Walter Scott
tells us that the first stanza of the Ballad of Cumnor
Hall used to do in his. It had a peculiar species of
enchantment for his youthful ear, the force of which
was not entirely spent when he wrote Kenilworth.
And it is this wonderful power of affecting others, as
if with the wand of a magician, which is the triumph
and glory of genius, transmuting into gold everything
that it touches. Take Comus, for instance, and a
writer in the *Quarterly* shall unfold to us how this
mighty magician deals with the most unpromising
subject. 'A young girl and her brothers are be-
nighted and separated as they pass through a forest
in Herefordshire. How meagre is this solitary fact!
—how barren a paragraph would it have made for
the Herefordshire journal, had such a journal been
then in existence! Submit it to Milton, and beautiful is the form which it assumes. Then rings that
wood with the jocund revelry of Comus and his company, and the maiden draws near in the strength of
unblemished chastity, and her courage waxes strong
as she sees

"A sable cloud
Turn forth her silver lining on the night,"

and she calls upon Echo to tell her of the flowery
cave which hides her brothers, and Echo betrays her
to the enchanter. Then comes the spirit from the
" starry threshold of Jove's court," and in shepherd
weeds leads on the brothers to her rescue ; and the
necromancer is put to flight, but not till he has bound
up the lady in fetters of stone ; and Sabrina hastens
from under her " translucent wave " to dissolve the
spell, and again they all three bend their happy steps
back to the roof of their fathers.'

And here we cannot refrain from quoting that exquisite passage with which the great Whig historian
concludes his critique, which cannot fail to strike a respondent chord in the heart of every lover of Milton.
' While this book '—his posthumous Treatise on Christian doctrine—' lies on our table, we seem to be contemporaries of the writer. We are transported a
hundred and fifty years back. We can almost fancy
that we are visiting him in his small lodging ; that we
see him sitting at the old organ beneath the faded
green hangings ; that we can catch the quick twinkle
of his eyes, rolling in vain to find the day ; that we
are reading in the lines of his noble countenance the
proud and mournful history of his glory and his affliction. We imagine to ourselves the breathless silence
in which we should listen to his slightest word, the
passionate veneration with which we should kneel to
kiss his hand and weep upon it, the earnestness with

which we should endeavour to console him, if indeed
such a spirit could need consolation, for the neglect of
an age unworthy of his talents and his virtues; the
eagerness with which we should contest with his
daughters, or with his Quaker friend Elwood, the
privilege of reading Homer to him, or of taking down
the immortal accents which flowed from his lips. The
sight of his books, the sound of his name, are pleasant
to us.   His thoughts are powerful not only to delight,
but to elevate and purify.   Nor do we envy the man
who can study either the life or the writings of the
great poet and patriot, without aspiring to emulate, not
indeed the sublime works with which his genius has
enriched our literature, but the zeal with which he
laboured for the public good, the fortitude with which
he endured every private calamity, the lofty disdain
with which he looked down on temptations and dangers, the deadly hatred which he bore to bigots and
tyrants, and the faith which he so sternly kept with
his country and with his fame.'

It is worthy of remark that for twenty years of his
life Milton wrote no poetry, except a few sonnets; 'simple but majestic records of the feelings of the poet.'
His various prose works, with one or two unimportant
exceptions, were all composed between the year 1641
and 1660; and this marks the period of his political
life, *i.e.*, from his thirty-third to his fifty-second year.
Strange that after writing such a piece as Comus, which

he produced in his twenty-sixth year, he ever should
have stooped to humble prose, and not have found
out, till the best of his life was past, that poetry was
his proper and heaven-appointed vocation. It was
left to mature years, and blindness, and disappointment, and suffering, to teach him that the closet not
the senate was his proper field of action—that there
God had a work for him to perform, the noblest that
ever fell to the lot of a mortal man, and in which we
look upon him as truly inspired, though not to the
some degree and extent, or for the same purpose, as
were St. Paul and St. John. It was, however, a stern
sense of duty, and the noblest patriotism and self-ab-
negation, which turned him from poetry to prose. How
much must he have sacrificed! All the fond aspirations of his earliest years! For that grand Epic, which
he was destined to accomplish, from first to last ever
loomed before him. At the age of nineteen he was
conscious of

> " Thoughts that rove about
> And loudly knock to have their passage out."

However " naked " he felt them then to be, he knew
ere long they would be decked in the richest robes
and gayest attire of his native language. To the eye
of his young mind the chiefest treasure of her wardrobe had all been displayed. He longed to " clothe
his fancy in fit sound," and to be employed in " graver
subjects " than the " new-fangled toys," which de-

lighted his fellow-collegians.   From the task before
him, his " deep transported mind " soared far " above
wheeling poles," and "looked in at heaven's door,"
and listening there longed

> " To sing of secret things that come to pass
> When beldame Nature in her cradle was."

At thirty he writes to a dear friend, " Do you ask
what I am meditating?   By the help of heaven, an
immortality of fame. But what am I doing? πτεροφυῶ
I am letting my wings grow, and preparing to fly ;
but my Pegasus has not yet feathers enough to soar
aloft in the fields of air."   Twenty-seven years after
writing this, in the fifty-seventh year of his age, at
Chalfont, in Buckinghamshire, whither he had retired
when the great plague was raging in London, in
1665, he finished that work which has for ever dis-
tanced him from all competitors, and, indeed, conferred upon him an immortality of fame.   It was
published two years after, in 1667, and sold for an
immediate payment of five pounds, with an agree-
ment for fifteen pounds more when a certain number
of copies should be sold.   Simmonds was the pur-
chaser, who afterwards made over the original copy-
right to Jacob Tonson.   'Tonson, and all his family,
rode in their carriages from the profits of the five-
pound Epic.'   So long time elapsed before he saw
the cherished aspirations of his heart fulfilled, and
this must ever be to us a matter of deep regret. Yes,

in spite of the splendid passages which occur in his prose works—in spite of that only readable one in its entirety, the Areopagitica, which we so much admire, we cannot help regretting that Milton should have spent so many years in courting 'the muse of prose literature,' engaged in controversial and political warfare. What self-denial, what stern and indomitable self-control, these long years must have cost him! How uncongenial for such a man to write nothing but dry despatches, manifestoes, letters of state, treatises and tracts in defence and praise of the present government! We are surprised to find so much genuine gold amongst this dross, when Parliament, not the heavenly muse, inspires him. A mistaken patriotism "damps his intended wing depressed." He is no longer " smit with the love of sacred song." No longer his celestial patroness, Urania (the meaning, not the name), brings nightly to his ear his easy unpremeditated verse. But darker days follow; neglected by his pet party, paid as a hireling to write at the bidding of Parliament, yet no hireling he, thrust aside, uncourted, unpreferred, sick at heart, and broken in body, blind, and afflicted with gout, proscribed and outlawed, he bethinks himself of his long-neglected but still loved lyre; searches for some heroic subject; thinks he has found a fitting hero in King Arthur; abandons him for a more terrible one—we had almost said for a far grander one—and, " long choos-

ing and beginning late," at last fixes upon Paradise
Lost.   Surely he chose wisely and well!   He did
not wait in vain ; he did not wait a moment too long.
It was well for him and well for us that he had

> " Fall'n on evil days,
> On evil days had fall'n, and evil tongues,
> In darkness, and with dangers compass'd round,
> And solitude,"

or he might have gone on writing prose to the end of
his days.   Would this have been a calamity?   Yes,
if it had deprived the world of his immortal poem,
which is 'not the greatest of heroic poems, only because it was not the first.'   But then perhaps his
prose works would have been better appreciated, for,
after all, they are worthier of a deeper study than
they have usually met with.   They are full of magnificent passages, such as no one but himself could have
written, resplendent with the magic touch and stamp
of genius, and, in the words of a competent judge,
'written as if an angel had held the pen.'

We will proceed to cull from his prose works, arranged in their chronological order, the most striking
of these 'disjecta membra poetæ,' these prose-poems,
what he himself so well calls " sentences of a venturous edge, uttered in the height of zeal ; and who
knows whether they might not be the dictates of a
Divine Spirit?"   Our extracts will necessarily be
somewhat fragmentary and unconnected, but we trust
that they will include all that ordinary readers would

consider as valuable, interesting, and worthy of preservation in the prose works of John Milton, the friend and lover, the champion and martyr of " white-robed truth "—" sincerely good and perfectly divine."

It only remains to say that we have given entire, and without multilation, his great masterpiece, the Areopagitica : a Speech for the Liberty of Unlicensed Printing. 'The glory of this battle is all his own. Thousands among his contemporaries raised their voices against ship-money and the star-chamber. But there were few indeed who discerned the more fearful evils of moral and intellectual slavery, and the benefits which would result from the liberty of the press and the unfettered exercise of private judgment. These were the objects which Milton had in view when he attacked the licensing system, in that sublime treatise which every statesman should wear as a sign upon his hand, and as frontlets between his eyes.'

Much Cowarne, February, 1870.

MILTON'S PROSE WORKS

ARRANGED IN CHRONOLOGICAL ORDER.

THERE is great advantage to be derived from reading and studying the works of an author in the order in which they have been written. Editors have long made this discovery, and our best editions of the classics are those in which this chronological order is observed; such as Bentley's Horace, Scholefield's Æschylus, and Bekker's Aristophanes. To read the ancient tragedies and comedies in the order in which they were acted, as far as it can be ascertained, must add very much to their interest and historical value. And in nothing is the benefit of chronological arrangement more evident than in St. Paul's Epistles, which, as arranged by Bishop Wordsworth in his scholarly and invaluable Greek Testament, are seen to form one connected and consistent whole, setting forth a complete system of Doctrine and Discipline, which they can hardly be said to do in their disjointed and usual order.

These remarks will be found true with regard to Milton's controversial writings, and in some measure with regard to his poetry.

1641. Of Reformation in England.
1641. Of Prelatical Episcopacy.
1641. The Reason of Church Government urged against Prelaty.
1641. Animadversions upon the Remonstrant's Defence.
1642. An Apology for Smectymnus.
1644. The Doctrine and Discipline of Divorce.
1644. On Education.
1644. Areopagitica.
1645. The Judgment of Martin Bucer concerning Divorce.
1645. Tetrachordon.
1645. Colasterion.
1650. The Tenure of Kings and Magistrates.
1650. The History of Britain to the Norman Conquest. First Four
     Books.
1651. Iconoclastes.
1651. A Defence of the People of England. In Latin.
1654. The Second Defence. In Latin.
1655. Authoris pro se Defensio.
1655. Authoris ad Alexandri Mori Supplementum Responsio.
1655. A Manifesto of the Lord Protector.
1659. Considerations to remove Hirelings out of the Church.
1659. Of Civil Power in Ecclesiastical Causes.
1659. Letter on the Ruptures of the Commonwealth.
1649-1659. Letters of State.
1660. Mode of Establishing a Commonwealth.
1660. Brief Notes on Dr. Griffith's Sermon.
1625-1666. Familiar Letters. In Latin.
1670. Remainder of the History of Britain.
1672. Artis Logicæ Plenior Institutio.
1673. Of True Religion, Heresy, Schism, Toleration.
     Posthumous Treatise on the Christian Doctrine. In Two
       Books. In Latin. Discovered, in 1823, by Mr. Lemon,
       deputy keeper of the state papers, among the presses of
       his office, and translated by C. R. Sumner, late Bishop
       of Winchester.

With regard to the chronology of Milton's great
Poems, it may be interesting to bear in mind that he
wrote his Ode on the Nativity at twenty-one, his
Comus at twenty-six, his Lycidas at twenty-nine, his

Paradise Lost at fifty-seven, his Paradise Regained and Samson Agonistes at sixty-one.

Milton's three marriages took place in his thirty-fifth, fiftieth, and fifty-fourth year. He also fell in love when he was nineteen. See his seventh elegy, and Cowper's beautiful translation. It was love at first sight. That is the one face for me. He saw, but never spoke to the beloved object.

> " She was gone, and vanish'd, to appear no more."

He proceeded to solace himself with his Latin Muse.

The one face that was for Milton was Catharine Woodcock's, whom he married and lost in childbed within the year. If his sonnets mean anything, and are faithful records of the feelings of the poet, he was and would have been happy with her. Witness the eighteenth, like that on the Martyrs of Piedmont, a ' collect in verse.'

> " Methought I saw my late espoused saint
>   Brought to me, like Alcestis, from the grave,
>   Whom Jove's great son to her glad husband gave,
> Rescued from death by force, though pale and faint.
> Mine, as whom wash'd from spot of child-bed taint
>   Purification in the old law did save,
>   And such as yet once more I trust to have
> Full sight of her in heaven without restraint,
> Came vested all in white, pure as her mind :
>   Her face was veil'd ; yet to my fancied sight
> Love, sweetness, goodness, in her person shined
>   So clear as in no face with more delight.
> But, O ! as to embrace me she inclined
>   I waked ; she fled ; and day brought back my night !'"

INTRODUCTORY REMARKS.

THE Prose Works of Milton seem at first sight to be a very confused and miscellaneous series of compositions ; but they admit of an easy and simple classification, the key to which is seen at a glance in the Second Defence. In the highly interesting autobiography which he there gives, he mentions the origin and occasion of his most important works, the reasons which induced him to undertake them, and the aim and object which he had in view.

The passage itself will be quoted at length in its proper place, when we come to our selections from that portion of his productions. All his writings are in defence of that thing which he called Liberty—a subject on which he and some of his contemporaries literally went mad. He divides liberty into three species, essential to the happiness of social life—religious, domestic, and civil. On the first we have five great Treatises, four of which were published in 1641, viz., The Treatises of Reformation, of Prelatical Episcopacy, The Reason of Church Government, and some Animadversions; and in the following year he produced the fifth, his Apology. In the cause of domestic liberty, involving, as it does, three material questions, marriage, education, and the free publication of thought, he wrote three great Treatises, on Divorce (for all on that subject we class as one), on Education, and his Areopagitica, which deals with the freedom of the human mind, the most valuable but at that time least valued liberty of all. These eight Treatises he wrote without fee or reward, presenting gratuitously these fruits of his private studies to the Church and to the State. And lastly, in the cause of civil liberty, at the bidding and in the pay of Parliament, he penned the Iconoclastes, and his two, or rather three, Defences.

The origin of these several works was briefly this: In the course of his travels he had arrived at Rome, and was intending to visit Greece, when tidings of the civil commotions in his native country reached his ears. He determined at once to return and fight in the ranks of Liberty. Accordingly, he boldly throws himself into the breach, and wields his powerful pen, in those eight treatises we have mentioned, in the cause of religious and domestic liberty, leaving the third, as he says, to the care of the magistrates. It was then about the year 1650, and he expected an interval of literary ease, and began writing his History of England, from the earliest times to the period in which he was living. But ease and quietude were not to be. his lot. A command from the Council of State bade him compose an answer to the Icon Basiliké, which had just appeared. To this we owe the Iconoclastes, in which he declares how far his thoughts were from insulting fallen majesty, only professing to prefer Queen Truth to King Charles. Then follows his battle with Salmasius and Alexander More.

We have now mentioned the chief of his works, putting aside some minor and unimportant short pamphlets, and his voluminous but worthless posthumous work on Christian Doctrine. So, after all, they form a connected whole, consisting of twelve principal compositions—five in defence of what may be called religious liberty, three of domestic liberty, and four pre-eminently political and polemical.

The characteristic of the first series is his inveterate and implacable hatred to Prelatical Episcopacy—this is their sum and substance. His sentiments on the subject of Divorce and on Education are untenable, and simply absurd; and with those on the Great Rebellion, and on the execution of Charles, it is impossible to have any sympathy. His wretched squabbles with Salmasius and More excite our pity and contempt. We cannot but regret that circumstances should have led him to descant on such unfortunate and unpromising themes; but on these circumstances,

not on Milton himself, we would fain cast the blame.
So utterly visionary and Utopian are they in themselves, though propounded in majestic language, and
interspersed with the sublimest and noblest thoughts,
that there is no fear, and never was, of his finding
followers, or forming a sect.   And, in fact, he who
errs with him must be endued with the same gigantic
powers of soul and intellect as he possessed, which
will for ever preclude any danger that might arise
from studying his works.   We regard him as a much
misunderstood, ill-used, and disappointed man.   With
Hamlet, he might have exclaimed—

> ' The time is out of joint ;—O cursed spite,
> That ever I was born to set it right !'

But this was a work beyond even his powers.   Still,
he set about it manfully and resolutely, and, failing,
he delivered his own soul.

We can well understand why his works should be
unpopular, especially to those who do not penetrate
beneath the surface; and our desire is not so much to
direct attention to his opinions, but to the oftentimes
magnificent language in which they are clothed—not
to recommend all that he wrote, but certain parts,
which we would not willingly let die, or remain in an
undeserved and unjust oblivion.   We do not hesitate
to say that the reading of his works by those whose
principles are formed, however much they seem to
fall in with and foster republican views, would tend

to generate a healthy tone in these degenerate days, and that from the lofty, and majestic, and high-minded spirit which pervades them. Honesty of purpose and consistency of conduct, in the midst of severe temptation, are the characteristic marks and the true glory of Milton. He is the most splendid example which could be cited of the truth of that noble stanza of Horace (Carm. iii., 3).

> ' Justum ac tenacem propositi virum
> Non civium ardor prava jubentium,
> Non vultus instantis tyranni
> Mente quatit solida, neque Auster,
> Dux inquieti turbidus Adriæ,
> Nec fulminantis magna manus Jovis :
> Si fractus illabatur orbis,
> Impavidum ferient ruinæ.'

He was no reed shaken with the wind, but onward he pursued his course, through good report and evil report. He commands our respect even where we most differ from him. Take the simple fact that he took office under the usurper Cromwell, and refused to take office under the Restoration, though urged to do so, and we see how consistent and noble was that mind which excessive light alone led astray. In a word, he had grace to live

> "As ever in his great Taskmaster's eye ;"

not meaning that God is a hard taskmaster to anyone, but that He has given to everyone his allotted task to do in this world ; and this is what Milton desired to find out, and then did with all his might.

OF THE REFORMATION IN ENGLAND,

AND THE CAUSES THAT HITHERTO HAVE HINDERED IT.

WRITTEN TO A FRIEND.

WE are glad this work comes first under notice, because it furnishes a good specimen of Milton's peculiar style. The length of the sentences almost takes away one's breath, and the wonder is how those which occur in his speeches could have been spoken by him; just as we wonder how the actors in the ancient theatres madet hemselves heard by an audience of thirty thousand in the open air. Long as they are, they are built up most artistically, and we confess to liking them in Milton, though perhaps we should not in any one else.

The exordium and the peroration of this remarkable production are exceedingly grand and striking. The latter astonishes and enchants us by its powerful and matchless eloquence, and its richly musical cadences. It has never been surpassed in any language, and is a glorious specimen of impassioned prose. Such an outburst seems to us little less than direct inspiration. It is in fact a prose-poem, a patriotic lyric; and naturally prompts the question where does poetry begin and prose end, and what is the proper domain of each art? for here we see them invading each other. Macaulay doubtless had this celebrated passage in view when he spoke of his prose style as 'stiff with gorgeous embroidery—a perfect field of cloth of gold.' This burst of ' devotional and lyric rapture,' in which his excited feelings find a vent, and others, especially in the Areopagitica, seem to us to rival the poetry of the Paradise Lost. We have said so much that we think our readers will not thank us if we detain them any longer from the rich feast we propose to set before them.

"Amidst those deep and retired thoughts, which, with every man Christianity instructed, ought to be most frequent of God, and of His miraculous ways and works amongst men, and of our religion and works, to be performed to Him ; after the story of our Saviour Christ, suffering to the lowest bent of weakness in the flesh, and presently triumphing to the highest pitch of glory in the spirit, which drew up His body also, till we in both be united to Him in the revelation of His kingdom : I do not know of anything more worthy to take up the whole passion of pity on the one side, and joy on the other, than to consider first the foul and sudden corruption, and then, after many a tedious age,

the long deferred, but much more wonderful and
happy reformation of the church in these latter days.
Sad it is to think how that doctrine of the gospel,
planted by teachers divinely inspired, and by them
winnowed and sifted from the chaff of overdated ceremonies, and refined to such a spiritual height and
temper of purity, and knowledge of the Creator, that
the body, with all the circumstances of time and
place, were purified by the affections of the regenerate
soul, and nothing left impure but sin; faith needing
not the weak and fallible office of his senses, to be
either the ushers or interpreters of heavenly mysteries, save where our Lord Himself in His sacraments
ordained; that such a doctrine should, through the
grossness and blindness of her professors, and the
fraud of deceivable traditions, drag so downwards, as
to backslide one way into the Jewish beggary of old
cast rudiments, and stumble forward another way into
the new-vomited paganism of sensual idolatry, attri-
buting purity or impurity to things indifferent, that
they might bring the inward acts of the spirit to the
outward and customary eyeservice of the body, as if
they could make God earthly and fleshly, because they
could not make themselves heavenly and spiritual;
they began to draw down all the divine intercourse
betwixt God and the soul, yea, the very shape of God
Himself, into an exterior and bodily form, urgently
pretending a necessity and obligement of joining the

body in a formal reverence and worship circumscribed; they hallowed it, they fumed it, they sprink-
led it, they bedecked it, not in robes of pure inno-
cency, but of pure linen, with other deformed and
fantastic dresses, in palls and mitres, gold and gew-
gaws fetched from Aaron's old wardrobe, or the
flamen's vestry : then was the priest set to con his motions and his postures, his liturgies and his hurries, till
the soul by this means of overbodying herself, given
up justly to fleshly delights, bated her wing apace
downward : and finding the ease she had from her
visible and sensuous colleague, the body, in performance of religious duties, her pinions now broken, and
flagging, shifted off from herself the labour of high soaring any more, forgot her heavenly flight, and left the
dull and droiling carcase to plod on the old road, and
drudging trade of outward conformity. And here,
out of question from her perverse conceiting of God
and holy things, she had fallen to believe no God at
all, had not custom and the worm of conscience
nipped her incredulity : hence to all the duties of
evangelical grace, instead of the adoptive and cheerful boldness which our new alliance with God requires, came servile and thrall-like fear : for in very
deed the superstitious man, by his good will, is an
atheist ; but being scared from thence by the pangs
and gripes of a boiling conscience, all in a pudder
shuffles up to himself such a God and such a worship

as is most agreeable to remedy his fear ; which fear of his, as also is his hope, fixed only upon the flesh, renders likewise the whole faculty of his apprehension carnal ; and all the inward acts of worship, issuing from the native strength of the soul, run out lavishly to the upper skin, and there harden into a crust of formality. Hence men came to scan the Scriptures by the letter, and in the covenant of our redemption magnified the external signs more than the quickening power of the Spirit ; and yet, looking on them through their own guiltiness with a servile fear, and finding as little comfort, or rather terror, from them again, they knew not how to hide their slavish approach to God's behests, by them not understood nor worthily received, but by cloaking their servile crouching to all religious presentiments, sometimes lawful, sometimes idolatrous, under the name of humility, and terming the piebald frippery and ostentation of ceremonies, decency. Then was baptism changed into a kind of exorcism, and that feast of free grace to which Christ invited His disciples to sit as brethren and coheirs of the happy covenant, which at that table was to be sealed to them, even that feast of love and heavenly-admitted fellowship, the seal of filial grace, became the subject of horror, and glouting adoration, pageanted about like a dreadful idol, which sometimes deceives well-meaning men, and beguiles them of their reward by their voluntary humility—which, indeed, is fleshly pride—preferring a foolish sacrifice, and the rudiments of the world, as St. Paul to the Colossians explaineth, before a savoury obedience to Christ's example. Such was Peter's unseasonable humility, as then his knowledge was small, when Christ came to wash his feet, who at an impertinent time would needs strain courtesy with his master, and falling troublesomely upon the lowly, allwise, and unexaminable intention of Christ, in what He went with resolution to do, so provoked by his interruption the meek Lord, that he threatened to exclude him from his heavenly portion, unless he could be content to be less arrogant and stiff-necked in his humility.

"But to dwell no longer in characterizing the depravities of the church, and how they sprung, and how they took increase; when I recall to mind at last, after so many dark ages, wherein the huge overshadowing train of error had almost swept all the stars out of the firmament of the church, how the bright and blissful Reformation (by divine. power) struck through the black and settled night of ignorance and anti-Christian tyranny, methinks a sovereign and reviving joy must needs rush into the bosom of him that reads or hears, and the sweet odour of the returning gospel imbathe his soul with the fragrancy of heaven. Then was the sacred Bible sought out of the dusty corners, where profane falsehood and neg-

lect had thrown it, the schools opened, divine and
human learning raked out of the embers of forgotten
tongues, the princes and cities trooping apace to the
new-erected banner of salvation ; the martyrs, with
the unresistible might of weakness, shaking the powers
of darkness, and scorning the fiery rage of the old red
dragon.

"The pleasing pursuit of these thoughts hath ofttimes led me into a serious question and debatement
with myself, how it should come to pass that England
(having had this grace and honour from God to be
the first that should set up a standard for the recovery
of lost truth, and blow the first evangelic trumpet to
the nations, holding up, as from a hill, the new lamp
of saving light to all Christendom) should now be last
and most unsettled in the enjoyment of that peace,
whereof she taught the way to others ; although, indeed, our Wickliffe's preaching, at which all the succeeding reformers more effectually lighted their tapers,
was to his countrymen but a short blaze, soon damped
and stifled by the Pope and prelates for six or seven
kings' reigns ; yet methinks the precendency which
God gave this island, to be the first restorer of buried
truth, should have been followed with more happy
success, and sooner attained perfection, in which, as
yet, we are amongst the last : for, albeit in purity of
doctrine we agree with our brethren, yet in discipline,
which is the execution and applying of doctrine home,

we are no better than a schism from all the Reformation, and a sore scandal to them. Certainly it would be worth the while therefore, and the pains, to inquire more particularly what and how many the chief causes have been that have still hindered our uniform consent to the rest of the churches abroad, at this time especially when the kingdom is in a good propensity thereto, and all men in prayers, in hopes, or in disputes, either for or against it.

"Yet I will not insist on that which may seem to be the cause on God's part; as His judgment on our sins, the trial of His own, the unmasking of hypocrites: nor shall I stay to speak of the continual eagerness and extreme diligence of the pope and papists to stop the furtherance of reformation, which now have no hold or hope of England, their lost darling. But I shall chiefly endeavour to declare those causes that hinder the forwarding of true discipline, which are among ourselves. Orderly proceeding will divide our inquiry into our forefathers' days, and into our times. Henry VIII. was the first that rent this kingdom from the pope's subjection totally; but his quarrel being more about supremacy, than other faultiness in religion that he regarded, it is no marvel if he stuck where he did. The next default was in the bishops, who, though they had renounced the pope, still hugged the popedom. In Edward the Sixth's days, why a complete reformation was not effected, to any considerate man may appear. First, he no sooner entered his kingdom, but into a war with Scotland; rebellions on all sides, and other tumults; hereupon followed ambitious contentions among the peers, which ceased not but with the protector's death; the prelates were halting and timeserving, followers of this world, the least wry face of a politician hushed them. But it will be said these men (Cranmer, Ridley, and Latimer) were martyrs: what then? Though every true Christian will be a martyr when he is called to it, not presently does it follow, that every one suffering for religion is, without exception. St. Paul writes, that "a man may give his body to be burnt (meaning for religion,) and yet not have charity:" he is not therefore above all possibility of erring, because he burnt for some points of truth. Witness the Arians and Pelagians, which were slain by the heathen for Christ's sake, yet we take both these for no true friends of Christ."

We may infer from this passage that Milton was in his younger years untainted by Arianism.

"More tolerable it were for the church of God, that all these names were utterly abolished, like the brazen serpent, than that men's fond opinion should thus idolize them, and the heavenly and spotless truth be thus captivated.

"Lastly, all know by example, that exact reformation is not perfected at the first push. The hindering causes in Queen Elizabeth's time will be found to be common with those alleged for King Edward VI.: the greenness of the times, the weak estate which Queen Mary left the realm in, the great places and offices executed by papists, the bishops firm to Rome. They had found a good tabernacle, they sat under a spreading vine, their lot was fallen in a fair inheritance. Those that found fault with the decrees of the convocation were subjected to imprisonments, troubles, disgraces, and straight were branded with the name of puritans. From this period I count to begin our times. I shall distinguish such as I esteem to be the hinderers of reformation into three sorts, Antiquitàrians (for so I had rather call them than antiquaries, whose labours are useful and laudable); 2, Libertines; 3, Politicians.

"To the votarists of antiquity I shall think to have fully answered, if I shall be able to approve out of antiquity, First, that if they will conform our bishops to the purer times, they must mew their feathers. Secondly, that those purer times were corrupt, and their books corrupted soon after. Thirdly, that the best of those that then wrote disclaim that any man should repose on them, and send all to the scriptures.

"A fast friend of episcopacy, Camden, who cannot but love bishops as well as old coins, and his much lamented monasteries, for antiquity's sake.

"Doubtless that which led the fathers into fraud and

error was that they attended more to the near tradition of what they heard the apostles sometimes did, than to what they had left written, not considering that many things which they did were by the apostles themselves professed to be done only for the present, and of mere indulgence to some scrupulous converts of the circumcision ; but what they writ was of firm decree to all future ages."

In contrast with Milton's opinion of the Apostolical Fathers, we may cite the opinion of Archbishop Wake, of Dr. Waterland, and of the present Bishop of Lincoln, Dr. Wordsworth.

1. 'They were contemporary with the Apostles, and instructed by them. They were men not only of a perfect piety, but of great courage and constancy. Their writings were approved by the Church in those days, which could not be mistaken in its approbation of them.'

2. 'The ancient Fathers are useful for fixing the sense of Scripture in controverted texts. Those that lived in or near the Apostolical times might retain in memory what the Apostles themselves, or their immediate successors, said upon such and such points. The charismata, the extraordinary gifts of the Holy Spirit, were then frequent, and visibly rested in and upon the Church, and there only. The Fathers of the third and fourth centuries had the advantage of many

written accounts of the doctrine of the former ages, which have since been lost.'

3. 'The Ancient Interpreters are never flippant and familiar, they are never self-conceited and vainglorious—they are never scornful and profane. They handle Scripture with reverence; their tone is high and holy, produced by careful study of Scripture, with humble prayer for light to the Divine Author of Scripture. They reflect some of that light, and raise and spiritualize the thoughts of the reader, and do not depress them into the lower and more obscure regions of clouds, which hang over the minds of those who approach Scripture with presumption and irreverence, and which disable them from seeing its light, and, much more, from displaying it to others.'

" I am not of opinion to think the Church a vine in this respect, because, as they take it, she cannot subsist without clasping about the elm of worldly strength and felicity, as if the heavenly city could not support itself without the props and buttresses of secular authority.

" The very essence of truth is plainness and brightness ; the darkness and crookedness is our own. The wisdom of God created understanding, fit and proportionable to truth, the object and end of it, as the eye to the thing visible.

" 2. *Libertines.*—It will not be requisite to answer

these men, but only to discover them; for reason
they have none, but lust and licentiousness, and therefore answer can have none. It is not any discipline
they could live under—it is the corruption and remis-
sion of discipline that they seek. It is only the merry
friar in Chaucer can disple (disciple) them.

> " Full sweetly heard he confession,
> And pleasant was his absolution,
> He was an easy man to give penance."

And so I leave them, and refer the political discourse
of episcopacy to a second book."

THE SECOND BOOK.

"TO govern well is to train up a nation in true wisdom and virtue, and that which springs from thence, magnanimity, and that which is our beginning, regeneration, and happiest end, likeness to God, which in one word we call godliness; this is the true flourishing of a land—other things follow as the shadow does the substance. A commonwealth ought to be but as one huge Christian personage, one mighty growth and stature of an honest man, as big and compact in virtue as in body; for look what the grounds and causes are of single happiness to one man, the same ye shall find them to a whole state."

On the quotation which follows from Chaucer's Ploughman, we may observe that Tyrwhitt does not admit that tale into his edition. He says, ' I cannot understand that there is the least ground of evidence, either external or internal, for believing it to be a work of Chaucer's.' It has not the least resemblance to Chaucer's manner either of writing or thinking, in his other works. It is not at all probable that a Roman Catholic would be likely to rail and inveigh against the whole government of the Church in the style of this Ploughman's Tale. Nevertheless, we here see

Milton pressing him into the service of Protestantism.

We must not omit the Fable of the Wen, an imitation of the well-known Fable of the Stomach and the Members, with which "pretty tale" Menenius Agrippa pacified the insurrection of the Roman plebeians against the patricians, and obtained the appointment of the tribunes of the people, as beautifully related in Shakespeare's Coriolanus, act i., scene i.; also in Camden's Remains.

"Upon a time the body summoned all the members to meet in the guild, for the common good : the head by right takes the first seat, and next to it a huge and monstrous wen, little less than the head itself, growing to it by a narrower excrescency. The members, amazed, began to ask one another what he was that took place next their chief? None could resolve. Whereat the wen, though unwieldly, with much ado gets up, and bespeaks the assembly to this purpose: "That as in place he was second to the head, so by due of merit, that he was to it an ornament, and strength, and of special near relation; and that if the head should fail, none were fitter than himself to step into his place : therefore he thought it for the honour of the body that such dignities and rich endowments should be decreed him, as did adorn and set out the noblest members." To this was answered, that it should be consulted. Then was a wise and

learned philosopher sent for, that knew all the char-
ters, laws, and tenures of the body. On him it is imposed by all, as chief committee, to examine, and discuss the claim and petition of right put in by the
wen ; who soon perceiving the matter, and wondering at the boldness of such a swoln tumour, " Wilt
thou," quoth he, " that are but a bottle of vicious and
hardened excrements, contend with the lawful and
freeborn members, whose certain number is set by
ancient and unrepealable statute ? Head thou art
none, though thou receive this huge substance from
it. What office bearest thou ? What good canst thou
show by thee done to the commonweal ? The wen,
not easily dashed, replies that his office was his glory ;
for so oft as the soul would retire out of the head
from over the steaming vapours of the lower parts to
divine contemplation, with him she found the purest
and quietest retreat, as being most remote from soil
and disturbance. "Lourdan," (or Lurdan, an old
word for blockhead) quoth the philosopher, " thy
folly is as great as thy filth : know that all the faculties of the soul are confined of old to their several
vessels and ventricles, from which they cannot part
without dissolution of the whole body ; and that thou
containest no good thing in thee, but a heap of hard
and loathsome uncleanness, and art to the head a foul
disfigurement and burden, when I have cut thee off,
and opened thee, as by the help of these implements
I will do, all men shall see."

"The prelates took the ready way to despoil us
both of manhood and grace at once, and that in the
shamefullest and ungodliest manner, upon that day
which God's law, and even our own reason hath con-
secrated, that we might have one day at least of seven
set apart wherein to examine and increase our knowledge of God, to meditate and commune of our faith,
our hope, our eternal city in heaven, and to quicken
withal the study and exercise of charity; at such a
time that men should be plucked from the soberest
and saddest thoughts, and by bishops instigated and
pushed forward to gaming, jigging, wassailing, and
mixed dancing, is a horror to think !"

Milton here alludes to the celebrated Book of
Sports put forth by James I., 1618, and republished
with additions by Charles I., 1633, at the instigation
of Archbishop Laud ; and the bishops were ordered
to take care of its publication in all parish churches.
The Long Parliament, to their credit, ordered it to be
burnt by the hands of the common hangman 1643, two
years after Milton wrote this.

"Now I appeal to all wise men, what an excessive
waste of treasure hath been within these few years in
this land, not in the expedient, but in the idolatrous
erection of temples beautified exquisitely to outvie the
Papists, the costly and dear bought scandals and snares
of images, pictures, rich copes, gorgeous altar-cloths.
What can we suppose this will come to? If the

splendour of gold and silver begin to lord it once again in the Church of England, we shall see Antichrist shortly wallow here, though his chief kennel be at Rome. If they had but one thought on God's glory, and the advancement of Christian faith, they would be a means that with these expenses, thus profusely thrown away in trash, rather churches and schools might be built, where they cry out for want, and more added where too few are ; a moderate maintenance to every painful minister, that now scarce sustains his family with bread; which (I hope) the worthy men of our land will consider."

The word "painful" here means taking pains. Thus Fuller, ' O the holiness of their living, and the painfulness of their preaching.' 'Many things,' Archbishop French well observes ' would not be so painful in the present sense of the word, if they had been more painful in the earlier, as perhaps some sermons.' " They would rouse us up to a war fit for Cain to be the leader of, an abhorred, a cursed, a fraternal war. England and Scotland, dearest brothers both in nature and in Christ, must be set to wade in one another's blood; and Ireland, our free denizen, upon the back of us both, as occasion should serve : a piece of service that the pope and all his factors have been compassing to do ever since the Reformation.

" But ever-blessed be He, and ever glorified, that

from His high watch-tower in the heavens, discerning
the crooked ways of perverse and cruel men, hath
hitherto maimed and infatuated all their inventions,
and deluded their great wizards with a delusion fit
for fools and children : had God been so minded, he
could have sent a spirit of mutiny amongst us, as He
did between Abimelech and the Sechemites, to have
made our funerals ; but He, when we least deserved,
sent out a gentle gale and message of peace from the
wings of those His cherubims that fan His mercy-
seat.

"Go on both hand in hand, O nations, never to be
disunited ; be the praise and the heroic song of all
posterity; merit this, but seek only virtue, not to extend your limits (for what needs to win a fading tri-
umphant laurel out of the tears of wretched men ?) ;
but to settle the pure worship of God in His church
and justice in the state : then shall the hardest diffi-
culties smooth out themselves before ye ; envy shall
sink to hell, craft and malice be confounded, whether
it be homebred mischief or outlandish cunning : yea,
other nations will then covet to serve ye, for lordship
and victory are but the pages of justice and virtue ;
join your invincible might to do worthy and god-like
deeds ; and then he that seeks to break your union,
a cleaving curse be his inheritance to all generations."

"If the sacred and dreadful works of holy discipline, censure, penance, excommunication, and abso-

lution, where no profane thing ought to have access,
nothing to be assistant but sage and Christianly admonition, brotherly love, flaming charity and zeal;
and then, according to the effects, paternal sorrow, or
paternal joy, mild severity, melting compassion: if
such divine ministeries as these, wherein the angel of
the church represents the person of Christ Jesus,
must lie prostitute to sordid fees, and not pass to and
fro between our Saviour, that of free grace redeemed
us, and the submissive penitent, without the truckage
of perishing coin, then have the Babylonish merchants
of souls just excuse."

"This most mild, though withal dreadful and inviolable prerogative of Christ's diadem, excommunication, serves for nothing but to prog and pander for
fees. But in the evangelical and reformed use of this
sacred censure no such prostitution, no such Iscarioti-
cal drifts are to be doubted, as that spiritual doom
and sentence should invade worldly possession, which
is the rightful lot and portion even of the wickedest
men, as frankly bestowed upon them by the all-dis-
pensing bounty as rain and sunshine. No, no; it seeks
not to bereave or destroy the body; it seeks to save
the soul by humbling the body, not by imprisonment
or pecuniary mulct, much less by stripes, or bonds,
or disinheritance, but by fatherly admonishment and
Christian rebuke, to cast it into godly sorrow, whose
end is joy, and ingenuous bashfulness to sin: if that

cannot be wrought, then as a tender mother takes her child and holds it over the pit with scaring words, that it may learn to fear where danger is; so doth excommunication as dearly and as freely, without money, use her wholesome and saving terrors; she is instant, she beseeches, by all the dear and sweet promises of salvation she entices and woos; by all the threatenings and thunders of the law, and rejected gospel, she charges and adjures: this is all her armoury, her munition, her artillery; then she awaits with long sufferance, and yet ardent zeal. In brief, there is no act in all the errand of God's ministers to mankind wherein passes more lover-like contestation between Christ and the soul of a regenerate man lapsing, than before, and in, and after the sentence of excommunication. As for the fogging proctorage of money, with such an eye as struck Gehazi with leprosy and Simon Magus with a curse, so does she look, and so threaten her fiery whip against that banking den of thieves that dare thus baffle, and buy, and sell the awful and majestic wrinkles of her brow. He that is rightly and apostolically sped with her invisible arrow, if he can be at peace in his own soul, and not smell within him the brimstone of hell, may have fair leave to tell all his bags over undiminished of the least farthing, may eat his dainties, drink his wine, use his delights, enjoy his lands and liberties, not the least skin raised, not the least hair misplaced, for all that excommunication has done : much more may a king enjoy his rights and prerogatives unde-flowered, untouched, and be as absolute and complete a king as all his royalties and revenues can make him. But let us not for fear of a scarecrow, or else through hatred to be reformed, stand hankering and politizing, when God with spread hands testifies to us, and points us out the way to our peace."

We will conclude our selections from this remark-able first prose composition of Milton with its truly magnificent peroration.

"O, sir, I do now feel myself inwrapped on a sudden into those mazes and labyrinths of dreadful and hideous thoughts, that which way to get out, or which way to end, I know not, unless I turn mine eyes, and with your help lift up my hands to that eternal and propitious throne, where nothing is readier than grace and refuge to the distresses of mortal suppliants : and it were a shame to leave these serious thoughts less piously than the heathen were wont to conclude their graver discourses.

"Thou, therefore, that sittest in light and glory unapproachable, parent of angels and men ! next, Thee I implore, omnipotent King, Redeemer of that lost remnant whose nature Thou didst assume, ineffa-ble and everlasting Love ! and Thou, the third sub-sistence of divine infinitude, illumining Spirit, the joy and solace of created things! one Tripersonal Godhead! look upon this Thy poor and almost spent and expiring church, leave her not thus a prey to these unfortunate wolves that wait and think long till they devour Thy tender flock; these wild boars that have broken into Thy vineyard, and left the fruit of their polluting hoofs on the souls of Thy servants. O let them not bring about their designs, that stand now at the entrance of the bottomless pit, expecting the watchword to open, and let out those dreadful locusts and scorpions, to re-involve us in that pitchy cloud of infernal darkness, where we shall never more see the sun of Thy truth again, never hope for the cheerful dawn, never more hear the bird of morning sing. Be moved with pity at the afflicted state of this our shaken monarchy, that now lies labouring under her throes, and struggling against the grudges of more dreaded calamities.

" O Thou, that, after the impetuous rage of five bloody inundations, and the succeeding sword of intestine war, soaking the land in her own gore, didst pity the sad and ceaseless revolution of our swift and thick coming sorrows; when we were quite breathless, of Thy free grace didst motion peace, and terms of covenant with us; and having first well-nigh freed us from anti-Christian thraldom, didst build up this Britannic empire to a glorious and enviable height, with all her daughter islands about her; stay us in this felicity, let not the obstinacy of our half-obedience and will-worship bring forth that viper of sedition that for these fourscore years hath been breeding, to eat through the entrails of our peace: but let her cast her abortive spawn without the danger of this travailing and throbbing kingdom: that we still remember in our solemn thanksgivings how, for us, the northern ocean, even to the frozen Thule, was scattered with the proud shipwrecks of the Spanish armada, and the very maw of hell ransacked, and made to give up her concealed destruction, ere she could vent it in that horrible blast.

" O how much more glorious will those former deliverances appear, when we shall know them not only to have saved us from greatest miseries past, but to have reserved us for greatest happiness to come! Hitherto Thou hast but freed us, and that not fully, from the unjust and tyrannous claim of Thy foes; now unite us entirely, and appropriate us to Thyself, tie us everlastingly in willing homage to the prerogative of Thy eternal throne.

" And now we know, O Thou our most certain hope and defence, that Thine enemies have been consulting all the sorceries of the great whore, and have joined their plots with that sad intelligencing tyrant that mischiefs the world with his mines of Ophir, and lies thirsting to revenge his naval ruins that have larded our seas: but let them all take counsel together, and let it come to nought; let them decree, and do Thou

E

cancel it; let them gather themselves, and be scattered; let them embattle themselves, and be broken; let them embattle, and be broken, for Thou art with us.

"Then, amidst the hymns and hallelujahs of saints, some one may perhaps be heard offering at high strains, in new and lofty measure, to sing and celebrate Thy divine mercies and marvellous judgments in this land throughout all ages; whereby this great and warlike nation, instructed and inured to the fervent and continual practice of truth and righteousness, and casting far from her the rags of her whole vices, may press on hard to that high and happy emulation to be found the soberest, wisest, and most Christian people at that day when Thou, the eternal and shortly-expected King, shalt open the clouds to judge the several kingdoms of the world, and distributing national honours and rewards to religious and just commonwealths, shalt put an end to all earthly tyrannies, proclaiming Thy universal and mild monarchy through heaven and earth; where they, undoubtedly, that by their labours, counsels, and prayers have been earnest for the common good of religion and their country, shall receive, above the inferior orders of the blessed, the regal addition of principalities, legions, and thrones into their glorious titles, and in super-eminence of beatific vision, progressing the dateless and irrevoluble circle of eternity, shall clasp inseparable hands with joy and bliss, in over-measure for ever.

"But they contrary, that by the impairing and diminution of the true faith, the distresses and servitude
of their country, aspire to high dignity, rule, and promotion here, after a shameful end in this life, shall be
thrown down eternally into the darkest and deepest
gulf of hell, where they shall remain in that plight for
ever, the basest, the lowermost, the most dejected,
most underfoot, and downtrodden vassals of perdition."

OF PRELATICAL EPISCOPACY,

AND WHETHER IT MAY BE DEDUCED FROM THE APOSTO-
LICAL TIMES, BY VIRTUE OF THOSE TESTIMONIES
WHICH ARE ALLEGED TO THAT PURPOSE IN SOME
LATE TREATISES.

THE Treatises here referred to are those by Bishop Hall and by Archbishop Usher, who of course would maintain the divine origin of Prelatical Episcopacy. They would agree with Milton that "it is clear in Scripture that a bishop and presbyter is all one both in name and office," but they would disagree with his next proposition "that what was done by Timothy and Titus, executing an extraordinary place, as fellow-labourers with the Apostles, and of a universal charge in planting Christianity through divers regions, cannot be drawn into particular and daily example." Here we have *the thing itself* acknowledged, and the quarrel about names is profitless. Timothy and Titus are confessed to have executed an extraordinary office, as fellow-labourers of the Apostles, distinct from that of the two inferior Orders of presbyters or episcopi, as they were also called at first by reason of their being *overseers* of their respective

flocks, and of Deacons. The form of Church Government presented to our view in these epistles of St.
Paul is therefore threefold : first, individuals exercising
authority over all, both Clergy and Laity; secondly,
presbyters or bishops; thirdly, deacons. Afterwards
the title of bishops was transferred and confined to the
highest Order of the Clergy; and therefore the Preface to the Ordinal of the Church of England truly
says, " It is evident unto all men diligently reading
the Holy Scriptures and ancient Authors, that from
the Apostles' time there ever have been these Orders
of Ministers in Christ's Church, Bishops, Priests, and
Deacons.

The thing itself is found in Scripture, and the explanation of the change in name is easy and satisfac-
tory. From what has been said we may see the reason why this Treatise is entitled Of Prelatical Episcopacy. Milton's quarrel is not with the word " bishop "
as applied to the presbytery, but only with the word
" prelate." Accordingly, his first words explain what
he means by Prelatical Episcopacy.

" Episcopacy, as it is taken for an order in the
church above a presbyter, or, as we commonly name
him, the minister of a congregation, is either of divine
constitution or of human. If only of human, we have
the same human privilege that all men have ever had
since Adam, being born free, and in the mistress
island of all the British, to retain this episcopacy, or

to remove it. If it be of divine constitution, to satisfy us fully in that the Scripture only is able, it being the only book left us of divine authority, not in anything more divine than in the all-sufficiency it hath to furnish us, as with all other spiritual knowledge, so with this in particular, setting out to us a perfect man of God, accomplished to all the good works of his charge : through all which book can be nowhere, either by plain text or solid reasoning, found any difference between a bishop and a presbyter, save that they be two names to signify the same order. Notwithstanding this clearness, and that by all evidence of argument, Timothy and Titus had rather the vicegerency of an apostleship committed to them, than the ordinary charge of a bishopric, as being men of extraordinary calling ; yet to verify that which St. Paul foretold of succeeding times, when men began to have itching ears, then not contented with the plentiful and wholesome fountains of the gospel, they began after their own lusts to heap to themselves teachers, and as if the divine Scripture wanted a supplement, and were to be eked out, they cannot think any doubt resolved, and any doctrine confirmed ; unless they run to that indigested heap and fry of authors which they call antiquity. Whatsoever time, or the heedless hand of blind chance, hath drawn down from of old to this present, in her huge drag-net, whether fish or seaweed, shells or shrubs, unpicked, unchosen, those are the fathers."

Here we have much reckless assertion, and little
solid reasoning ; in fact, Milton begs the question,
and may be confuted from his own words. He allows
the very thing for which Prelatical Episcopalians contend, and their doctrine could not be better expressed than he has done it, namely, that "Timothy and
Titus had the vicegerency of an apostleship committed
to them, as being men of extraordinary calling."
What can this mean but that they held an office as
representatives of the Apostles, distinct, and apart
from, and superior to that exercised by those who
were indifferently designated bishops or presbyters ?
But our object is not to expose and refute the errors
which Milton entertained, but rather to cover them
with a reverential and loving hand, and to search for
those "sentences of a venturous edge, uttered in the
height of zeal"—zeal, however, mistaken and mis-
directed, which astonish and enchant us with their
matchless beauty and marvellous rhythm, and sublime and nervous rhetoric and elegance. 'God-
gifted organ-voice of England, O mighty-mouth'd
inventor of harmonies,' in prose as well as verse !
who would not sit at thy feet, and listen to the
melody and music of thy words, blind to thy faults,
the product not of thine own mighty, honest, and
truth-loving soul, but of those unhappy times in which
thy lot was cast ! O golden-mouthed prophet and
lover of truth, thy very errors are almost sacred, be-

cause of thy sincerity and honesty of intention, because of thine own pure and blameless life—we love thee too well to scan them severely. His honesty of purpose appears in this very attack on Prelatical Episcopacy. "It came into my thoughts to persuade myself, setting all distances and nice respects aside, that I could do religion and my country no better service for the time than doing my utmost endeavour to recall the people of God from this vain foraging after straw, and to reduce them to their firm stations under the standard of the gospel, by making appear to them, first the insufficiency, next the inconveniency, and lastly the impiety of these gay testimonies, that their great doctors would bring them to dote on."

"We do injuriously in searching among the verminous and polluted rags dropped overworn from the toiling shoulders of time, with these deformedly to quilt and interlace the entire, the spotless, and undecaying robe of truth, the daughter, not of time, but of Heaven, only bred up here below in Christian hearts, between two grave and holy nurses, the doctrine and discipline of the Gospel."

"Wherever a man, who had been anyway conversant with the Apostles, was to be found, thither flew all the inquisitive ears, although the exercise of right instructing was changed into the curiosity of impertinent fabling: where the mind was to be edified with solid doctrine, there the fancy was soothed with solemn stories : with less fervency was studied what St. Paul or St. John had written, than was listened to one that could say, Here he taught, here he stood, this was his stature, and thus he went habited ; and, O happy this house that harboured him, and that cold stone whereon he rested, this village wherein he wrought such a miracle, and that pavement bedewed with the warm effusion of his last blood, that sprouted up into eternal roses to crown his martyrdom. Thus, while all their thoughts were poured out upon circumstances, and the gazing after such men as had sat at table with the Apostles (many of which Christ hath professed, yea, though they had cast out devils in His name, He will not know at the last day), by this means they lost their time, and truanted in the fundamental grounds of saving knowledge, as was seen shortly by their writings."

The same beautifully-expressed thought occurs in Paradise Lost, chap. xi. :

" Here I could frequent
With worship place by place where He vouchsaf'd
Presence Divine ; and to my sons relate,
On this mount He appear'd ; under this tree
Stood visible ; among these pines his voice
I heard ; here with Him at this fountain talk'd."

" It will next behove us to consider the inconvenience we fall into, by using ourselves to be guided by these kind of episcopal testimonies. He that thinks it the part of a well-learned man to have read diligently the ancient stories of the church, and to be no stranger in the volumes of the fathers, shall have all judicious men consenting with him ; not hereby to control and new-fangle the Scripture—God forbid !— but to mark how corruption and apostasy crept in by degrees, and to gather up wherever we find the remaining sparks of original truth, wherewith to stop the mouths of our adversaries, and to bridle them with their own curb, who willingly pass by that which is orthodoxal in them, and studiously call out that which is commentitious, and best for their turns, not weighing the fathers in the balance of scripture, but scripture in the balance of the fathers. If we, therefore, making first the gospel our rule and oracle, shall take the good which we light on in the fathers, and set it to oppose the evil which other men seek from them, in this way of skirmish we shall easily master all superstition and false doctrine ; but if we turn this our discreet and wary usage of them into a blind devotion towards them, and whatsoever we find written by them ; we forsake our own grounds and reasons which led us at first to part from Rome, that is, to hold to the scriptures against all antiquity, and must be constrained to take upon ourselves a thousand superstitions and falsities."

We heartily concur in these admirable sentiments, and wish our author had always borne them in mind, and acted upon them.

"Lastly, I do not know, it being undeniable that

there are but two ecclesiastical orders, bishops and
deacons, mentioned in the gospel, how it can be less
than impiety to make a demur at that, which is there
so perspicuous."

Such is Milton's dictum, but we maintain that
scripture nowhere says that there are but two orders,
or the controversy would be at once decided; in that
case it would be impossible but to acquiesce in his
next beautiful words, which are based on this false
assumption. " Certainly, if Christ's apostle have set
down but two,"—again we ask where has He done
this ?—" then according to his own words, though he
himself should unsay it, and not only the angel of
Smyrna, but an angel from heaven, should bear us
down that there be three, St. Paul has doomed him
twice : "let him be accursed ;" for Christ has pronounced that no tittle of His word shall fall to the
ground ; and if one jot be alterable, it is as possible
that all should perish ; and this shall be our righteousness, our ample warrant, and strong assurance,
both now and at the last day, never to be ashamed
of, against all the heaped names of angels and martyrs, councils and fathers, urged upon us, if we have
given ourselves up to be taught by the pure and living
precept of God's word only ; which, without more additions, nay, with a forbidding of them, hath within
itself the promise of eternal life, the end of all
our wearisome labours,. and all our sustaining hopes."

THE REASON OF CHURCH GOVERNMENT
URGED AGAINST PRELATY.

THE preface to the second book of this Treatise is especially interesting from his subject leading him to speak of himself, his studies, intentions, and aspirations, and why they were now interrupted and postponed.

" In the publishing of human laws, to set them barely forth to the people without reason or preface or only with threatenings, in the judgment of Plato was thought to be done neither generously nor wisely. His advice was, that there should be used as an induction some well-tempered discourse, showing how good, how gainful, how happy it must needs be to live according to honesty and justice ; which being uttered with those native colours and graces of speech, as true eloquence, the daughter of virtue, can best bestow upon her mother's praises, would so incite, and in a manner charm the multitude into the love of that which is really good, as to embrace it ever after, not of custom and awe, but of choice and purpose, with true and constant delight. But this practice we may learn from a better and more ancient author-

ity than any heathen writer hath to give us; and indeed being a point of so high wisdom and worth, how
could it be but we should find it in that book, within
whose sacred context all wisdom is unfolded. Moses,
therefore, the only law-giver that we can believe to
have been visibly taught of God, knowing how vain it
was to write laws to men whose hearts were not
first seasoned with the knowledge of God and of
His works, began from the book of Genesis, as a pro-
logue to His laws; that the nation of the Jews, reading therein the universal goodness of God to all creatures in the creation, and His peculiar favour to them
in His election of Abraham, their ancestor, might be
moved to obey sincerely, by knowing so good a reason of their obedience: how much more then ought
the members of the church, under the gospel, seek to
inform their understanding in the reason of that government which the church claims to have over them! But
because about the manner and order of this government, whether it ought to be presbyterial or prelatical,
such endless question, or rather uproar, is arisen in this
land, as may be justly termed the eternal reproach of
our divines: I shall in the meanwhile not cease to hope
through the mercy and grace of Christ, the head and
husband of His church, that England shortly is to belong, neither to see patriarchal, nor see prelatical, but
to the faithful feeding and disciplining of that ministerial order, which the blessed apostles constituted

throughout the churches; and this, I shall essay to prove, can be no other than that of presbyters and deacons. And if any man incline to think I undertake a task too difficult for my years, I trust through the supreme enlightening assistance far otherwise; for my years, be they few or many, what imports it? So they bring reason, let that be looked on; and for the task, I conclude it must be easy; God having to this end ordained His gospel to be the revelation of His power and wisdom in Christ Jesus. And this is one depth of His wisdom, that He could so plainly reveal so great a measure of it to the gross distorted apprehension of decayed mankind. Let others, therefore, dread and shun the scriptures for their darkness; I shall wish I may deserve to be reckoned among those who admire and dwell upon them for their clearness. And this seems to be the cause why, in those places of holy writ, wherein is treated of church government, the reasons thereof are not formally and professedly set down, because to him that heeds attentively the drift and scope of Christian profession, they easily imply themselves." Most undoubedly.

"The first and greatest reason of church government we may securely, with the assent of many on the adverse part, affirm to be because we find it so ordained and set out to us by the appointment of God in the Scriptures; but whether this be presbyterial or prelatical, it cannot be brought to the scanning, until

I have said what is meet to some who do not think it for the ease of their inconsequent opinions to grant that church discipline is platformed in the Bible, but that it is left to the discretion of men. To this conceit of theirs I answer that it is both unsound and untrue; for there is not that thing in the world of more grave and urgent importance throughout the whole life of man than is discipline. What need I instance? He that hath read with judgment of nations and commonwealths, of cities and camps, of peace and war, sea and land, will readily agree that the flourishing and decaying of all civil societies, all the moments and turnings of human occasions, are moved to and fro as upon the axle of discipline. So that whatsoever power or sway in mortal things weaker men have attributed to fortune, I durst with more confidence (the honour of Divine Providence ever saved) ascribe either to the vigour or the slackness of discipline. Nor is there any sociable perfection in this life, civil or sacred, that can be above discipline; but she is that which, with her musical chords, preserves and holds all the parts thereof together. Hence in those perfect armies of Cyrus in Xenophon, and Scipio in the Roman stories, the excellence of military skill was esteemed, not by the not needing, but by the readiest submitting to the edicts of their commander. And certainly discipline is not only the removal of disorder, but if any visible shape can be given to divine things, the very visible shape and image of virtue, whereby she is not only seen in the regular gestures and motions of her heavenly paces as she walks, but also makes the harmony of her voice audible to mortal ears. Yea, the angels themselves, in whom no disorder is feared, as the apostle that saw them in his rapture describes, are distinguished and quaternioned into their celestial princedoms and satrapies, according as God Himself has writ his imperial decrees through the great provinces of Heaven. The state also of the blessed in paradise, though never so perfect, is not, therefore, left without discipline, whose golden surveying-reed marks out and measures every quarter and circuit of New Jerusalem. Yet is it not to be conceived, that those eternal effluences of sanctity and love in the glorified saints should by this means be confined and cloyed with repetition of that which is prescribed, but that our happiness may orb itself into a thousand vagancies of glory and delight, and with a kind of eccentrical equation be, as it were, an invariable planet of joy and felicity; how much less can we believe that God would leave his frail and feeble, though not less beloved church, here below, to the perpetual stumble of conjecture and disturbance in this our dark voyage, without the card and compass of discipline! Which is so hard to be of man's making, that we may see, even in the guidance of a civil state to worldly happiness, it is not for every learned, or every wise man, though many of them consult in common, to invent or frame a discipline; but if it be at all the work of man, it must be of such a one as is a true knower of himself, and in whom contemplation and practice, wit, prudence, fortitude, and eloquence, must be rarely met, both to comprehend the hidden causes of things, and span in his thoughts all the various effects that passion or complexion can work in man's nature; and hereto must his hand be at defiance with gain, and his heart in all virtues heroic; so far is it from the ken of these wretched projectors of ours that bescrawl their pamphlets every day with new forms of government for our church. And therefore all the ancient lawgivers were either truly inspired, as Moses, or were such men as with authority enough might give it out to be so, as Minos, Lycurgus, Numa, because they wisely forethought that men would never quietly submit to such a discipline as had not more of God's hand in it than man's. To come within the narrowness of household government, observation will show us many deep counsellors of state, and judges, to demean themselves incorruptibly in the settled course of affairs, and many worthy preachers upright in their lives, powerful in their audience: but look upon either of these men, where they are left to their own disciplining at home, and you shall soon perceive, for all their single knowledge and uprightness, how deficient they are in the

F

regulating of their own family; not only in what may concern the virtuous and decent composure of their minds in their several places, but that which is a lower and easier performance, the right possessing of the outward vessel, their body, in health or sickness, rest or labour, diet or abstinence, whereby to render it more pliant to the soul, and useful to the common-wealth: which if men were but as good to discipline themselves as some are to tutor their horses and hawks, it could not be so gross in most households."

Here let us pause a moment to notice how truly Milton describes his own case, though perhaps without intending it. He knew well how to discipline himself, but was utterly incapable of governing his own household. Great as a statesman, great in managing the public affairs, great as Cromwell's secretary and adviser, great in his various plans and suggestions for the better government of church and state, in domestic life he miserably failed, both as a husband and father. How unhappy and wretched were his hearth and home is evident from the following extract from his last will and testament: "The portion due to me from Mr. Powell, my former wife's father, I leave to the unkind children I had by her, having received no part of it: but my meaning is, they shall have no other benefit of my estate than the said portion, and what I have besides done for them, they having been very undutiful to me. All the residue of my estate

I leave to the disposal of Elizabeth, my loving wife."
This Elizabeth was his third wife, whom he married
in his fifty-fourth year, being blind and infirm, and
requiring a nurse. She, we are told, was a termagant, and used frequently to tease him for his carelessness or ignorance about money matters, but on
the whole treated him with kindness and tenderness.
His three daughters by his first wife—the only children he ever had, fortunately, perhaps—Mary, Deborah, and Anne, contested this will, and gained their
cause. The documents relating to this trial are given
by Warton, and incidentally reveal curious and interesting circumstances of Milton's domestic life, but
full of melancholy and wretchedness. But to return
from this digression.

"If then it appear so hard, and so little known
how to govern a house well, which is thought of so
easy discharge, and for every man's undertaking,
what skill of man, what wisdom, what parts can be
sufficient to give laws and ordinances to the elect
household of God? If we could imagine that He
had left it at random without His provident and gra-
cious ordering, who is he so arrogant, so presumptuous, that durst dispose and guide the living ark of the
Holy Ghost, though he should find it wandering in
the field of Bethshemesh, without the conscious warrant of some high calling? Certainly, if God be the
father of his family the church, wherein could He

express that name more than in training it up under
His own all-wise and dear economy, not turning it
loose to the havoc of strangers and wolves? Again,
if Christ be the church's husband, expecting her to be
presented before Him a pure unspotted virgin, in
what could He shew His tender love to her more
than in prescribing His own ways, which He best
knew would be to the improvement of her health
and beauty? For of any age or sex, most unfitly
may a virgin be left to an uncertain and arbitrary
education. Yea, though she be well instructed, yet
is she still under a more strait tuition, especially if
betrothed. In like manner the church, bearing the
same resemblance, it were not reason to think she
should be left destitute of that care which is as necessary and proper to her as instruction. For public
preaching, indeed, is the gift of the Spirit, working as
best seems to His secret will; but discipline is the
practic work of preaching directed and applied, as is
most requisite, to particular duty; without which it
were all one to the benefit of souls, as it would be
to the cure of bodies, if all the physicians in London
should get into the several pulpits of the city, and as-
sembling all the diseased in every parish, should
begin a learned lecture of pleurisies, palsies, lethar-
gies, to which, perhaps, none there present were inclined; and so, without so much as feeling one pulse,
or giving the least order to any skilful apothecary,

should dismiss them from time to time, some groaning, some languishing, some expiring, with this only charge, to look well to themselves, and do as they hear. Of what excellence and necessity, then, church discipline is—how beyond the faculty of man to frame, and how dangerous to be left to man's invention, who would be every foot turning it to sinister ends ; how properly, also, it is the work of God as Father, and of Christ as Husband of the church, we have by this much heard." So also says the Episcopalian.

The remaining chapters of this first book are uninteresting, and will not detain us long.

"One of these two, prelaty or presbytery, *and none other*, is of God's ordaining; and if it be, that ordinance must be evident in the gospel." Observe here that Milton differs from those who hold that *no* form of church government is prescribed in Scripture, that as much is to be said for one form as another; which is Dean Alford's erroneous opinion, as expressed lately in " Good Words."

" With as good a plea (as that prelaty prevents schism) might the dead-palsy boast to a man : It is I that free you from stitches and pains, and the troublesome feeling of cold and heat, of wounds and strokes : if I were gone all these would molest you. The winter might as well vaunt itself against the spring : I destroy all noisome and rank weeds, I keep down all pestilent vapours. Yes, and all wholesome herbs, and all fresh dews, by your violent and hide-bound frost : but when the gentle west winds shall open the fruitful bosom of the earth, thus overgirded by your imprisonment, then the flowers put forth and spring, and then the sun shall scatter the mists, and the manuring hand of the tiller shall root up all that burdens the soil without thank to your bondage."

Milton's prose works are interesting, as containing many words which since his day have altogether changed their meaning; as, for instance, the two words "noisome" and "manuring" in the last quoted passage. The former word we now use in the sense of offensive, causing disgust; but the old meaning here, and wherever it occurs in the authorised translation of the Bible, is that of noxious or actually hurtful; it is used again a little further on, "And thus they are so far from hindering dissensions, that they have made unprofitable, and even *noisome*, the chiefest remedy we have to keep Christendom at one, which is by councils." The second word, "manuring," is now confined to one branch of agriculture, in Milton's time it was applied to the whole art of cultivating the soil, and meant any work with the hand, being derived from the French 'manœuvre.' It occurs in this old sense in the Paradise Lost,

> " branches overgrown
> That mock our scant manuring."

In the preface to the second book of this treatise

he digresses to explain the right he had to meddle in these matters, how he had relinquished and interrupted his own more favourite studies at the call of his country and of duty, but yet had not for ever abandoned them, as he purposed in happier times writing an epic poem. Thus at the age of thirty-three the idea of his Paradise Lost, though not in that or in any definite form, was floating before his mind; and twenty-five long years elapsed ere the aspirations so dearly cherished throughout his life were realized. The whole of this preface is far too valuable, too eloquent, and too interesting to be curtailed.

"How happy were it for this frail, and, as it may be called, mortal life of man, since all earthly things which have the name of good and convenient in our daily use, are withal so cumbersome and full of trouble, if knowledge, yet which is the best and lightsomest possession of the mind, were, as the common saying is, no burden; and that what it wanted of being a load to any part of the body, it did not with a heavy advantage overlay upon the spirit! For not to speak of that knowledge that rests in the contemplation of natural causes and dimensions, which must needs be a lower wisdom, as the object is low, certain it is that he who hath obtained in more than the scantiest measure to know anything distinctly of God, and of His true worship, and what is infallibly good and happy in the state of man's life, what is in itself evil and miser-

able, though vulgarly not so esteemed; he that hath
obtained to know this, the only high valuable wisdom
indeed, remembering also that God, even to a strictness, requires the improvement of these His entrusted
gifts, cannot but sustain a sorer burden of mind, and
more pressing than any supportable toil or weight
which the body can labour under, how and in what
manner he shall dispose and employ those sums of
knowledge and illumination, which God hath sent him
into this world to trade with. And that which
aggravates the burden more, is, that having received
amongst his allotted parcels certain precious truths, of
such an orient lustre as no diamond can equal, which
nevertheless he has in charge to put off at any cheap
rate, yea, for nothing, to them that will, the great
merchants of this world, fearing that this course would
soon discover and disgrace the false glitter of their
deceitful wares, wherewith they abuse the people,
like poor Indians with beads and glasses, practise by
all means how they may suppress the vending of such
rarities, and at such a cheapness as would undo them,
and turn their trash upon their hands. Therefore, by
gratifying the corrupt desires of men in fleshly doctrines, they stir them up to persecute with hatred and
contempt all those that seek to bear themselves up-
rightly in this their spiritual factory: which they,
foreseeing, though they cannot but testify of truth,
and the excellency of that heavenly traffic which they

bring, against what opposition or danger soever, yet needs must it sit heavily upon their spirits, that being, in God's prime intention and their own, selected heralds of peace, and dispensers of treasure inestimable, without price, to them that have no peace, they find in the discharge of their commission, that they are made the greatest variance and offence—a very sword and fire both in house and city over the whole earth. This is that which the sad prophet Jeremiah laments, "Woe is me, my mother, that thou hast borne me, a man of strife and contention!" And although divine inspiration must certainly have been sweet to those ancient prophets, yet the irksomeness of that truth which they brought was so unpleasant unto them, that everywhere they call it a burden. Yea, that mysterious book of revelation, which the great evangelist was bid to eat, as it had been some eye-brightening electuary of knowledge and foresight, though it were sweet in his mouth, and in the learning, it was bitter in his belly, bitter in the denouncing. Nor was this hid from the wise poet Sophocles, who in that place of his tragedy where Tiresias is called to resolve King Œdipus in a matter which he knew would be grievous, brings him in bemoaning his lot, that he knew more than other men. For surely to every good and peaceable man, it must in nature needs be a hateful thing to be the displeaser and molester of thousands: much better

would it like him doubtless to be the messenger of
gladness and contentment, which is his chief intended
business to all mankind, but that they resist and
oppose their own true happiness. But when God
commands to take the trumpet, and blow a dolorous
or a jarring blast, it lies not in man's will what he
shall say, or what he shall conceal. If he shall think
to be silent as Jeremiah did, because of the reproach
and derision he met with daily, " and all his familiar
friends watched for his halting," to be revenged on
him for speaking the truth, he would be forced to
confess as he confessed : " His word was in my heart
as a burning fire shut up in my bones ; I was weary
with forbearing, and could not stay." Which might
teach these times not suddenly to condemn all things
that are sharply spoken or vehemently written as
proceeding out of stomach, virulence, and ill-nature ;
but to consider rather, that no man can be justly
offended with him that shall endeavour to impart and
bestow, without any gain to himself, those sharp but
saving words which would be a terror and a torment
in him to keep back. For me, I have determined to
lay up as the best treasure and solace of a good old
age, if God vouchsafe it me, the honest liberty of free
speech from my youth, where I shall think it available
in so dear a concernment as the Church's good. For
if I be, either by disposition or what other cause, too
inquisitive or suspicious of myself and mine own

doings, who can help it? But this I foresee, that should the church be brought under heavy oppression, and God have given me ability the while to reason against that man that should be the author of so foul a deed; or should she, by blessing from above on the industry and courage of faithful men, change this her distracted estate into better days, without the least furtherance or contribution of those few talents which God at that present had lent me; I foresee what stories I should hear within myself all my life after, of discourage and reproach. Timorous and ungrateful, the church of God is now again at the foot of her insulting enemies, and thou bewailest. What matters it for thee, or thy bewailing? When time was, thou couldst not find a syllable of all that thou hast read, or studied, to utter in her behalf. Yet ease and leisure was given thee for thy retired thoughts, out of the sweat of other men. Thou hast the diligence, the parts, the language of a man, if a vain subject were to be adorned or beautified; but when the cause of God and His church was to be pleaded, for which purpose that tongue was given thee which thou hast, God listened if He could hear thy voice among His zealous servants, but thou wert dumb as a beast; from henceforward be that which thine own brutish silence hath made thee. Or else I should have heard on the other ear: Slothful, and ever to be set light by, the church hath now overcome her late dis-

tresses after the unwearied labours of many her true
servants that stood up in her defence; thou also
wouldst take upon thee to share amongst them of
their joy: but wherefore thou? Where canst thou
show any word or deed of thine which might have
hastened her peace? Whatever thou dost now talk,
or write, or look, is the alms of other men's active
prudence and zeal. Dare not now to say or do anything better than thy former sloth and infancy; or if
thou darest, thou dost impudently to make a thrifty
purchase of boldness to thyself, out of the painful
merits of other men; what before was thy sin,
is now thy duty, to be abject and worthless.
These, and such like lessons as these, I know would
have been my matins duly, and my even-song. But
now by this little diligence, mark what a privilege I
have gained with good men and saints, to claim my
right of lamenting the tribulations of the church, if
she should suffer, when others, that have ventured
nothing for her sake, have not the honour to be admitted mourners. But if she lift up her drooping
head and prosper, among those that have something
more than wished her welfare, I have my charter and
freehold of rejoicing to me and my heirs. Concerning, therefore, this wayward subject against prelaty,
the touching whereof is so distasteful and disquietous
to a number of men, as by what hath been said I
may deserve of charitable readers to be credited, that

· neither envy nor gall hath entered me upon this controversy, but the enforcement of conscience only, and
a preventive fear lest the omitting of this duty should
.be against me, when I would store up to myself the
good provision of peaceful hours; so, lest it should
be still imputed to me, as I have found it hath been,
that some self-pleasing humour of vain-glory hath in-
cited me to contest with men of high estimation, now
while green years are upon my head; from this need-
less surmisal I shall hope to dissuade the intelligent
and equal auditor, if I can but say successfully that
which in this exigent behoveth me; although I would
be heard only, if it might be, by the elegant and
learned reader, to whom principally for a while I
shall beg leave I may address myself. To him it will
be no new thing, though I tell him that if I hunted
after praise, by the ostentation of wit and learning, I
should not write thus out of mine own season, when
I have neither yet completed to my mind the full
circle of my private studies, although I complain not
of any insufficiency to the matter in hand; or were I
ready to my wishes, it were a folly to commit anything elaborately composed to the careless and interrupted listening of these tumultuous times. Next, if
I were wise only to my own ends, I would certainly
take such a subject as of itself might catch applause,
whereas this hath all the disadvantages, on the contrary, and such a subject as the publishing whereof

might be delayed at pleasure, and time enough to pencil it over with all the curious touches of art, even to the perfection of a faultless picture; whereas in this argument the not deferring is of great moment to the good speeding, that if solidity have leisure to do her office, art cannot have much. Lastly, I should not choose this manner of writing, wherein knowing myself inferior to myself, led by the genial power of nature to another task, I have the use, as I may account, but of my left hand. And though I shall be foolish in saying more to this purpose, yet, since it will be such a folly, as wisest men go about to commit, having only confessed and so committed, I may trust with more reason, because with more folly, to have courteous pardon. For although a poet, soaring in the high reason of his fancies, with his garland and singing robes about him, might, without apology, speak more of himself than I mean to do, yet for me, sitting here below in the cool element of prose, a mortal thing among many readers of no empyreal conceit, to venture and divulge unusual things of myself, I shall petition to the gentler sort, it may not be envy to me. I must say, therefore, that after I had for my first years, by the ceaseless diligence and care of my father (whom God recompense!) been exercised to the tongues, and some sciences, as my age would suffer, by sundry masters and teachers, both at home and at the schools, it was found that whether aught was imposed me by them that had the over-looking, or betaken to of mine own choice in English, or other tongue, prosing or versing, but chiefly by this latter, the style, by certain vital signs it had, was likely to live. But much latelier, in the private academies of Italy, whither I was favoured to resort, perceiving that some trifles which I had in memory, composed at under twenty or thereabout (for the manner is, that everyone must give some proof of his wit and reading there), met with acceptance above what was looked for ; and other things which I had shifted in scarcity of books and conveniences to patch up amongst them, were received with written encomiums, which the Italian is not forward to bestow on men of this side of the Alps. I began thus far to assent both to them and divers of my friends here at home, and not less to an inward prompting which now grew daily upon me, that by labour and intense study (which I take to be my portion in this life), joined with the strong propensity of nature, I might perhaps leave something so written to after-times, as they should not willingly let it die. These thoughts at once possessed me, and these other ; that if I were certain to write as men buy leases, for three lives and downward, there ought no regard be sooner had than to God's glory, by the honour and instruction of my country. For which cause, and not only for that I knew it would be hard to arrive at the

second rank among the Latins, I applied myself to
that resolution, which Ariosto followed against the
persuasions of Bembo, to fix all the industry and art
I could unite to the adorning of my native tongue ;
not to make verbal curiosities the end (that were a
toilsome vanity), but to be an interpreter and relater
of the best and sagest things among mine own citizens
throughout this island in the mother dialect. That
what the greatest and choicest wits of Athens, Rome,
or modern Italy, and those Hebrews of old did for
their country, I, in my proportion, with this over and
above, of being a Christian, might do for mine ; not
caring to be once named abroad, though perhaps I
could attain to that, but content with these British
islands as my world ; whose fortune hath hitherto
been, that if the Athenians, as some say, made their
small deeds great and renowned by their eloquent
writers, England hath had her noble achievements
made small by the unskilful handling of monks and
mechanics.

"Time serves not now, and perhaps I might seem
too profuse to give any certain account of what the
mind at home, in the spacious circuits of her musing,
hath liberty to propose to herself, though of highest
hope and hardest attempting ; whether that epic form
whereof the two poems of Homer, and those other
two of Virgil and Tasso, are a diffuse, and the book
of Job a brief model : or whether the rules of

Aristotle herein are strictly to be kept, or nature to be followed, which in them that know art, and use judgment, is no transgression, but an enriching of art : and lastly, what king or knight before the Conquest, might be chosen in whom to lay the pattern of a Christian hero? And as Tasso gave to a prince of Italy his choice whether he would command him to write of Godfrey's expedition against the Infidels, or Belisarius against the Goths, or Charlemain against the Lombards ; if to the instinct of nature, and the emboldening of art aught may be trusted, and that there be nothing adverse in our climate, or the fate of this age, it haply would be no rashness, from an equal diligence and inclination, to present the like offer in our own ancient stories ; or whether those dramatic constitutions, wherein Sophocles and Euripides reign, shall be found more doctrinal and exemplary to a nation. The Scripture also affords us a divine pastoral drama in the Song of Solomon, consisting of two persons, and a double chorus, as Origen rightly judges. And the Apocalypse of St. John is the majestic image of a high and stately tragedy, shutting up and intermingling her solemn scenes and acts with a sevenfold chorus of hallelujahs and harping symphonies; and this my opinion the grave authority of Pareus, commenting that book, is sufficient to confirm. Or if occasion shall lead, to imitate those magnific odes and hymns, wherein Pindarus and

G

Callimachus are in most things worthy, some others
in their frame judicious, in their matter most an end
faulty.   But those frequent songs throughout the law
and prophets beyond all these, not in their divine
argument alone, but in the very critical art of composition, may be easily made appear over all the kinds
of lyric poesy to be incomparable. These abilities,
wheresoever they be found, are the inspired gift of
God, rarely bestowed, but yet to some (though most
abuse) in every nation ; and are of power, beside the
office of a pulpit, to imbreed and cherish in a great
people the seeds of virtue and public civility, to allay
the perturbations of the mind, and set the affections in
right tune ; to celebrate in glorious and lofty hymns
the throne and equipage of God's almightiness, and
what He works, and what He suffers to be wrought
with high providence in His church, to sing victorious
agonies of martyrs and saints, the deeds and triumphs
of just and pious nations, doing valiantly through
faith against the enemies of Christ; to deplore the
general relapses of kingdoms and states from justice
and God's true worship.   Lastly, whatsoever in religion is holy and sublime, in virtue amiable or grave,
whatsoever hath passion or admiration in all the
changes of that which is called fortune from without,
or the wily subtleties and refluxes of man's thoughts
from within ; all these things with a solid and treat-
able smoothness to paint out and describe.   Teaching

over the whole book of sanctity and virtue, through
all the instances of example, with such delight to
those especially of soft and delicious temper, who will
not so much as look upon truth herself, unless they
see her elegantly dressed; that whereas the paths of
honesty and good life appear now rugged and difficult, though they be indeed easy and pleasant, they will
then appear to all men both easy and pleasant, though
they were rugged and difficult indeed. And what a
benefit this would be to our youth and gentry, may
be soon guessed by what we know of the corruption
and bane which they suck in daily from the writings
and interludes of libidinous and ignorant poetasters,
who, having scarce ever heard of that which is the
main consistence of a true poem, the choice of such
persons as they ought to introduce, and what is moral
and decent to each one, do for the most part lay up
vicious principles in sweet pills to be swallowed down,
and make the taste of virtuous documents harsh and
sour. But because the spirit of man cannot demean
itself lively in this body, without some recreating in-
termission of labour and serious things, it were happy
for the commonwealth if our magistrates, as in those
famous governments of old, would take into their
care not only the deciding of our contentious law-
cases and brawls, but the managing of our public
sports and festival pastimes; that they might be, not
such as were authorised a while since, the provoca-

tions of drunkenness and lust, but such as may inure
and harden our bodies by martial exercises to all
warlike skill and performance; and may civilize,
adorn, and make discreet our minds by the learned
and affable meeting of frequent academies, and the
procurement of wise and artful recitations, sweetened
with eloquent and graceful enticements to the love
and practice of justice, temperance, and fortitude,
instructing and bettering the nation at all opportuni-
ties, that the call of wisdom and virtue may be heard
everywhere, as Solomon saith : " She crieth without,
she uttereth her voice in the streets, in the top of high
places, in the chief concourse, and in the openings of
the gates." Whether this may not be, not only in
pulpits, but after another persuasive method, at set
and solemn paneguries, in theatres, porches, or what
other place or way may win most upon the people to
receive at once both recreation and instruction, let
them in authority consult."

From this remarkable passage we see that the idea
of our popular Penny Readings occurred to the mind
of Milton more than two hundred years ago.

"The thing which I had to say, and those intentions which have lived within me ever since I could
conceive myself anything worth to my country, I return to crave excuse that urgent reason hath plucked
from me, by an abortive and foredated discovery.
And the accomplishment of them lies not but in a

power above man's to promise; but that none hath by
more studious ways endeavoured, and with more unwearied spirit that none shall, that I dare almost aver
of myself, as far as life and free leisure will extend.
Neither do I think it shame to covenant with any
knowing reader, that for some few years yet I may go
on trust with him toward the payment of what I am
now indebted, as being a work not to be raised from
the heat of youth, or the vapours of wine ; nor to be
obtained by the invocation of dame memory and her
siren daughters, but by devout prayer to that eternal
Spirit, who can enrich with all utterance and knowledge, and sends out His seraphim, with the hallowed
fire of His altar, to touch and purify the lips of whom
He pleases : to this must be added industrious and
select reading, steady observation, insight into all
seemly and generous arts and affairs ; till which in
some measure be compassed, at mine own peril and
cost, I refuse not to sustain this expectation from
as many as are not loth to hazard so much credulity
upon the best pledges that I can give them. Although it nothing content me to have disclosed thus
much beforehand, but that I trust hereby to make it
manifest with what small willingness I endure to interrupt the pursuit of no less hopes than these, and
leave a calm and pleasing solitariness, fed with cheerful and confident thoughts, to embark in a troubled
sea of noises and hoarse disputes, put from beholding

the bright countenance of truth in the quiet and still
air of delightful studies, to come into the dim reflection of hollow antiquities sold by the seeming bulk,
and there be fain to club quotations with men whose
learning and belief lies in marginal stuffings, who, when
they have, like good sumpters, laid ye down their
horse-loads of citations and fathers at your door, with
a rhapsody of who and who were bishops here or
there, ye may take off their pack-saddles, their day's
work is done, and episcopacy, as they think, stoutly
vindicated. Let any gentle apprehension, that can
distinguish learned pains from unlearned drudgery,
imagine what pleasure or profoundness can be in this,
or what honour to deal against such adversaries. But
were it the meanest under-service, if God by His secretary conscience enjoin it, it were sad for me if I should
draw back; for me especially, now when all men
offer their aid to help, ease, and lighten the difficult
labours of the church, to whose service, by the intentions of my parents and friends, I was destined of a
child, and in mine own resolutions: till coming to
some maturity of years, and perceiving what tyranny
had invaded the church, that he who would take
orders must subscribe slave, and take an oath withal,
which, unless he took with a conscience that would
retch, he must either straight perjure, or split his
faith; I thought it better to prefer a blameless silence
before the sacred office of speaking, bought and begun

with servitude and forswearing. Howsoever, thus church-outed by the prelates, hence may appear the right I have to meddle in these matters, as before the necessity and constraint appeared."

"After this digression, I shall add another reason. Albeit I must confess to be half in doubt whether I should bring it forth or no, it being so contrary to the eye of the world, and the world so potent in most men's hearts, that I shall endanger either not to be regarded, or not to be understood; for who is there almost that measures wisdom by simplicity, strength by suffering, dignity by lowliness? Who is there that counts it first to be last, something to be nothing, and reckons himself of great command in that he is a servant? Yet God, when He meant to subdue the world and hell at once, part of that to salvation, and this wholly to perdition, made choice of no other weapons or auxiliaries than these, whether to save or to destroy. It had been a small mastery for Him to have drawn out His legions into array, and flanked them with His thunder; therefore He sent foolishness to confute wisdom, weakness to bind strength, despisedness to vanquish pride: and this is the great mystery of the gospel made good in Christ Himself, who, as He testifies, came not to be ministered to, but to minister; and must be fulfilled in all His ministers till His second coming."

"But let them chant while they will of prerogatives, we shall tell them of scripture; of custom, we of scripture; of acts and statutes, still of scripture; till the quick and piercing word enter to the dividing of their souls, and the mighty weakness of the gospel throw down the weak mightiness of man's reasoning."

"Truth, I know not how, hath this unhappiness fatal to her, ere she can come to the trial and inspection of the understanding; being to pass through many little wards and limits of the several affections and desires, she cannot shift it, but must put on such colours and attire. as those pathetic handmaids of the soul please to lead her in to their queen : and if she find so much favour with them, they let her pass in her own likeness; if not, they bring her into the presence habited and coloured like a notorious falsehood. And contrary, when any falsehood comes that way, if they like the errand she brings, they are so artful to counterfeit the very shape and visage of truth, that the understanding not being able to discern the fucus (paint) which these enchantresses with such cunning have laid upon the feature, sometimes of truth, sometimes of falsehood interchangeably, sentences for the most part one for the other at the first blush, according to the subtle imposture of these sensual mistresses, that keep the ports and passages between her and the object."

"Now if the Roman censor could, without this juridical sword or saw, strike such a reverence of itself into the most undaunted hearts, as with one single dash of ignominy to put all the senate and knighthood of Rome into a tremble; surely much rather might the heavenly ministry of the evangel bind herself about with far more piercing beams of majesty and awe, by wanting the beggarly help of halings and amercements in the use of her powerful keys. For when the church without temporal support is able to do her great works upon the unforced obedience of men, it argues a divinity about her. But when she thinks to credit and better her spiritual efficacy, and to win herself respect and dread by strutting in the false vizard of worldly authority, it is evident that God is not there, but that her apostolic virtue is departed from her, and hath left her keycold."

The church, though now under the Presbyterian form of government, still retained, in Milton's opinion, the power of the keys—the power of exercising church discipline and administering ecclesiastical censure, and even excommunication. She possessed an apostolic virtue, was still a divine institution. It is curious to see here and elsewhere our great Puritan contending for that godly discipline which prevailed in the primitive church, but which has long been lost to us—a fact which the Church of England acknowledges and deplores year by year in her Commination Service. The truth is, he never wholly shook off the

Church of England training he received in his youth,
and up to the time that he had abandoned all intention of taking Holy Orders. It appears equally in
his poetry and his prose. In better times, and had
he been better treated and appreciated, we should
have seen him Deacon, Priest, and Bishop; and what
a Bishop would he have made!—a second, and, if
possible, still more eloquent Jeremy Taylor!

But we must pass on to his interesting theory of
church discipline, as expressed in this book.

"The minister of each congregation" is to be
"God's spiritual deputy" in this matter, "who, being
best acquainted with his own flock, hath best reason
to know all the secretest diseases likely to be there.
Sometimes, also, not the elders alone, but the whole
body of the church is interested in the work of discipline, as oft as public satisfaction is given by those
that have given public scandal. If anything may be
done to imbreed in us a generous and Christianly
reverence one of another, the very nurse and guardian of piety and virtue, it cannot sooner be than by
such a discipline in the church, as may use us to have
in awe the assemblies of the faithful, and to count it
a thing most grievous, next to the grieving of God's
Spirit, to offend those whom He hath put in authority. And this will be accompanied with a religious
dread of being outcast from the company of saints,
and from the fatherly protection of God in His

church, to consort with the devil and his angels. But there is yet a more ingenuous and noble degree of honest shame, whereby men bear an inward reverence toward their own persons. And if the love of God, as a fire sent from heaven to be ever kept alive upon the altars of our hearts, be the first principle of all godly and virtuous actions in men, this pious and just honouring of ourselves is the second, and may be thought as the radical moisture and fountain-head, whence every laudable and worthy enterprise issues forth. Something I confess it is to be ashamed of evil-doing in the presence of any; and to reverence the opinion and the countenance of a good man rather than a bad, fearing most in his sight to offend, goes so far as almost to be virtuous; yet this is but still the fear of infamy, and many such, when they find themselves alone, saving their reputation, will compound with other scruples, and come to a close treaty with their dearer vices in secret. But he that holds himself in reverence and due esteem, both for the dignity of God's image upon him, and for the price of his redemption, which he thinks is visibly marked upon his forehead, accounts himself both a fit person to do the noblest and godliest deeds, and much better worth than to deject and defile, with such a debasement, and such a pollution as sin is, himself so highly ransomed and ennobled to a new friendship and filial relation with God. Nor can he fear so much the offence and reproach of others, as he dreads and would blush at the reflection of his own severe and modest eye upon himself, if it should see him doing or imagining that which is sinful, though in the deepest secresy. How shall a man know to do himself this right, how to perform his honourable duty of estimation and respect towards his own soul and body? Which way will lead him best to this hill-top of sanctity and goodness, above which there is no higher ascent but to the love of God, which from this self-pious regard cannot be asunder? No better way, doubtless, than to let him duly understand that as he is called by the high calling of God, to be holy and pure, so is he by the same appointment ordained, and by the church's call admitted to such offices of discipline in the church, to which his own spiritual gifts, by the example of apostolic institution, have authorized him. They who have an unworthy and abject opinion of themselves, approach to holy duties with a slavish fear, and to unholy doings with a familiar boldness. For seeing such a wide and terrible distance between religious things and themselves, they fear religion with such a fear as loves not, and think the purity of the gospel too pure for them, and that any uncleanness is more suitable to their unconsecrated estate."

"Thus, therefore, the minister assisted attends his heavenly and spiritual cure. His end is to recover all that is of man, both soul and body, to an everlasting health. Two heads of evil he has to cope with, ignorance and malice. Against the former he provides the daily manna of incorruptible doctrine, not at those set meals only in public, but as oft as he shall know that each infirmity or constitution requires. Against the latter, with all the branches thereof, he, beginning at the prime causes and roots of the disease, sends in those two divine ingredients of most cleansing power to the soul, admonition and reproof. And he that will not let these pass into him, though he be the greatest king, must be thought to remain impure within. As soon, therefore, as it may be discerned that the Christian patient hath disordered his diet, and spread an ill-humour through his veins, immediately disposing to a sickness, the minister speeds him betimes to overtake that diffused malignance with some gentle potion of admonishment. This not succeeding after once or twice, or oftener, in the presence of two or three his faithful brethren appointed thereto, he advises him to be more careful of his dearest health, and what it is that he so rashly hath let down into the divine vessel of his soul, God's temple. If this obtain not, he then, with the counsel of more assistants, who are informed of what diligence hath been already used, with more speedy remedies lays nearer to the entrenched causes of his distemper, not sparing such fervent and well-aimed reproofs as may best give him to see the dangerous estate wherein he is. To this also his brethren and friends entreat, exhort, adjure; and all these endeavours, as there is hope left, are more or less repeated. But if neither the regard of himself, nor the reverence of his elders and friends prevail with him to leave his vicious appetite, then as the time urges, such engines of terror God hath given into the hand of his minister, as to search the tenderest angles of the heart: one while he shakes his stubbornness with racking convulsions nigh despair; other whiles with deadly corrosive he gripes the very roots of his faulty liver to bring him to life through the entry of death. Hereto the whole church beseech him, beg of him, deplore him, pray for him. After all this performed with what patience and attendance is possible, and no relenting on his part, having done the utmost of their cure, in the name of God and of the church they dissolve their fellowship with him, and holding forth the dreadful sponge of excommunion, pronounce him wiped out of the list of God's inheritance, and in the custody of Satan till he repent. Which horrid sentence, though it touch neither life nor limb, nor any worldly possession, yet has it such a penetrating force, that swifter than any chemical sulphur, or that lightning which harms not the skin, and rifles the entrails, it scorches the inmost soul. Yet even this terrible denouncement is left to the church for no other cause but to be as a rough and vehement cleansing medicine, where the malady is obdurate, a mortifying to life, a kind of saving by undoing. And it may be truly said, that as the mercies of wicked men are cruelties, so the cruelties of the church are mercies. For if repentance sent from heaven meet this lost wanderer, and draw him out of that steep journey wherein he was hasting towards destruction, to come and reconcile to the church, if he bring with him his bill of health, and that he is now clear of infection, and of no danger to the other sheep; then with incredible expressions of joy, all his brethren receive him, and set before him those perfumed banquets of Christian consolation; with precious ointments bathing and fomenting the old, and now to be forgotten stripes, which terror and shame had inflicted; and thus with heavenly solaces they cheer up his humble remorse, till he regain his first health and felicity. This is the approved way, which the gospel prescribes, these are the spiritual weapons of holy censure, and ministerial warfare, not carnal, but mighty through God to the pulling down of strongholds, casting down imaginations, and every high thing that exalteth itself against the knowledge of God, and bringing into captivity every thought to the obedience of Christ."

This is a specimen of Milton's complete mastery of the English language, of his own peculiar method of building his lofty prose, piling up elaborate sentence upon sentence interlaced with simile upon simile, rearing and constructing with consummate skill and perseverance, a stately and gorgeous edifice of matchless strength and beauty. But curious, instructive, and suggestive as is the remarkable passage just cited, for all practical purposes it is utterly impracticable, extravagant, and visionary, as almost all his projects and schemes of reformation undoubtedly were ; and in this way we account for his unpopularity even with the scholar and antiquarian.   .

Let us take another passage from the conclusion of this treatise, equally striking, grand, imaginative, and curious, but to which we are able to attach little meaning and less practical worth. We gather from it his hatred to prelacy, but nothing more. Here let us call to mind how, in his early days, prelates, instead of calling forth his hatred, inspired his muse. His third elegy is a tribute of praise to the memory of Lancelot Andrewes, Bishop of Winchester, who died in 1826 ; and his third piece in his Sylvarum Liber is another graceful tribute on the death of Nicholas Felton, Bishop of Ely, which happened not many days after.

" I cannot better liken the state and person of a king than to that mighty Nazarite Samson, who being disciplined from his birth in the precepts and the practice of temperance and sobriety, without the strong drink of injurious and excessive desires, grows

up to a noble strength and perfection with his illustrious and sunny locks, the laws, waving and curving
about his godlike shoulders. And while he keeps
them about him undiminished and unshorn, he may
with the jawbone of an ass, that is, with the word of
his meanest officer, suppress and put to confusion
thousands of those that rise against his just power.
But laying down his head among the strumpet flatteries of prelates, while he sleeps and thinks no harm,
they wickedly shaving off all those bright and
weighty tresses of his law, and just prerogatives,
which were his ornament and strength, deliver him
over to indirect and violent counsels, which, as those
Philistines, put out the fair and far-sighted eyes of his
natural discerning, and make him grind in the prison-
house of their sinister ends and practices upon him;
till he, knowing this prelatical rasor to have bereft
him of his wonted might, nourish again his puissant
hair, the golden beams of law and right; and they
sternly shook, thunder with ruin upon the heads of
those his evil counsellors, but not without great
affliction to himself. This is the sum of their loyal
service to kings; yet these are the men that still cry,
The king, the king, the Lord's anointed! We grant
it; and wonder how they came to light upon anything so true; and wonder more, if kings be the
Lord's anointed, how they dare thus oil over and
besmear so holy an unction with the corrupt and

H

putrid ointment of their base flatteries; which while
they smooth the skin, strike inward and envenom the
lifeblood."

The next and last passage we shall quote for the
sake of the old and unusual word which occurs in it,
giving Archbishop Trench's explanation of it from his
Select Glossary.

"Prelaty seems to have had this fatal gift in her
nativity, that whatsoever she should touch, it should
turn, not to gold, but to the dross and scum of
slavery, breeding and settling both in the bodies and
the souls of all such as do not in time, with the sovereign *treacle* of sound doctrine, provide to fortify
their hearts against her hierarchy." 'At present
'treacle' means only the sweet syrup of molasses, but
was a word once of far wider reach and far nobler
significance, having come to us from afar, and by steps
which are curious to be traced. They are these: the
Greeks, in anticipation of modern homœopathy, called
a supposed antidote to the viper's bite, which was
composed of the viper's flesh, θηριακή, from θηρίον, a
name often given to the viper, as in Acts xxviii., 5;
of this came the Latin 'theriaca,' and our 'theriac,' of
which, or rather of the Latin form, 'treacle' is but a
popular corruption.' He does not cite this passage
from Milton, but in one from Gurnall we find even
the same epithet applied, 'The saints' experiences
help them to a *sovereign treacle* made of the scorpion's

own flesh (which they through Christ have slain), and that hath a virtue above all other to expel the venom of Satan's temptations from the heart.'—*The Christian in Complete Armour*, c. ix., § 2.

ANIMADVERSIONS UPON THE REMONSTRANT'S DEFENCE AGAINST SMECTYMNUUS.

THIS, the least pleasing of Milton's earlier contro-versial works, was the fourth Treatise which he put forth in 1641. It is arranged in the form of a dialogue, and is coarse and commonplace. Smectym-nuus was a pamphlet written by five Presbyterian divines, the initial letters of whose names form the appellation, Smectymnuus, namely, Stephen Marshal, Edmund Calamy, Thomas Young, who was Milton's tutor, Matthew Newcomen, and William Spurstow. Bishop Hall replied to it, and he is the Remonstrant against whom our author enters the lists. The work before us was answered by a son of Bishop Hall, assisted by his father, in the 'Modest Confutation against a slanderous and scurrilous Libel,' which in turn called forth the Apology for Smectymnuus in 1642, 'a noble and justifiable burst of egotism, richly teeming with beautiful thoughts, full of youthful and cheering reminiscences, and vehemently eloquent.' So writes one of his editors. To this we shall pro-ceed, passing by the Animadversions as containing nothing meriting observation or preservation, in spite of Lord Macaulay's extraordinary assertion that there are magnificent passages occurring in it. We are at a loss to conceive which he refers to. Probably that at the close of the fourth Section, an apostrophe to the Deity, but how unlike the one with which he concludes his Treatise of Reformation, which we have already given. We have read it more than once, and can discover in it no "sentence of a venturous edge, uttered in the height of zeal"—nothing that touches a respondent chord in the soul—nothing that exalts, invigorates, or inspires. Perhaps we ought to except one sentence, which we regard as a prophetic allusion to the Paradise Lost, and is therefore interesting, and worth quoting. It is this, referring to the time when God shall have settled peace in the church and righteous judgment in the kingdom. "And he, that now for haste snatches up a plain ungarnished present as a thank-offering to Thee, which could not be deferred in regard of Thy so many late deliverances wrought for us one upon another, may then perhaps take up a harp, and sing Thee an elaborate song to generations."

AN APOLOGY FOR SMECTYMNUUS.

THIS Treatise is valuable for that noble egotism and justifiable self-assertion which are its characteristics. Thus, parenthetically, as it were, and incidentally, we are made acquainted, on the very best authority, with many anecdotes, circumstances, habits, thoughts, and feelings connected with the life of Milton, which are most interesting, instructive, and essential to everyone who would rightly understand the complex character of this truly wonderful man. Even when the connexion with the matter immediately in hand hardly seems to justify it, he passes on to speak of himself, his intentions, hopes, and aspirations, and reveals his most secret and private thoughts with an ingenuous and enchanting simplicity. Never was any man more transparent. He had nothing to conceal ; he lived and acted in the spirit of his own noble sonnet, composed on arriving at his twenty-third year—

> " All is, if I have grace to use it so,
> As ever in my great Taskmaster's eye."

" If to that same great difficulty of well-doing what we certainly know were not added in most men as great a carelessness of knowing what they and others ought to do, we had been long ere this much further on our way to some degree of peace and happiness in this kingdom. But since our sinful neglect of practising that which we know to be undoubtedly true and good hath brought forth among us so great a difficulty now to know that which otherwise might be soon learnt; I resolved (of what small moment soever I might be thought) to stand on that side where I saw both the plain authority of Scripture leading, and the reason of justice and equity persuading; with this opinion, which esteems it more unlike a Christian to be a cold neuter in the cause of the church, than the law of Solon made it punishable after a sedition in the State."

So Dryden

> '—— neuters in their middle way of steering,
> Are neither fish, nor flesh, nor good red herring.'

" And because I observe that fear and dull disposition, lukewarmness and sloth, are not seldomer wont to cloak themselves under the affected name of moderation, than true and lively zeal is customably disparaged with the term of indiscretion, bitterness, and choler; I could not to my thinking honour a good cause more from the heart than by defending it earnestly, as oft as I could judge it to behove me, notwithstanding any false name that could be invented to wrong or undervalue an honest meaning.

Wherein if it be lawful to attribute somewhat to gifts of God's imparting, which I boast not, but thankfully acknowledge, and fear also lest at my certain account they be reckoned to me rather many than few; or if it be but justice not to defraud of due esteem the wearisome labours and studious watchings, wherein I have spent and tired out almost a whole youth, I shall not distrust to be acquitted of presumption. However, now against the rancour of an evil tongue, I must be forced to proceed from the unfeigned and diligent inquiry of my own conscience at home to give a more true account of myself abroad than this modest confuter, as he calls himself, hath given of me. Albeit, that in doing this I shall be sensible of two things, which to me will be nothing pleasant; the one is, that not unlikely I shall be thought too much a party in mine own cause, and therein to see least: the other, that I shall be put unwillingly to molest the public view with the vindication of a private name; as if it were worth the while that the people should care whether such a one were thus or thus. Yet those I entreat who have found the leisure to read that name, however of small repute, unworthily defamed, would be so good and so patient as to hear the same person not unneedfully defended."

"I will not deny but that the best apology against false accusers is silence and sufferance, and honest deeds set against dishonest words. But when I discerned the intent of this confuter was not so much to smite at me, as through me to render odious the truth which I had written, I conceived myself to be now not as mine own person, but as a member incorporate into that truth whereof I was persuaded, and whereof I had declared openly to be a partaker. Whereupon I thought it my duty not to leave on my garment the least spot or blemish in good name, so long as God should give me to say that which might wipe it off, lest those disgraces which I ought to suffer, if it so befall me, for my religion, through my default religion be made liable to suffer for me."

" For doubtless that indeed according to art is most eloquent, which turns and approaches nearest to nature, from whence it came; and they express nature best, who in their lives least wander from her safe leading. So that how he should be truly eloquent who is not withal a good man, I see not."

" I must be thought, if this libeller (for now he shows himself to be so) can find belief, after an inordinate and riotous youth spent at the university, to have been at length ' vomited out thence.' For which commodious lie I thank him, for it hath given me an apt occasion to acknowledge publicly with all grateful mind, that more than ordinary favour and respect, which I found above any of my equals at the hands of those courteous and learned men, the fellows of that college wherein I spent some years : who at my parting, after I had taken two degrees, as the manner is, signified many ways how much better it would content them that I would stay; as by many letters full of kindness and loving respect, both before that time, and long after, I was assured of their singular good affection towards me."

We have here Milton's flat denial of what some of his biographers have too easily asserted that he was ever rusticated or expelled from college.

"But he follows me to the city, 'and where my morning haunts are he wisses not.' I will tell him. Those morning haunts are where they should be, at home; not sleeping, or concocting the surfeits of an irregular feast, but up and stirring, in winter often ere the sound of any bell awake men to labour, or to devotion; in summer as oft with the bird that first rouses, or not much tardier, to read good authors, or cause them to be read, till the attention be weary, or memory have its full fraught; then, with useful and generous labours preserving the body's health and hardiness to render lightsome, clear, and not lumpish obedience to the mind, to the cause of religion, and our country's liberty, when it shall require firm hearts in sound bodies to stand and cover their stations, rather than to see the ruin of our protestation, and the enforcement of a slavish life.

"These are the morning practices: proceed now to the afternoon; 'in playhouses,' he says, 'and the

bordelloes.' Your intelligence, unfaithful spy of
Canaan ?"

His opponent has before confessed that he had
no certain notice of him further than what he gathers
from his writings. "In the Animadversions, saith he,
I find the mention of old cloaks, false beards, and
night-walkers; therefore the animadverter haunts
playhouses and bordelloes; for if he did not how
could he speak of such gear?" Having turned the
tables on the confuter he proceeds to say, "Since
there is such necessity to the hearsay of a tire, a peri-
wig, or a vizard, that plays must have been seen,
what difficulty was there in that? when in the col-
leges so many of the young divines, and those in next
aptitude to divinity, have been seen so often upon the
stage. There, while they acted and overacted, among
other young scholars, I was a spectator; they thought
themselves gallant men, and I thought them fools;
they made sport, and I laughed ; they mispronounced
and I disliked; and, to make up the atticism, they
were out, and I hissed." Milton seems to have been
always unpopular both in boyhood and manhood ; he
had little or no humour in his composition, and his
attempts at it are ludicrous. He then rebuts the
absurd and unfounded charges, and "in a way not
often trod discovers his inmost thoughts, through the
course of his years and studies."   .

"I had my time, as others have, who have good

learning bestowed upon them, to be sent to those
places where, the opinion was, it might be soonest attained ; and as the manner is, was not unstudied in
those authors which are most commended. Whereof
some were grave orators and historians, whose matter
methought I loved indeed, but as my age then was,
so I understood them ; others were the smooth elegiac
poets, whom both for the pleasing sound of their
numerous writing, which in imitation I found most
easy, and most agreeable to nature's part in me, and
I was so allured to read, that no recreation came to
me better welcome. I thought with myself by every
instinct and presage of nature, which is not wont to
be false, that what emboldened them to this task,
might with such diligence as they used embolden me.
And if I found those authors anywhere speaking unworthy things of themselves, or unchaste of those
names which before they had extolled ; this effect it
wrought with me, from that time forward their art I
still applauded, but the men I deplored ; and above
them all, preferred the two famous renowners of
Beatrice and Laura (Dante and Petrarch), who never
write but honour of them to whom they devote their
verse, displaying sublime and pure thoughts, without
transgression. And, long it was not after, when I
was confirmed in this opinion, that he who would not
be frustrate of his hope to write well hereafter in
laudable things, ought himself to be a true poem ;

that is, a composition and pattern of the best and honourablest things; not presuming to sing high praises of heroic men, or famous cities, unless he have in himself the experience and the practice of all that which is praiseworthy."

This magnificent and glorious sentence reminds us of those lines in Cowley's Ode on Liberty (he was Milton's junior by ten years),

> ' If life should a well-order'd Poem be
>   (In which he only hits the white,
> Who joins true Profit with the best Delight),
> The more Heroic strain let others take,
>   Mine the Pindaric way I'll make.
> The matter shall be grave, the numbers loose and free.'

But let us proceed with the interesting autobiography before us of one who was indeed himself a true poem, and of the most heroic strain.

" Next, readers, that I may tell ye whither my younger feet wandered; I betook me among those lofty fables and romances which recount in solemn cantos the deeds of knighthood founded by our victorious kings, and from hence had in renown over all Christendom. There I read it in the oath of every knight, that he should defend, to the expense of his best blood, the honour and chastity of virgin or matron; from whence even then I learned what a noble virtue chastity sure must be, to the defence of which so many worthies, by such a dear adventure of themselves, had sworn. And if I found in the story afterward, any of them, by word or deed, breaking that oath, I judged it the same fault of the poet, as that which is attributed to Homer, to have written indecent things of the gods. Only this my mind gave me, that every free and gentle spirit, without that that oath, ought to be born a knight, nor needed to expect the gilt spur, or the laying of a sword upon his shoulder to stir him up, both by his counsel and his arms, to secure and protect the weakness of any attempted chastity. So that even these books, which to many others have been the fuel of wantonness and loose living, I cannot think how, unless by divine indulgence, proved to me so many incitements to the love and stedfast observation of virtue.

"Thus, from the laureat fraternity of poets, riper years, and the ceaseless round of study and reading, led me to the shady spaces of philosophy ; but chiefly to the divine volumes of Plato, and his equal Xenophon : where, if I should tell ye what I learnt of chastity and love, I mean that which is truly so, whose charming cup is only virtue, which she bears in hand to those who are worthy (the rest are cheated with a thick intoxicating potion, which a certain sorceress, the abuser of love's name, carries about) ; and how the first and chiefest office of love begins and ends in the soul, producing those happy twins of her divine generation, knowledge and virtue. With such abstracted sublimities as these, it might be worth your listening, readers, as I may one day hope to have ye in a still time, when there shall be no chiding, not in these noises.

"Last of all, not in time, but as perfection is last, that care was ever had of me, with my earliest capacity, not to be negligently trained in the precepts of the Christian religion : this that I have hitherto related hath been to show that though Christianity had been but slightly taught me, yet a certain reservedness of natural disposition, and moral discipline, learnt out of the noblest philosophy, an honest haughtiness, and self-esteem, either of what I was, or what I might be (which let envy call pride), were enough to keep me still above all low descents of mind, and in disdain of vice."

David Masson says, ' Were we to define in one word our impression of the prevailing tone, the characteristic mood and disposition of Milton's mind, even in his early youth, we should say, that it consisted in a deep and habitual *seriousness.* We doubt not he is thinking of himself and his own childhood, at all events, the lines well describe his own youth, when he says, in the first book of Paradise Regained—

> " When I was yet a child, no childish play
> To me was pleasing ; all my mind was set
> Serious to learn and know, and thence to do
> What might be public good ; myself I thought
> Born to that end, born to promote all truth,
> All righteous things : therefore, above my years,
> The law of God I read, and found it sweet,
> Made it my whole delight."

'The outward manifestation of this seriousness,' again to use the words of Masson, ' of this solemn and even austere demeanour of mind, was a life of pure and devout observance. He who does not lay stress on this, knows not and loves not Milton !' But we proceed with our extract.

" But having had the doctrine of holy scripture unfolding those chaste and high mysteries, with timeliest care infused, that " the body is for the Lord, and the Lord for the body ;" thus also I argued to myself, that if unchastity in a woman, whom St. Paul terms the glory of man, be such a scandal and dishonour, then certainly in a man, who is both the image and glory of God, it must, though commonly not so thought, be much more deflouring and dishonourable ; in that he sins both against his own body, which is the perfecter sex, and his own glory, which is in the woman ; and, that which is worst, against the image and glory of God, which is in himself. Nor did I slumber over that place expressing such high rewards of ever accompanying the Lamb, with those celestial songs to others inapprehensible, but not to those who were not defiled with women, which doubtless means fornication ; for marriage must not be called a defilement."

He next defends the vehement style of these Animadversions, which he wrote against the Remonstrant in defence of Smectymnuus.

"Doth not Christ Himself teach the highest things
by the similitude of old bottles and patched clothes?
Doth He not illustrate best things by things most
evil? His own coming to be as a thief in the night,
and the righteous man's wisdom to that of an unjust
steward? In the teaching of men diversely tempered,
different ways are to be tried. The Baptist, we know,
was a strict man, remarkable for austerity and set
order of life. Our Saviour, who had all gifts in Him,
was Lord to express His indoctrinating power in
what sort Him best seemed; sometimes by a mild
and familiar converse; sometimes with plain and im-
partial home-speaking, regardless of those whom the
auditors might think he should have had in more respect; otherwhile, with bitter and ireful rebukes, if
not teaching, yet leaving excuseless those His wilful
impugners. What was all in Him was divided among
many others, the teachers of His church; some to be
severe, and ever of a sad gravity, that they may win
such, and check sometimes those who be of nature
over-confident and jocund; others were sent more
cheerful and free, that they who are so tempered
may have by whom they might be drawn to salvation,
and they who are too scrupulous, and dejected of
spirit, might be often strengthened with wise consola-
tions and revivings: no man being forced wholly to
dissolve that groundwork of nature which God created
in him, the sanguine to empty out all his sociable

I

liveliness, the choleric to expel quite the unsinning predominance of his anger ; but that each radical humour and passion, wrought upon and corrected as it ought, might be made the proper mould and foundation of every man's peculiar gifts and virtues. Some also were indued with a staid moderation and soundness of argument, to teach and convince the rational and sober-minded ; yet not therefore that to be thought the only expedient course of teaching, for in times of opposition, when either against new heresies arising, or old corruptions to be reformed, this cool, unpassionate mildness of positive wisdom is not enough to damp and astonish the proud resistance of carnal and false doctors, then (that I may have leave to soar awhile as the poets use) Zeal, whose substance is ethereal, arming in complete diamond, ascends his fiery chariot, drawn with two blazing meteors, figured like beasts, but of a higher breed than any the zodiac yields, resembling two of those four which Ezekiel and St. John saw ; the one visaged like a lion, to express power, high authority, and indignation ; the other of countenance like a man, to cast derision and scorn upon perverse and fraudulent seducers : with these the invincible warrior, Zeal, shaking loosely the slack reins, drives over the heads of scarlet prelates, and such as are insolent to maintain traditions, bruising their stiff necks under his flaming wheels.

"Thus did the true prophets of old combat with

the false : thus Christ Himself, the fountain of meekness, found acrimony enough to be still galling and
vexing the Pharisees. But ye will say these had immediate warrant from God to be thus bitter ; and I
say, so much the plainer is it proved that there may
be a sanctified bitterness against the enemies of
truth."

"The Spirit of God, who is purity itself, when He
would reprove any fault severely, or but relate things
done or said with indignation by others, abstains not
from some words not civil at other times to be
spoken. But these, they will say, were honest words
in that age when they were spoken. Which is more
than any rabbin can prove ; and certainly had God
been so minded, He could have picked such words as
should never have come into abuse. And thus I take
it to be manifest that indignation against men and
their actions notoriously bad hath leave and authority ofttimes to utter such words and phrases, as in
common talk were not so mannerly to use : that ye
may know, not only as the historian speaks, " that all
those things for which men plough, build, or sail,
obey virtue," but that all words, and whatsoever may
be spoken, shall at some time in an unwonted manner
wait upon her purposes."

A similar passage to this occurs in the "Authoris
pro se Defensio," vol. ii., p. 240, Dr. Birch's edition.

" But he proceeds, ' a rich widow, or a lecture, or

both, would content me :' whereby I perceive him to
be more ignorant in his art of divining than any
gipsy. For this I cannot omit without ingratitude to
that Providence above, who hath ever bred me up in
plenty, although my life hath not been unexpensive
in learning, and voyaging about ; so long as it shall
please Him to lend me what He hath hitherto thought
good, which is enough to serve me in all honest and
liberal occasions, and something over besides, I were
unthankful to that highest bounty, if I should make
myself so poor as to solicit needily any such kind of
rich hopes as this fortune-teller dreams of. And that
he may further learn how his astrology is wide all
the houses of heaven in spelling marriages, I care not
if I tell him thus much professedly, though it be the
losing of my rich hopes, as he calls them, that I think
with them who, both in prudence and elegance of
spirit, would choose a virgin of mean fortunes, honest-
ly bred, before the wealthiest widow."

Here we may remark that Milton selected his three
wives out of the virgin state.

 " His next venom he utters against a prayer which
he found in the Animadversions ; he dislikes it, and
I therefore like it the better. Neither was it a
prayer, so much as a hymn in prose, frequent both in
the prophets, and in human authors ; therefore, the
style was greater than for an ordinary prayer." 'The
muse of prose-literature,' observes David Masson

' has been very hardly dealt with. We see not why, in prose, there should not be much of that mighty licence in the fantastic, that measured riot, that unabashed dalliance with the extreme and the beautiful, which the world allows, by prescription to verse. All speed, then, to the prose invasion of the peculiar realm of verse; and the farther the conquest can proceed, perhaps the better in the end for both parties. The time is perhaps coming when the best prose shall be more like verse than it now is, and the best verse shall not disdain a certain resemblance to prose.'

"If we have indeed given a bill of divorce to popery and superstition, why do we not say as to a divorced wife, "Those things which are yours take them all with you, and they shall sweep after you"? Why were we not thus wise at our parting from Rome? Ah! like a crafty adulteress, she forgot not all her smooth looks and enticing words at her parting: "Yet keep these letters, these tokens, and these few ornaments; I am not all so greedy of what is mine, let them preserve with you the memory"—of what I am? No, but—"of what I was; once fair and lovely in your eyes." Thus did those tenderhearted reformers dotingly suffer themselves to be overcome. And she, like a witch, but with a contrary policy, did not take something of theirs, that she still might have power to bewitch them, but for the same

intent left something of her own behind her."   " But
now, readers, we have the port within sight; his last
section, which is no deep one, remains only to be
forded, and then the wished shore."

" I that was erewhile the ignorant, on the sudden
by his permission am now granted "to know something."   And that " such a volley of expressions" he
hath met withal, " as he would never desire to have
them better clothed."   For me, readers, although I
cannot say that I am utterly untrained in those rules
which best rhetoricians have given, or unacquainted with
those examples which the prime authors of eloquence
have written in any learned tongue; yet true eloquence I find to be none, but the serious and hearty
love of truth: and that whose mind soever is fully
possessed with a fervent desire to know good things,
and with the dearest charity to infuse the knowledge
of them into others, when such a man would speak,
his words, like so many nimble and airy servitors,
trip about him at command, and in well-ordered files,
as he would wish, fall aptly into their own places."

THE DOCTRINE AND DISCIPLINE OF DIVORCE;

RESTORED TO THE GOOD OF BOTH SEXES.

In Two Books.

To the Parliament of England with the Assembly.

IN the year 1644 Milton produced this extraordinary work, his brief Treatise on Education, and his incomparable Areopagitica. He had a short time previously been married to his first wife, who, after one month of wedded life, suddenly returned to her father, and stayed with him three years. On hearing that he meditated a divorce, she as suddenly threw herself at his feet and obtained his forgiveness. It was to justify his resolution of being divorced that he wrote the present work, which will not detain us long, but we shall hope to rescue from out this mass of trash a few sentences of transcendant beauty. He professes " with much labour to have first found out, or at least first published, to the manifest good of Christendom, that which, calling to witness everything mortal and immortal, he believes unfeignedly to be true; and then he doubts not but with one gentle stroking to wipe away ten thousand tears out of the

life of man." Such was his sincerity even when most
erring. 'This elaborate discussion,' writes Warton
on his eleventh sonnet which is entitled "On the
detraction which followed upon my writing certain
Treatises," 'unworthy in many respects of Milton,
and in which much acuteness of argument, and com-
prehension of reading, were idly thrown away, was
received with contempt, or rather ridicule. He held
that disagreement of mind was a better cause of separation than adultery. Here was a fair opening for
the laughers. For this doctrine our author was summoned before the Lords. But they not approving
his accusers, the presbyterian clergy, or thinking the
business too speculative, he was quickly dismissed.
On this occasion Milton commenced hostilities against
the presbyterians,' and joined the independents. His
conjugal life is anything but pleasant to contemplate.
Perhaps so laborious a student, so sensitive, and stern,
and unbending a character had better have remained
single. That he was not averse to marriage is evident
from his essaying it three times. It was not every
woman who could be a help-meet for such a mind as
his, or make him happy. But Mary Powell was the
last person we should have expected him to choose.
No wonder such a marriage proved an unhappy one.
He entertained the most exalted views of love, marriage, and domestic felicity, regarding a true woman
with the utmost reverence as the companion of man's

intellect, the remedy of loneliness, "another self, a second self, a very self itself." "Cleave to a wife, but let her be a wife, let her be a meet help, a solace, not a nothing, not an adversary, not a desertrice." The prime end of marriage is, 'the mutual society, help, and comfort, that the one ought to have of the other, both in prosperity and adversity.' This failing, divorce became a duty in Milton's opinion. Our surprise is that a mind so rightly constituted as was his could go wrong in this matter. That he was extremely susceptible of the softer passions is evident from the general tenour of his writings, and from the fact that he was in love when he was nineteen, as we learn from his seventh Latin Elegy. Who the object of this boyish passion was it is impossible to say. It seems to have been unreturned, and her heart to have been created of hard adamant. She was quickly and for ever separated from him, but he felt it most keenly, as these verses show; and the lovesick youth laments, ·

"Nescio cur, miser est suaviter omnis amans."

"I know not why, every lover is sweetly wretched." Henceforth he prays, if ever it should be his lot to love again, that one dart may pierce the breast of two lovers. Alas! his prayer was doomed never to be answered, except, perhaps, for one short year. It was about this time, while at Cambridge, the following adventure, which, however, is a mere tradition, and rests on no authority, happened to him. And we cannot do better than describe it in the words of 'Satan' Montgomery.

> ' There is a tale—and let it live
> Such life as fond romance can give,—
> That once as slumb'ring Milton lay
> In umbrage from the noon-warm day,
> Beneath the twilight of a tree,
> That arch'd its waving canopy,
> A maiden saw his sleeping face,
> And, spell-bound with its beauteous grace,
> Her wonder in sweet song express'd,
> And placed it on the poet's breast :—
> "If eyes when *shut* the heart can take,
> How bright their vict'ry when *awake !*"
> Oh! who can tell what beauty flowed
> From feelings by such words bestow'd ?
> The Eve of his enchanted thought,
> From hues of nature's heaven was wrought,
> And she, of Paradise the queen,
> Embodied what his soul had seen.'

But we must pass on to our selections, which will prove the truth of these remarks.

"If it were seriously asked (and it would be no untimely question), renowned parliament, select assembly! who, of all teachers and masters that have ever taught, hath drawn the most disciples after him, both in religion and in manners? it might be not untruly answered, custom. Though virtue be commended for the most persuasive in her theory, and conscience, in the plain demonstration of the spirit, finds most evincing; yet whether it be the secret of divine will, or the original blindness we are born in, so it happens for the most part that custom still is

silently received for the best instructor. Except it
be because her method is so glib and easy, in some
manner like to that vision of Ezekiel, rolling up her
sudden book of implicit knowledge, for him that will
to take and swallow down at pleasure, which puffs up
unhealthily a certain big face of pretended learning,
and not only in private mars our education, but also
in public is the common climber into every chair,
where either religion is preached, or law reported;
filling each estate of life and profession with abject
and servile principles, depressing the high and heaven-
born spirit of man far beneath the condition wherein
either God created him or sin hath sunk him. To
pursue the allegory, custom being but a mere face,
as echo is a mere voice, rests not in her unaccomplish-
ment, until by secret inclination she accorporate herself with error, who, being a blind and serpentine
body, without a head, willingly accepts what he wants,
and supplies what her incompleteness went seeking.
Hence it is that error supports custom, custom coun-
tenances error; and these two between them would
persecute and chase away all truth and solid wisdom
out of human life, were it not that God, rather than
man, once in many ages calls together the prudent
and religious counsels of men, deputed to repress the
encroachments, and to work off the inveterate blots
and obscurities wrought upon our minds by the subtle
insinuating of error and custom. Against which no-

torious injury and abuse of man's free soul, to testify
and oppose the utmost that study and true labour can
attain, the duty and the right of an instructed Christian calls me through the chance of good or evil report, to be the sole advocate of a discountenanced truth:
a high enterprise, lords and commons, a high enterprise and a hard, and such as every seventh son of a
seventh son does not venture on."

Brand, in his *Popular Antiquities*, vol. iii, p. 265,
says, 'The seventh son of a seventh son is accounted
an infallible doctor, having an intuitive knowledge of
the art of curing all disorders.'

"Nor have I, amidst the clamour of so much envy
and impertinence whither to appeal, but to the concourse of so much piety and wisdom here assembled.
Bringing in my hands an ancient and most necessary,
most charitable, and yet most injured statute of Moses:
not repealed ever by Him who only had the authority,
but thrown aside with much inconsiderate neglect ; as
once the whole law was in Josiah's time.   And he
who shall endeavour the amendment of any old neglected grievance in church or state, or in the daily
course of life, shall be boarded presently by the ruder
sort, with a thousand idle descants and surmises.   But
were they not more busy and inquisitive than the
apostle commends, they would hear him at least,
"rejoicing so the truth be preached, whether of envy
or other pretence whatsoever:" for truth is as impos-

sible to be soiled by any outward touch as the sun-beam."

A fine parallel passage occurs in the conclusion of the fifth of the Prolusiones Oratoriæ, " Satis enim superque suo Marte valet ad se defendendam invicta semper Veritas; nec ad id alienis indiget adminiculis; et licet nobis aliquando superari, et pessum premi videatur, inviolatam tamen perpetuò servat se, et in-tactam ab erroris unguibus; in hoc soli non absimilis, qui sæpe involutum se, et quasi inquinatum nubibus ostendit humanis oculis, cum tamen collectis in se radiis, totoque ad se revocato splendore purissimus ab omni labe colluceat."

" What though the brood of Belial, to whom no liberty is pleasing, but unbridled and vagabond lust without pale or partition, will laugh broad perhaps, to see so great a strength of scripture mustering up in favour, as they suppose, of their debaucheries; they will know better when they shall hence learn, that honest liberty is the greatest foe to dishonest licence. He who wisely would restrain the reasonable soul of man within due bounds, must first himself know per-fectly, how far the territory and dominion extends of just and honest liberty. As little must he offer to bind that which God hath loosened, as to loosen that which He hath bound. The ignorance and mistake of this high point hath heaped up one huge half of all the misery that hath been since Adam. In the gospel we shall read a supercilious crew of masters, whose holiness, or rather whose evil eye, grieving that God should be so facile to man, was to set straiter limits to obedience than God hath set, to enslave the dignity of man, to put a garrison upon his neck of empty and over-dignified precepts: and we shall read our Saviour never more grieved and troubled than to meet with such a peevish madness among men against their own freedom. How can we expect Him to be less offended with us, when much of the same folly shall be found yet remaining where it least ought, to the perishing of thousands? The greatest burden in the world is superstition, not only of ceremonies in the church, but of imaginary and scarecrow sins at home. What greater weakening, what more subtle stratagem against our Christian warfare, when besides the gross body of real transgressions to encounter, we shall be terrified by a vain and shadowy menacing of faults that are not? When things indifferent shall be set to overfront us under the banners of sin, what wonder if we be routed, and by this art of our adversary, fall into the subjection of worst and deadliest offences?"

"No place in heaven or earth, except hell, where charity may not enter: yet marriage, the ordinance of our solace and contentment, the remedy of our loneliness, will not admit now either of charity or mercy, to come in and mediate, or pacify the fierceness of this gentle ordinance, the unremedied loneliness of this remedy."

"Man is the occasion of his own miseries in most of those evils which he imputes to God's inflicting. Though it were granted us by divine indulgence to be exempt from all that can be harmful to us from without, yet the perverseness of our folly is so bent, that we should never cease hammering out of our own hearts, as it were out of a flint, the seeds and sparkles of new misery to ourselves, till all were in a blaze again. And no marvel if out of our own hearts, for they are evil; but even out of those things which God meant us, either for a principal good, or a pure contentment, we are still hatching and contriving upon ourselves matter of continual sorrow and perplexity."

He hopes "to restore the much-wronged and over-sorrowed state of matrimony, not only to those merciful and life-giving remedies of Moses, but, as much as may be, to that serene and blissful condition it was in at the beginning."

Is it possible that a sane man could use such language as the following—"that some conscionable and tender pity might be had of those who have unwarily, in a thing they never practised before, made themselves the bondmen of a luckless and helpless matrimony:" and again—"to redeem and restore such as are the object of compassion, having in an ill hour hampered themselves, to the utter dispatch of all their most beloved comforts and repose for this life's term?" This surely is utter nonsense; and if the beautiful exhortation in our marriage service were properly attended to, no further legislature on the subject would be needed—'this holy estate is not by any to be enterprised, nor taken in hand, unadvisedly, lightly, or wantonly, like brute beasts that have no understanding; but reverently, discreetly, advisedly, soberly, and in the fear of God, duly considering the causes for which matrimony was ordained.' Had Milton weighed this sentence of the Liturgy he hated, he would have had no occasion to write this Treatise on Divorce, for he never would have married his first wife, whom he so lightly and unadvisedly chose.

It is curious that about this time, and previous to the Reformation in the wilder districts of Scotland, there actually prevailed a lawless and iniquitous custom called 'handfasting'—exactly the state of things which Milton seems here to desiderate. It is thus described in the Monastery of Sir Walter Scott. 'We Border-men are more wary than your inland clowns of Fife and Lothian—no jump in the dark for us—no clenching the fetters around our wrists till we know how they will wear with us—we take our wives like our horses, upon trial. When we are handfasted, as we term it, we are man and wife for a year and day—

that space gone by, each may choose another mate,
or, at their pleasure, may call the priest to marry
them for life—and this we call handfasting.' We
cannot forbear quoting the passage which follows in
the novel, a complete answer, if answer were needed,
to the theory of Divorce propounded by Milton.
'Then, said the preacher, I tell thee, noble Baron, in
brotherly love to thy soul, it is a custom licentious,
gross, and corrupted, and, if persisted in, dangerous,
yea damnable. It binds thee to the frailer being
while she is the object of desire—it relieves thee
when she is most the subject of pity—it gives all to
brutal sense, and nothing to generous and gentle
affection. I say to thee, that he who can meditate
the breach of such an engagement is worse than the
birds of prey. Above all, it is contrary to the pure
Christian doctrine, which assigns woman to man as
the partner of his labour, the soother of his evil, his
helpmate in peril, his friend in affliction ; not as the
toy of his looser hours, or as a flower, which, once
cropped, he may throw aside at pleasure.'

The concluding sentence of the Preface is perhaps
worth transcribing. " But if we shall obstinately dislike this new overture of unexpected ease and recovery, what remains but to deplore the frowardness
of our hopeless condition, which neither can endure
the estate we are in, nor admit of remedy either
sharp or sweet? Sharp we ourselves distaste ; and

K

sweet, under whose hands we are, is scrupled and suspected as too luscious. In such a posture Christ found the Jews, who were neither won with the austerity of John the Baptist, and thought it too much licence to follow freely the charming pipe of Him who sounded and proclaimed liberty and relief to all distresses: yet truth in some age or other will find her witness, and shall be justified at last by her own children."

"In God's intention a meet and happy conversation is the chiefest and the noblest end of marriage, the prevention of loneliness to the mind and spirit of man. What hinders the solace and peaceful society of the married couple more than the unfitness and defectiveness of an unconjugal mind? This is that desire which God put into Adam in Paradise, the desire and longing to put off an unkindly solitariness, by uniting another body, but not without a fit soul to his, in the cheerful society of wedlock. Which, if it were so needful before the fall, when man was much more perfect in himself, how much more is it needful now against all the sorrows and casualties of this life, to have an intimate and speaking help, a ready and reviving associate in marriage? Whereof who misses, by chancing on a mute and spiritless mate, remains more alone than before. But all ingenuous men will see that the dignity and blessing of marriage is placed in the mutual enjoyment of that which the wanting

soul needfully seeks. Hence it is that Plato in his
festival discourse brings in Socrates relating what he
feigned to have learned from the prophetess Diotima,
how Love was the son of Penury, begot of Plenty in
the garden of Jupiter. Which divinely sorts with
that which in effect Moses tells us, that Love was the
son of Loneliness, begot in Paradise by that sociable
and helpful aptitude which God implanteth between
man and woman toward each other."

"When he shall find himself bound fast to an un-
complying discord of nature, or, as it oft happens, to
an image of earth and phlegm, with whom he looked
to be the co-partner of a sweet and gladsome society,
and sees withal that his bondage is now inevitable, he
will be ready to mutiny against Divine Providence :
and this doubtless is the reason of those lapses, and
that melancholy despair, which we see in many
wedded persons, though they understand it not, or
pretend other causes, because they know no remedy."

"Marriage is a covenant, the very being whereof
consists not in a forced cohabitation, and counterfeit
performance of duties, but in unfeigned love and
peace : and of matrimonial love, no doubt but that
was chiefly meant, which by the ancient sages was
thus parabled ; that Love, if he be not twin-born, yet
hath a brother wondrous like him, called Anteros ;
whom, while he seeks all about, his chance is to meet
with many false and feigning desires, that wander

singly up and down in his likeness : by them in their
borrowed garb, Love, though not wholly blind, as
poets wrong him, yet having but one eye, as being
born an archer aiming, and that eye not the quickest
in this dark region here below, which is not Love's
proper sphere, partly out of the simplicity and credulity which is native to him, often deceived, embraces
and consorts him with these obvious and suborned
striplings, as if they were his mother's own sons ; for
so he thinks them, while they subtilly keep themselves
most on his blind side. But after a while, as his
manner is, when soaring up into the high tower of his
Apogæum, above the shadow of the earth, he darts
out the direct rays of his then most piercing eyesight
upon the impostures and trim disguises that were
used with him, and discerns that this is not his genuine brother, as he imagined ; he has no longer the
power to hold fellowship with such a personated
mate : for straight his arrows lose their golden heads,
and shed their purple feathers, his silken braids un-
twine, and slip their knots, and that original and
fiery virtue given him by fate all on a sudden goes
out, and leaves him undeified and despoiled of all his
force ; till finding Anteros at last, he kindles and re-
pairs the almost faded ammunition of his deity by the
reflection of a co-equal and homogeneal fire. Thus
mine author sung it to me : and by the leave of those
who would be counted the only grave ones, this is no

mere amatorious novel (though to be wise and skilful
in these matters, men heretofore of greatest name in
virtue have esteemed it one of the highest arcs, that
human contemplation circling upwards can make from
the globy sea whereon she stands); but this is a deep
and serious verity, showing us that love in marriage
cannot live nor subsist unless it be mutual; and where
love cannot be, there can be left of wedlock nothing
but the empty husk of an outside matrimony."

"As those priests of old were not to be long in
sorrow, or if they were, they could not rightly execute their function; so every true Christian in a
higher order of priesthood is a person dedicate to joy
and peace, offering himself a lively sacrifice of praise
and thanksgiving; and there is no Christian duty that
is not to be seasoned and set off with cheerishness;
which in a thousand outward and intermitting crosses
may yet be done well, as in this vale of tears: who
sees not therefore how much more Christianity it
would be to break by divorce that which is more
broken by forcible keeping, rather than ' to cover the
altar of the Lord with continual tears, so that He
regardeth not the offering any more,' rather than that
the whole duty of serving God should be blurred and
tainted with a sad unpreparedness and dejection of
spirit, wherein God has no delight."

"There is a certain scale of duties, there is a certain hierarchy of upper and lower commands, which

for want of studying in right order, all the world is in confusion."

"The author of Ecclesiasticus, whose wisdom hath set him next the Bible." We quote the next passage for the sake of the word 'assassinated,' used in the sense of 'extremely maltreated,' here and in Samson Agonistes,

> "Such usage as your honourable lords
> Afford me, *assassinated* and betrayed."

"As for the custom that some parents and guardians have of forcing marriages, it will be better to say nothing of such a savage inhumanity, but only thus; that the law which gives not all freedom of divorce to any creature endued with reason so *assassinated*, is next in cruelty."

"To banish for ever into a local hell, whether in the air or in the centre, or in that uttermost and bottomless gulf of chaos, deeper from holy bliss than the world's diameter multiplied." This is the germ of the description of the site of hell in the commencement of Paradise Lost,

> "Such place eternal justice had prepared
> For those rebellions; here their prison ordain'd
> In utter darkness, and their portion set
> As far removed from God and light of heaven,
> As from the centre thrice to the utmost pole."

Here also is found the germ of the title of that his greatest work, the immortal syllables though transposed.

" It will best behove our soberness to follow rather what moral Sinai prescribes equal to our strength, than fondly to think within our strength all that LOST PARADISE relates."

" Last of all, to those whose mind is still to maintain textual restrictions, I would ever answer by putting them in remembrance of a command above all commands, which they seem to have forgot, and Who spake it; in comparison whereof this which they so exalt is but a petty and subordinate precept. " Let them go, therefore," and consider well what this lesson means, " I will have mercy and not sacrifice:" for on that " saying all the law and prophets depend;" much more the gospel, whose end and excellence is mercy and peace. Or if they cannot learn that, how will they hear this? which yet I shall not doubt to leave with them as a conclusion, that God the Son hath put all other things under His own feet, but His commandments He hath left all under the feet of charity."

THE JUDGMENT OF MARTIN BUCER,
CONCERNING DIVORCE.

IT may be convenient, before we proceed with our Selections from the Treatise on Education, and the Areopagitica, which follow next in chronological order, to pass on to the three parasitical Treatises, which grow out of, and are intimately connected with the elaborate work which has just been before us, namely the Judgment of Martin Bucer, Tetrachordon, and Colasterion, for under such uncouth and repelling titles did Milton put forth his several performances. They were published in the year 1645, the following year to that in which the Doctrine and Discipline of Divorce appeared; and together they exhaust all that can be said on the subject, and we may ask, What are all these reasonings worth, whereas the words of Christ are plainly against all divorce, " except in case of fornication"?　We believe that no one would care to read more of these Treatises than we have here set down.　We light upon few sentences of a venturous edge, uttered in the height of zeal indeed, but not of a zeal according to knowledge, and therefore shall dismiss this part of our subject very quickly.

The first Treatise is said in the title to be "written to Edward the Sixth, and now Englished; wherein a late book, restoring the "Doctrine and Discipline of Divorce," is here confirmed and justified by the authority of Martin Bucer." It is not our purpose to transcribe any of Bucer's arguments, and we care not any more for his opinion on Divorce than we do for Milton's; the preface and postscript of the latter are all that we have to do with.

"Certainly if it be in man's discerning to sever providence from chance, I could allege many instances wherein there would appear cause to esteem of me no other than a passive instrument under some power and counsel higher and better than can be human, working to a general good in the whole course of this matter. For that I owe no light or leading received from any man in the discovery of this truth, what time I first undertook it in the "Doctrine and Discipline of Divorce," and had only the infallible grounds of scripture to be my guide, He who tries the inmost heart, and saw with what severe industry and examination of myself I set down every period, will be my witness. When I had almost finished the first edition, I chanced to read in the notes of Hugo Grotius upon the fifth of Matthew. Glad, therefore, of such an able assistant, however at much distance, I resolved at length to put off into this wild and calumnious world. For God, it seems, intended to prove me, whether I durst alone take up a rightful cause against a world of disesteem, and found I durst."

"Thus far Martin Bucer:—others may read him in his own phrase on the First to the Corinthians, and ease me who never could delight in long citations, much less in whole traductions; whether it be natural disposition or education in me, or that my mother bore me a speaker of what God made mine own, and not a translator." He had epitomized his author, not "giving an inventory of so many words, but weighing their force."

TETRACHORDON :

EXPOSITIONS UPON THE FOUR CHIEF PLACES IN SCRIPTURE
WHICH TREAT OF MARRIAGE, OR NULLITIES IN MARRIAGE.

ON

GEN. I. 27, 28, COMPARED AND EXPLAINED BY GEN. II. 18, 23, 24.
DEUT. XXIV. 1, 2.
MATT. V. 31, 32, WITH MATT. XIX. 3-11.
1 COR. VII. 10-16.

To the Parliament.

THE immediate cause of his writing this Treatise
was the clamour which was raised on the
publication of his Doctrine and Discipline of Divorce;
and a sermon appears to have been preached before
the Lords and Commons on a day of humiliation, in
which it was said that 'there was a wicked book
abroad'—'uncensured, and deserving to be burnt;'
and 'impudence' was charged upon the author, who
durst 'set his name to it and dedicate it to Parliament.'
To this Milton replies, but not very forcibly. He seems
also to have had recourse to his Muse, and wrote his
eleventh and twelfth sonnets, entitled, "On the Detraction which followed upon my writing certain Treatises." The one begins,

> " A book was writ of late call'd Tetrachordon,
> And woven close, both matter, form, and style;
> The subject new : it walk'd the town awhile,
> Numb'ring good intellects ; now seldom por'd on."

The rest of this sonnet is poor, as he attempts humour, of which he was utterly destitute ; the other is far more interesting, and we insert it entire, as illustrative of his unpopularity.

> " I did but prompt the age to quit their clogs
> By the known rules of ancient liberty,
> When straight a barbarous noise environs me
> Of owls, and cuckoos, asses, apes, and dogs :
> As when those hinds that were transform'd to frogs
> Rail'd at Latona's twin-born progeny,
> Which after held the sun and moon in fee.
> But this is got by casting pearls to hogs ;
> That bawl for freedom in their senseless mood,
> And still revolt when truth would set them free.
> Licence they mean when they cry Liberty ;
> For who loves that, must first be wise and good ;
> But from that mark how far they rove we see,
> For all this waste of wealth, and loss of blood."

GEN. I. 27, 28.

" It is enough determined, that this image of God, wherein man was created, is meant wisdom, purity, justice, and rule over all creatures. All which, being lost in Adam, was recovered with gain by the merits of Christ."

" Man, the portraiture of God."

" Had the image of God been equally common to them both, it had no doubt been said, " In the image of God created He them." But St. Paul ends the controversy by explaining that the woman is not primarily and immediately the image of God, but in reference to the man : "The head of the woman," saith he, 1 Cor. xi., "is the man"; he the image and glory of God, she the glory of the man; he not for her, but she for him. Therefore his precept is, "Wives, be subject to your husbands, as is fit in the Lord," Col. iii., 18; "in everything," Eph. v., 24. Nevertheless man is not to hold her as a servant, but receives her into a part of that empire which God proclaims him to, though not equally, yet largely, as his own image and glory : for it is no small glory to him, that a creature so like him should be made subject to him. Not but that particular exceptions may have place, if she exceed her husband in prudence and dexterity, and he contentedly yield : for then a superior and more natural law comes in, that the wiser should govern the less wise, whether male or female."

"Moreover, if man be the image of God, which consists in holiness, and woman ought in the same respect to be the image and companion of man, in such wise to be loved as the church is beloved of Christ; and if, as God is the head of Christ, and Christ the head of man, so man is the head of woman; I cannot see, by this golden dependence of headship and subjection, but that piety and religion is the main tie of Christian matrimony."

GEN. II. 18, 23, 24.

"Hitherto all things that have been named were

approved of God to be very good: loneliness is the
first thing which God's eye named not good.   And
here "alone" is meant alone without woman; otherwise Adam had the company of God himself, and
angels to converse with; all creatures to delight him
seriously, or to make him sport.   God could have
created him out of the same mould a thousand friends
and brother Adams to have been his consorts; yet for
all this, till Eve was given him, God reckoned him to
be alone."

"Austin contests that manly friendship had been a
more becoming solace for Adam, than to spend so
many secret years in an empty world with one woman.
But our writers deservedly reject this crabbed opinion;
and defend that there is a peculiar comfort in the
married state, which no other society affords.   No
mortal nature can endure, either in the actions of religion, or study of wisdom, without sometime slacken-
ing the cords of intense thought and labour, which,
lest we should think faulty, God Himself conceals us
not his own recreations before the world was built:
"I was," saith the Eternal Wisdom, "daily his delight,
playing always before Him."   And to Him, indeed,
wisdom is as a high tower of pleasure, but to us a steep
hill, and we toiling ever about the bottom.   He exe-
cutes with ease the exploits of His omnipotence, as
easy as with us it is to will, but no worthy enterprise
can be done by us without continual plodding and

wearisomeness to our faint and sensitive abilities. We cannot, therefore, always be contemplative, or pragmatical" (busy, we only employ the word in an ill sense) "abroad, but have need of some delightful intermissions, wherein the enlarged soul may leave off awhile her severe schooling, and like a glad youth in wandering vacancy, may keep her holidays to joy and harmless pastime ; which as she cannot well do without company, so in no company so well as where the different sex in most resembling unlikeness, and most unlike resemblance, cannot but please best, and be pleased in the aptitude of that variety."

" Here the heavenly institutor contents not Himself to say, I will make him a wife ; but resolving to give us first the meaning before the name of a wife, saith, graciously, "I will make him a help-meet for him." The original is more expressive than other languages word for word can render it; but all agree effectual conformity of disposition and affection to be hereby signified; which God, as it were, not satisfied with the naming of a help, goes on describing another self, a second self, a very self itself."

"That there was a nearer alliance between Adam and Eve than could be ever after between man and wife, is visible to any. For no other woman was ever moulded out of her husband's rib, but of mere strangers for the most part they come to have that consanguinity which they have by wedlock. And if we look nearly upon the matter, though marriage be most agreeable to holiness, to purity, and justice, yet is not a natural, but a civil and ordained relation. For if it were in nature, no law or crime could disannul it, to make a wife or husband otherwise than still a wife or husband, but only death; as nothing but that can make a father no father, or a son no son.—Adam spake like Adam the words of flesh and bones, the shell and rind of matrimony; but God spake like God, of love, and solace, and meet help, the soul both of Adam's words and of matrimony."

We find nothing worthy of Milton in the remainder of this tedious and heavy Treatise, which may deservedly be consigned to oblivion; as also may the next, entitled Colasterion, which means a scourge or instrument of chastisement; a favourite title at this period; thus we have Burton's Flagellum Pontificis et Episcoporum Latialium, and the celebrated Histriomastix of William Prynne, who was sentenced to a fine of £5,000, and imprisonment for life, by the Starchamber, in 1634, for an alleged libel on the Queen in the said book. It was he, who again in 1637, condemned to have his ears cut off in the pillory (for they had been sewn on in prison), and to be branded on both cheeks, with the letters S. L.—Seditious Libeller, cried out to the executioner, 'Cut me, tear me; I fear thee not; I fear the fire of hell.'

ON EDUCATION.

OUR author is a wholesale root-and-branch Reformer; he would reform everything, church, government, marriage, and now education; but all his systems and schemes happily proved abortive, visionary, vague, and vain. Instead of our public schools and universities, against which he seems to have been deeply prejudiced, he would have in every city " a spacious house and ground about it fit for an academy, which should be at once both school and university, and big enough to lodge a hundred and fifty persons." He objects to " forcing the empty wits of children to compose themes, verses, and orations, which are the acts of ripest judgment, and not matters to be wrung from poor striplings like the plucking of untimely fruit." Vacations are to be abolished, but he lays down rules for exercise and diet as well as study. We cannot sum up this absurd and impracticable scheme of " the reforming of education " better than in the sarcastic words of a Quarterly Reviewer. ' Here will every stripling, by the time he is one and twenty, have read more Latin and Greek authors than, perhaps, the most veteran scholar in these de-

L

generate days : he will besides have mastered the
Italian, the Hebrew, the Chaldee, and Syrian at "odd
hours." He will have made himself, in his school-
room and playground, a complete farmer, architect,
engineer, sportsman, apothecary, anatomist, law-giver,
philosopher, general officer of cavalry, skilled in " em-
battling, marching, encamping, fortifying, besieging,
and battering," equal to the command of an army,
the moment he has escaped from the rod; and thus
will he prove himself, "in a dangerous fit of the
commonwealth, no poor, shaken, uncertain reed, of
such a tottering conscience as many great counsellors
show themselves, but a stedfast pillar of the state."
This is hardly an exaggeration, and Milton himself
seems not to have had much faith in the very scheme
he propounds, for in conclusion he says, "Only I
believe that this is not a bow for every man to shoot
in, that counts himself a teacher ; but will require
sinews almost equal to those which Homer gave
Ulysses." One or two sentences are all that are worth
selecting.

" The end of learning is to repair the ruin of our first
parents by regaining to know God aright, and out of that
knowledge to love Him, to imitate Him, to be like Him,
as we may the nearest by possessing our souls of true
virtue, which being united to the heavenly grace of
faith, makes up the highest perfection. But because
our understanding cannot in this body found itself but

on sensible things, nor arrive so clearly to the knowledge of God and things invisible, as by orderly
conning over the visible and inferior creature, the
same method is necessarily to be followed in all
discreet teaching. Language is but the instrument
conveying to us things useful to be known. And
though a linguist should pride himself to have all the
tongues that Babel cleft the world into, yet if he have
not studied the solid things in them, as well as the
words and lexicons, he were nothing so much to be
esteemed a learned man, as any yeoman competently
wise in his mother dialect only."

He would allow an hour and a half, ere they ate, at
noon for exercise, and due rest afterwards. The exercise he commends is the exact use of their weapon,
and practice in wrestling, "wherein Englishmen were
wont to excel."

"The interim of unsweating themselves regularly,
and convenient rest before meat, may, both with profit
and delight, be taken up in recreating and composing
their travailed spirits with the solemn and divine harmonies of music, heard or learned; either whilst the
skilful organist plies his grave and fancied descant in
lofty fugues, or the whole symphony with artful and
unimaginable touches, adorn and grace the well-
studied chords of some choice composer; sometimes
the lute or soft organ-stop waiting on elegant voices,
either to religious, martial, or civil ditties; which, if

wise men and prophets be not extremely out, have a great power over dispositions and manners, to smooth and make them gentle from rustic harshness and distempered passions. The like also would not be inexpedient after meat, to assist and cherish nature in her first concoction, and send their minds back to study in good time and satisfaction. Where having followed it close under vigilant eyes, till about two hours before supper, they are, by a sudden alarum or watchword, to be called out to their military motions, under sky or covert, according to the season, as was the Roman wont; first on foot, then, as their age permits, on horseback, to all the arts of cavalry. Besides these constant exercises at home, there is another opportunity of gaining experience to be won from pleasure itself abroad; in those vernal seasons of the year when the air is calm and pleasant, it were an injury and sullenness against nature, not to go out and see her riches, and partake in her rejoicing with heaven and earth. I should not, therefore, be a persuader to them of studying much then, after two or three years that they have well laid their grounds, but to ride out in companies, with prudent and staid guides, to all the quarters of the land: learning and observing all places of strength, all commodities of building and of soil, for towns and tillage, harbours and ports for trade. Sometimes taking sea as far as to our navy, to learn there also what they can in the practical knowledge of sailing and of sea-fight."

AREOPAGITICA.

A SPEECH FOR THE LIBERTY OF UNLICENCED PRINTING.

To the Parliament of England.

WE have now arrived at Milton's masterpiece in prose-composition, the Areopagitica, so named after the Areopagiticus of "that old man eloquent," Isocrates, which towers aloft above the rest, as much as Comus does above his minor poems, and Paradise Lost above all his works, poetical or prose. The elder Disraeli characterises it as 'an unparalleled effusion.' It is a work of love and inspiration, breathing the most enlarged spirit of literature; separating, at an awful distance from the multitude, that character "who was born to study and to love learning for itself, not for lucre, or any other end, but perhaps for that lasting fame and perpetuity of praise, which God and good men have consented shall be the reward of those whose PUBLISHED LABOURS advance the good of mankind." Macaulay speaks of its 'sublime wisdom'; and, indeed, it deserves to be the manual and model of the statesman ; 'which every statesman,' to quote the glowing words of that great writer, 'should wear as a sign upon his hand, and as frontlets between his eyes.'

Our author nowhere shows higher rhetorical skill than in the manner in which he conducts his argument. He does not rush *in medias res* at once, but cautiously and circuitously approaches his subject with much tact and delicacy. His mildness and modesty at the beginning of this admirable and noble speech are as conspicuous as his boldness and vehemence when he is once fairly launched on the current of his eloquence. Then he carries all before him, warming as he advances with his theme, and pouring forth 'those vivid, inspiring,' and inspired 'flashes of eloquence which find their way to the very heart and root of all our noblest sympathies. Nothing can be more replete with grandeur than that creative, life-infusing spirit, which breathes through the whole, kindling up an intense love of the good and the beautiful; and awakening in every breast a devout admiration for those possessors of virtue and genius commissioned by heaven to reveal to us how much of the great and God-like there is in man.' He commences with a moderate yet manly and telling encomium on the parliament. The very fact of his making this speech proves that his country is free. He regards it as a certain testimony and trophy of freedom, and insinuates how desirable and beneficial it would be, both to literature and the country at large, to call in one of their published orders which he hints at, but does not yet name. Thus they would deserve and win the praise and gratitude of all men. They would further be imitating "the old and elegant humanity of Greece." Isocrates and others had done what he was now doing. From his private house, "that old man eloquent," whom "that dishonest victory at Chæronea, fatal to liberty, killed with report," wrote his Areopagitic discourse to the parliament of Athens, and boldly advised them to abandon that form of democracy which was then established. Such an honour he now seeks at their hands, and appealing to their love of truth, uprightness of judgment, prudent spirit, and meek demeanour, he at length presents them with a fit instance wherein to show their superiority, even to the polished Athenians, by rescinding their late order, and according to the nation the liberty of unlicenced printing. He then orderly arranges the several heads of his own incomparable Areopagitic discourse, and the torrent of his eloquence bursts forth with inimitable grandeur and magnificence. We will, as we promised, ' follow the stream in the great original.'

Before, however, we do this, it may be interesting to quote from Disraeli's Curiosities of Literature, his remarks on the literary fate of Milton in this respect. ' His genius was castrated alike by the monarchical and republican government. The royal licenser expunged

several passages from Milton's history, in which Milton
had painted the superstition, the pride, and the cunning of the Saxon monks, which the sagacious Licenser
applied to Charles II. and the bishops; but Milton
had before suffered as merciless a mutilation from his
old friends the republicans, who suppressed a bold
picture, taken from life, which he had introduced into
his History of the Long Parliament and Assembly of
Divines. Milton gave the unlicensed passages to the
Earl of Anglesey, the editor of Whitelock's Memorials.
It is a quarto tract, entitled, 'Mr. John Milton's
Character of the Long Parliament and Assembly of
Divines in 1641; omitted in his other works, and
never before printed, and very seasonable for these
times—1681.' It is inserted in the uncastrated edition
of Milton's prose works in 1738. (Dr. Birch's edition.)
It is a retort on the *Presbyterian* Clement Walker's
History of the *Independents;* and Warburton, in his
admirable characters of the historians of this period,
alluding to Clement Walker, says, 'Milton was even
with him in the fine and severe character he draws of
the Presbyterian administration.'

The ignorance and stupidity of these censors were
often, indeed, as remarkable as their exterminating
spirit. The noble simile of Milton, of Satan with the
rising sun, in the first book of the Paradise Lost, had
nearly occasioned the suppression of our national
epic: it was supposed to contain a treasonable allusion.

> " as when the sun, new risen,
> Looks through the horizontal misty air
> Shorn of his beams ; or from behind the moon,
> In dim eclipse, disastrous twilight sheds
> On half the nations, and with fear of change
> Perplexes monarchs."

This office seems to have lain dormant a short time under Cromwell, from the scruples of a conscientious licenser, who desired the council of state in 1649, for reasons given, to be discharged from that employment. This Mabot, the licenser, was evidently deeply touched by Milton's address for " the Liberty of unlicensed Printing." The office was, however, revived on the restoration of Charles II. ; and through the reign of James II. the abuses of licensers were unquestionably not discouraged; for in reprinting Gage's ' Survey of the West Indies,' the twenty-second chapter being obnoxious for containing particulars of the artifices of " the papalins," so Milton calls the Papists, in converting the author, was entirely chopped away by the licenser's hatchet. The castrated chapter, as usual, was preserved afterwards separately. Literary despotism at least is short-sighted in its views, for the expedients it employs are certain of overturning themselves. At the revolution in England, licences for the press ceased; but its liberty did not commence till 1694, when every restraint was taken off by the firm and decisive tone of the commons.'

As it will tend materially to the elucidation of the great speech before us, we will venture to quote further from the valuable observations of Isaac Disraeli on Licensers of the Press.

'In the history of literature, and perhaps in that of the human mind, the institution of THE LICENSERS OF THE PRESS, and CENSORS OF BOOKS, was a bold invention, designed to counteract that of the Press itself; and even to convert this newly-discovered instrument of freedom into one which might serve to perpetuate that system of passive obedience, which had so long enabled modern Rome to dictate her laws to the universe.   It was thought possible in the subtilty of Italian *astuzia* and Spanish monachism, to place a sentinel on the very thoughts, as well as on the persons of authors; and in extreme cases, that books might be condemned to the flames, as well as heretics.

'Of this institution, the beginnings are obscure, for it originated in caution and fear; but as the work betrays the workman, and the national physiognomy the native, it is evident that so inquisitorial an act could only have originated in the inquisition itself. Feeble or partial attempts might previously have existed, for we learn that the monks had a part of their libraries called the *inferno*, which was not the part which they least visited, for it contained all the prohibited books which they could smuggle into it. But this inquisitorial power assumed its most formidable shape in the Council of Trent, when Pius IV. was presented with a catalogue of condemned books. His bull not only confirmed this list, but added rules how books should be judged. Subsequent popes enlarged these catalogues and rules. Inquisitors of books were appointed; at Rome they consisted of certain cardinals, and "the master of the holy palace." These catalogues were called *Indexes*. The simple *Index* is a list of condemned books never to be opened; but the *Expurgatory Index* indicates those only prohibited till they have undergone a purification. No book was to be allowed on any subject, or in any language, which contained a single position, an ambiguous sentence, even a word, which, in the most distant sense, could be construed opposite to the doctrines of the supreme authority of this Council of Trent.

'The results of these indexes were somewhat curious. As they were formed in different countries, the opinions were often diametrically opposite to each other. Men who began by insisting that all the world should not differ from their opinions, ended by not agreeing with themselves. A civil war raged among the Index-makers; and if one criminated, the other retaliated. The expurgatory Indexes excited louder complaints; because the purgers and castrators as they were termed, or, as Milton calls them, "the executioners of books," by omitting, or interpolating passages, made an author say, or unsay, what the inquisitors chose. The whole process of these expurgatory Indexes that "rakes through the entrails of many an old good author, with a violation worse than any could be offered to his tomb," as Milton says, must inevitably draw off the life blood, and leave an author a mere spectre! A book in Spain and Portugal passes through six or seven courts before it can be published, and is supposed to recommend itself by the information, that it is published with *all* the necessary privileges. One case is said to have occupied them during forty years.

'When the insertions in the Index were found of no other use than to bring the peccant volumes under the eyes of the curious, they employed the secular arm in burning them in public places. They had yet to learn that burning was not confuting, and that these literary conflagrations were an advertisement by proclamation. The publisher of Erasmus's Colloquies intrigued to procure the burning of his book, which raised the sale to twenty-four thousand! In the reign of Henry VIII. we seem to have burnt books on both sides; it was an age of unsettled opinions; in Edward's the Catholic works were burnt; and Mary had her pyramids of Protestant volumes; in Elizabeth's, political pamphlets fed the flames; and libels in the reign of James I. and his sons.

' France cannot exactly fix on the æra of her *Censeurs de Livres;* and we ourselves, who gave it its death-blow, found the custom prevail without any authority from our statutes. The laws of England have never violated the freedom and the dignity of its press. Proclamations were occasionally issued against authors and books; and foreign works were, at times, prohibited. Elizabeth, as despotic in *deeds* as the pacific James was in *words*, condemned one author to have the hand cut off which wrote his book; and she hanged another. The regular establishment of licensers of the press appeared under Charles I. It must be placed among the projects of Laud, and the king, I suspect, inclined to it. The presbyterian party in parliament who thus found the press closed on them, vehemently cried out for its freedom ; and it was imagined, that when they had ascended into power, the odious office of a licenser of the press would have been abolished ; but these pretended friends of freedom, on the contrary, discovered themselves as tenderly alive to the office as the old government, and maintained it with the extremest vigour. Such is the political history of mankind.'

This last observation of Disraeli will account for the otherwise strange fact that this noble work of Milton's, to which we now proceed, had little or no effect upon the Presbyterians, if perhaps we except the case of Mabot.

AREOPAGITICA.

" THEY, who to states and governors of the commonwealth direct their speech, high court of parliament! or wanting such access in a private condition, write that which they foresee may advance the public good; I suppose them, as at the beginning of no mean endeavour, not a little altered and moved inwardly in their minds; some with doubt of what will be the success, others with fear of what will be the censure; some with hope, others with confidence of what they have to speak. And me perhaps each of these dispositions, as the subject was whereon I entered, may have at other times variously affected; and likely might in these foremost expressions now also disclose which of them swayed most, but that the very attempt of this address thus made, and the thought of whom it hath recourse to, hath got the power within me to a passion, far more welcome than incidental to a preface.

" Which though I stay not to confess ere any ask, I shall be blameless, if it be no other than the joy and gratulation which it brings to all who wish to promote their country's liberty; whereof this whole discourse proposed will be a certain testimony, if not a trophy. For this is not the liberty which we can hope, that no grievance ever should rise in the commonwealth : that let no man in this world expect; but when complaints are freely heard, deeply considered, and speedily reformed, then is the utmost bound of civil liberty obtained that wise men look for. To which if I now manifest by the very sound of this which I shall utter, that we are already in good part arrived, and yet from such a steep disadvantage of tyranny and superstition grounded into our principles, as was beyond the manhood of a Roman recovery, it will be attributed first, as is most due, to the strong assistance of God, our deliverer; next, to your faithful guidance and undaunted wisdom, lords and commons of England ! Neither is it in God's esteem, the diminution of His glory, when honourable things are spoken of good men, and worthy magistrates; which if I now first should begin to do, after so fair a progress of your laudable deeds, and such a long obligement upon the whole realm to your indefatigable virtues, I might be justly reckoned among the tardiest and the unwillingest of them that praise ye.

"Nevertheless there being three principal things, without which all praising is but courtship and flattery : first, when that only is praised which is solidly worth praise ; next, when greatest likelihoods are brought, that such things are truly and really in those persons to whom they are ascribed; the other, when he who praises, by showing that such his actual persuasion is of whom he writes, can demonstrate that he flatters not; the former two of these I have heretofore endeavoured, rescuing the employment from him who went about to impair your merits with a trivial and malignant encomium; the latter as belonging chiefly to my own acquittal, that whom I so extolled I did not flatter, hath been reserved opportunely to this occasion. For he who freely magnifies what hath been nobly done, and fears not to declare as freely what might be done better, gives ye the best covenant of his fidelity; and that his loyalest affection and his hope waits on your proceedings. His highest praising is not flattery, and his plainest advice is a kind of praising; for though I should affirm and hold by argument, that it would fare better with truth, with learning, and the commonwealth, if one of your published orders, which I should name, were called in; yet at the same time it could not but much redound to the lustre of your mild and equal government, when as private persons are hereby animated to think ye better pleased with public advice than other statists have been delighted heretofore with public flattery. And men will then see what difference there is between the magnanimity of a triennial parliament, and that jealous haughtiness of prelates and cabin counsellors that usurped of late,

whenas they shall observe ye in the midst of your
victories and successes more gently brooking written
exceptions against a voted order, than other courts,
which had produced nothing worth memory but the
weak ostentation of wealth, would have endured the
least signified dislike at any sudden proclamation.

" If I should thus far presume upon the meek demeanour of your civil and gentle greatness, lords and
commons! as what your published order hath directly
said, that to gainsay, I might defend myself with ease,
if any should accuse me of being new or insolent, did
they but know how much better I find ye esteem it
to imitate the old and elegant humanity of Greece,
than the barbaric pride of a Hunnish and Norwegian
stateliness. And out of those ages, to whose polite
wisdom and letters we owe that we are not yet Goths
and Jutlanders, I could name him who from his private house wrote that discourse to the parliament of
Athens, that persuades them to change the form of
democracy which was then established. Such honour
was done in those days to men who professed the
study of wisdom and eloquence, not only in their own
country, but in other lands, that cities and signiories
heard them gladly, and with great respect, if they
had aught in public to admonish the state. Thus did
Dion Prusæus, a stranger and a private orator, counsel the Rhodians against a former edict; and I abound
with other like examples, which to set here would be

M

superfluous. But if from the industry of a life wholly
dedicated to studious labours, and those natural endowments haply not the worst for two and fifty degrees
of northern latitude, so much must be derogat-
ed, as to count me not equal to any of those who had
this privilege, I would obtain to be thought not so inferior, as yourselves are superior to the most of them
who received their counsel; and how far you excel
them, be assured, lords and commons! there can no
greater testimony appear, than when your prudent
spirit acknowledges and obeys the voice of reason,
from what quarter soever it be heard speaking, and
renders ye as willing to repeal any act of your own
setting forth as any set forth by your predecessors.

" If ye be thus resolved, as it were injury to think
ye were not, I know not what should withhold me
from presenting ye with a fit instance wherein to show
both that love of truth which ye eminently profess,
and that uprightness of your judgment which is not
wont to be partial to yourselves; by judging over again
that order which ye have ordained " to regulate
printing: that no book, pamphlet, or paper shall be
henceforth printed, unless the same be first approved
and licensed by such, or at least one of such, as shall
be thereto appointed." For that part which preserves
justly every man's copy to himself, or provides for
the poor, I touch not; only wish they be not made
pretences to abuse and persecute honest and painful

men, who offend not in either of these particulars.
But that other clause of licensing books which we
thought had died with his brother quadragesimal and
matrimonial when the prelates expired, I shall now
attend with such a homily, as shall lay before ye,
first, the inventors of it to be those whom ye will be
loath to own ; next, what is to be thought in general
of reading, whatever sort the books be ; and that this
order avails nothing to the suppressing of scandalous,
seditious, and libellous books, which were mainly intended to be suppressed ; last, that it will be primely
to the discouragement of all learning, and the stop of
truth, not only by disexercising and blunting our
abilities, in what we know already, but by hindering
and cropping the discovery that might be yet further
made, both in religious and civil wisdom.

" I deny not but that it is of greatest concernment
in the church and commonwealth to have a vigilant
eye how books demean themselves, as well as men ;
and thereafter to confine, imprison, and do sharpest
justice on them as malefactors ; for books are not absolutely dead things, but do contain a progeny of life
in them to be as active as that soul was whose progeny they are ; nay, they do preserve as in a vial the
purest efficacy and extraction of that living intellect
that bred them. I know they are as lively, and as
vigorously productive, as those fabulous dragon's
teeth : and being sown up and down, may chance to

M 2

spring up armed men. And yet, on the other hand, unless wariness be used, as good almost kill a man as kill a good book: who kills a man kills a reasonable creature, God's image; but he who destroys a good book kills reason itself—kills the image of God, as it were, in the eye. Many a man lives a burden to the earth, but a good book is the precious life-blood of a master spirit, embalmed and treasured up on purpose to a life beyond life. It is true no age can restore a life, whereof, perhaps, there is no great loss; and revolutions of ages do not oft recover the loss of a rejected truth, for the want of which whole nations fare the worse. We should be wary, therefore, what persecution we raise against the living labours of public men, how we spill that seasoned life of man, preserved and stored up in books; since we see a kind of homicide may be thus committed, sometimes a martyrdom; and if it extend to the whole impression, a kind of massacre, whereof the execution ends not in the slaying of an elemental life, but strikes at the ethereal and fifth essence, the breath of reason itself; slays an immortality rather than a life. But lest I should be condemned of introducing licence, while I oppose licensing, I refuse not the pains to be so much historical, as will serve to show what hath been done by ancient and famous commonwealths, against this disorder, till the very time that this project of licensing crept out of the inquisition, was catched up by our prelates, and hath caught some of our presbyters.

"In Athens, where books and wits were ever busier than in any other part of Greece, I find but only two sorts of writings which the magistrate cared to take notice of; those either blasphemous and atheistical, or libellous. Thus the books of Protagoras were by the judges of Areopagus commanded to be burnt, and himself banished the territory for a discourse, begun with his confessing not to know " whether there were gods, or whether not." And against defaming, it was agreed that none should be traduced by name; as was the manner of Vetus Comœdia, whereby we may guess how they censured libelling ; and this course was quick enough, as Cicero writes, to quell both the desperate wits of other atheists, and the open way of defaming, as the event showed. Of other sects and opinions, though tending to voluptuousness, and the denying of divine Providence, they took no heed. Therefore we do not read that either Epicurus, or that libertine school of Cyrene, or what the Cynic impudence uttered, was ever questioned by the laws. Neither is it recorded that the writings of those old comedians were suppressed, though the acting of them were forbid; and that Plato commended the reading of Aristophanes, the loosest of them all, to his royal scholar, Dionysius, is commonly known, and may be excused, if holy Chrysostom, as is reported, nightly studied so much the same author, and had the art to cleanse a scurrilous vehemence into the style of a rousing sermon.

"That other leading city of Greece, Lacedæmon, considering that Lycurgus, their lawgiver, was so addicted to elegant learning as to have been the first that brought out of Ionia the scattered works of Homer, and sent the poet Thaletas from Crete, to prepare and mollify the Spartan surliness with his smooth songs and odes, the better to plant among them law and civility; it is to be wondered how museless and unbookish they were, minding nought but the feats of war. There needed no licensing of books among them, for they disliked all but their own laconic apophthegms, and took a slight occasion to chase Archilochus out of their city, perhaps for composing in a higher strain than their own soldiery ballads and roundels could reach to ; or if it were for his broad verses, they were not therein so cautious, but they were as dissolute in their promiscuous conversing ; whence Euripides affirms, in Andromache, that their women were all unchaste.

"This much may give us light after what sort of books were prohibited among the Greeks. The Romans, also, for many ages trained up only to a military roughness, resembling most the Lacedæmonian guise, knew of learning little but what their twelve tables and the pontific college with their augurs and flamens taught them in religion and law ;

so unacquainted with other learning, that when Carneades and Critolaus, with the Stoic Diogenes, coming ambassadors to Rome, took thereby occasion to give the city a taste of their philosophy, they were suspected for seducers by no less a man than Cato the Censor, who moved it in the senate to dismiss them speedily, and to banish all such Attic babblers out of Italy. But Scipio and others of the noblest senators withstood him and his old Sabine austerity; honoured and admired the men ; and the Censor himself at last, in his old age, fell to the study of that whereof before he was so scrupulous. And yet, at the same time, Nævius and Plautus, the first Latin comedians, had filled the city with all the borrowed scenes of Menander and Philemon. Then began to be considered there also what was to be done to libellous books and authors ; for Nævius was quickly cast into prison for his unbridled pen, and released by the tribunes upon his recantation : we read also that libels were burnt, and the makers punished, by Augustus.

"The like severity, no doubt, was used, if aught were impiously written against their esteemed gods. Except in these two points, how the world went in books, the magistrate kept no reckoning. And therefore Lucretius, without impeachment, versifies his Epicurism to Memmius, and had the honour to be set forth the second time by Cicero, so great a father of the commonwealth ; although himself disputes against that opinion in his own writings. Nor was the satirical sharpness or naked plainness of Lucilius, or Catullus, or Flaccus, by any order prohibited. And for matters of state, the story of Titus Livius, though it extolled that part which Pompey held, was not therefore suppressed by Octavius Cæsar, of the other faction. But that Naso was by him banished in his old age, for the wanton poems of his youth, was but a mere covert of state over some secret cause; and besides, the books were neither banished nor called in. From hence we shall meet with little else but tyranny in the Roman Empire, that we may not marvel, if not so often bad as good books were silenced. I shall therefore deem to have been large enough, in producing what among the ancients was punishable to write, save only which, all other arguments were free to treat on.

" By this time the emperors were become Christians, whose discipline in this point I do not find to have been more severe than what was formerly in practice. The books of those whom they took to be grand heretics were examined, refuted, and condemned in the general councils; and not till then were prohibited, or burnt, by authority of the emperor. As for the writings of heathen authors, unless they were plain invectives against Christianity, as those of Porphyrius and Proclus, they met with no interdict that can be cited, till about the year 400, in a Carthaginian council, wherein bishops themselves were forbid to read the books of Gentiles, but heresies they might read; while others long before them, on the contrary, scrupled more the books of heretics than of Gentiles. And that the primitive .councils and bishops were wont only to declare what books were not commendable, passing no further, but leaving it to each one's conscience to read or to lay by, till after the year 800, is observed already by Padre Paolo, the great unmasker of the Trentine Council. After which time the Popes of Rome, engrossing what they pleased of political rule into their own hands, extended their dominion over men's eyes, as they had before over their judgments; burning and prohibiting to be read what they fancied not; yet sparing in their censures, and the books not many which they so dealt with; till Martin the Fifth, by his bull, not only prohibited, but was the first that excommunicated the reading of heretical books; for about that time Wicliffe and Husse growing terrible, were they who first drove the papal court to a stricter policy of prohibiting. Which course Leo the Tenth and his successors followed, until the Council of Trent and the Spanish inquisition, engendering together, brought forth or perfected those catalogues and expurging indexes, that rake through the entrails of many an old good author with a violation worse than any could be offered to his tomb.

" Nor did they stay in matters heretical, but any

subject that was not to their palate, they either condemned in a prohibition, or had it straight into the new purgatory of an index. To fill up the measure of encroachment, their last invention was to ordain that no book, pamphlet, or paper should be printed (as if St. Peter had bequeathed them the keys of the press also as well as of Paradise) unless it were approved and licensed under the hands of two or three gluttonous friars. For example :—

"Let the chancellor Cini be pleased to see if in this present work be contained aught that may withstand the printing.

"VINCENT RABBATA
"*Vicar of Florence.*"

"I have seen this present work, and find nothing athwart the Catholic faith and good manners; in witness whereof I have given, &c.

"NICOLO CINI,
"*Chancellor of Florence.*"

"Attending the precedent relation, it is allowed that this present work of Davanzati may be printed.

"VINCENT RABBATA," &c.

"It may be printed, July 15.
"FRIAR SIMON MOMPEI D'AMELIA,
"*Chancellor of the Holy Office in Florence.*"

"Sure they have a concert, if he of the bottomless

pit had not long since broke prison, that this quad-
ruple exorcism would bar him down. I fear their
next design will be to get into their custody the licensing of that which they say Claudius intended, but
went not through with. Vouchsafe to see another of
their forms, the Roman stamp :—

"Imprimatur, If it seem good to the reverend master of the Holy Palace.

"BELCASTRO, *Vicegerent.*"

"Imprimatur,
"FRIAR NICHOLO RODOLPHI,
"*Master of the Holy Palace.*"

Sometimes five imprimaturs are seen together,
dialogue wise, in the piazza of one title-page, compli-
menting and ducking each to other with their shaven
reverences, whether the author, who stands by in perplexity at the foot of his epistle, shall to the press or to
the spunge. These are the pretty responsories, these
are the dear antiphonies, that so bewitched of late our
prelates and their chaplains, with the goodly echo they
made; and besotted us to the gay imitation of a lordly
imprimatur, one from Lambeth-house, another from
the west-end of Paul's; so apishly romanizing, that the
word of command was still set down in Latin; as if
the learned grammatical pen that wrote it would cast
no ink without Latin; or perhaps, as they thought, no
vulgar tongue was worthy to express the pure conceit

of an imprimatur: but rather, as I hope, for that our English, the language of men ever famous and foremost in the achievements of liberty, will not easily find servile letters enow to spell such a dictatory presumption Englished.

"And thus ye have the inventors and the original of book licensing ripped up, and drawn as lineally as any pedigree. We have it not, that can be heard of, from any ancient state, or polity, or church, nor by any statute left us by our ancestors elder or later; nor from the modern custom of any reformed city or church abroad; but from the most anti-christian council, and the most tyrannous inquisition that ever inquired. Till then books were ever as freely admitted into the world as any other birth; the issue of the brain was no more stifled than the issue of the womb: no envious Juno sat cross-legged over the nativity of any man's intellectual offspring; but if it proved a monster, who denies but that it was justly burnt, or sunk into the sea? But that a book, in worse condition than a peccant soul, should be to stand before a jury ere it be born to the world, and undergo yet in darkness the judgment of Radamanth and his colleagues, ere it can pass the ferry backward into light, was never heard before, till that mysterious iniquity, provoked and troubled at the first entrance of reformation, sought out new limboes and new hells wherein they might include our books also within the number of their damned. And this was the rare morsel so officiously snatched up, and so ill-favourably imitated by our inquisiturient bishops, and the attendant minorites, their chaplains. That ye like not now these most certain authors of this licensing order, and that all sinister intention was far distant from your thoughts, when ye were importuned the passing it, all men who know the integrity of your actions, and how ye honour truth, will clear ye readily.

" But some will say, what though the inventors were bad, the thing for all that may be good. It may be so ; yet if that thing be no such deep invention, but obvious and easy for any man to light on, and yet best and wisest commonwealths through all ages and occasions have forbore to use it, and falsest seducers and oppressors of men were the first who took it up, and to no other purpose but to obstruct and hinder the first approach of reformation ; I am of those who believe it will be a harder alchymy than Lullius ever knew, to sublimate any good use out of such an invention. Yet this only is what I request to gain from this reason, that it may be held a dangerous and suspicious fruit, as certainly it deserves; for the tree that bore it, until I can dissect one by one the properties it has. But I have first to finish, as was propounded, what is to be thought in general of reading books, whatever sort they be, and whether be more the benefit, or the harm that thence proceeds.

"Not to insist upon the examples of Moses, Daniel, and Paul, who were skilful in all the learning of the Egyptians, Chaldeans, and Greeks, which could not probably be without reading their books of all sorts, in Paul especially, who thought it no defilement to insert into Holy Scripture the sentences of three Greek poets, and one of them a tragedian; the question was, notwithstanding sometimes controverted among the primitive doctors, but with great odds on that side which affirmed it both lawful and profitable, as was then evidently perceived, when Julian the Apostate, and subtlest enemy of our faith, made a decree, forbiddding Christians the study of heathen learning; for, said he, they wound us with our own weapons, and with our own arts and sciences they overcome us. And indeed the Christians were so put to their shifts by this crafty means, and so much in danger to decline into all ignorance, that the two Apollinarii were fain, as a man may say, to coin all the seven liberal sciences out of the Bible, reducing into divers forms of orations, poems, dialogues, even to the calculating of a new Christian grammar.

"But, saith the historian Socrates, the providence of God provided better than the industry of Apollinarius and his son, by taking away that illiterate law with the life of him who devised it. So great an injury they then held it to be deprived of Hellenic learning; and thought it a persecution more undermining, and secretly decaying the church, than the open cruelty of Decius or Diocletian. And perhaps it was with the same politic drift that the devil whipped St. Jerome in a lenten dream, for reading Cicero; or else it was a phantasm, bred by the fever which had then seized him. For had an angel been his discipliner, unless it were for dwelling too much on Ciceronianisms, and had chastised the reading, not the vanity, it had been plainly partial, first, to correct him for grave Cicero, and not for scurril Plautus, whom he confesses to have been reading not long before; next to correct him only, and let so many more ancient fathers wax old in those pleasant and florid studies, without the lash of such a tutoring apparition; insomuch that Basil teaches how some good use may be made of Margites, a sportful poem, now extant, writ by Homer; and why not then of Morgante, an Italian romance much to the same purpose?

" But if it be agreed we shall be tried by visions, there is a vision recorded by Eusebius, far ancienter than this tale of Jerome, to the nun Eustochium, and besides, has nothing of a fever in it. Dionysius Alexandrinus was, about the year 240, a person of great name in the church for piety and learning, who had wont to avail himself much against heretics by being conversant in their books; until a certain presbyter laid it scrupulously to his conscience, how he durst venture himself among those defiling volumes. The

worthy man, loath to give offence, fell into a new
debate with himself, what was to be thought; when
suddenly a vision sent from God (it is his own epistle
that so avers it) confirmed him in these words: " Read
any books whatever come to thy hands, for thou art
sufficient both to judge aright, and to examine each
matter." To this revelation he assented the sooner,
as he confesses, because it was answerable to that of
the apostle to the Thessalonians: "Prove all things,
hold fast that which is good."

"And we might have added another remarkable
saying of the same author: "To the pure, all things
are pure;" not only meats and drinks, but all kind of
knowledge, whether of good or evil; the knowledge
cannot defile, nor consequently the books, if the will
and conscience be not defiled. For books are as
meats and viands are; some of good, some of evil
substance; and yet God in that unapocryphal vision
said without exception, "Rise, Peter, kill and eat,"
leaving the choice to each man's discretion. Wholesome meats to a vitiated stomach differ little or
nothing from unwholesome; and best books to a
naughty mind are not unapplicable to occasions of
evil. Bad meats will scarcely breed good nourish-
ment in the healthiest concoction; but herein the
difference is of bad books, that they to a discreet and
judicious reader serve in many respects to discover,
to confute, to forewarn, and to illustrate. Whereof

what better witness can ye expect I should produce, than one of your own now sitting in Parliament, the chief of learned men reputed in this land, Mr. Selden; whose volume of natural and national laws proves, not only by great authorities brought together, but by exquisite reasons and theorems almost mathematically demonstrative, that all opinions, yea, errors, known, read, and collated are of main service and assistance toward the speedy attainment of what is truest.

" I conceive, therefore, that when God did enlarge the universal diet of man's body (saving ever the rules of temperance), He then also, as before, left arbitrary the dieting and repasting of our minds; as wherein every mature man might have to exercise his own leading capacity. How great a virtue is temperance, how much of moment through the whole life of man ! Yet God commits the managing so great a trust, without particular law or prescription, wholly to the demeanour of every grown man. And therefore when He Himself tabled the Jews from heaven, that omer, which was every man's daily portion of manna, is computed to have been more than might have well sufficed the heartiest feeder thrice as many meals. For those actions which enter into a man, rather than issue out of him, and therefore defile not, God uses not to captivate under a perpetual childhood of pre-scription, but trusts him with the gift of reason to be his own chooser; there were but little work left for

N

preaching, if law and compulsion should grow so fast upon those things which heretofore were governed only by exhortation. Solomon informs us, that much reading is a weariness to the flesh; but neither he, nor other inspired author, tells us that such or such reading is unlawful; yet certainly had God thought good to limit us herein, it had been much more expedient to have told us what was unlawful, than what was wearisome.

" As for the burning of those Ephesian books by St. Paul's converts; it is replied, the books were magic, the Syriac so renders them. It was a private act, a voluntary act, and leaves us to a voluntary imitation : the men in remorse burnt those books which were their own; the magistrate by this example is not appointed; these men practised the books, another might perhaps have read them in some sort usefully. Good and evil we know in the field of this world grow up together almost inseparably; and the knowledge of good is so involved and interwoven with the knowledge of evil, and in so many cunning resemblances hardly to be discerned, that those confused seeds which were imposed upon Psyche as an incessant labour to cull out, and sort asunder, were not more intermixed. It was from out the rind of one apple tasted, that the knowledge of good and evil, as two twins cleaving together, leaped forth into the world. And perhaps this is that doom which Adam fell into of knowing good and evil; that is to say, of knowing good by evil.

"As therefore the state of man now is, what wisdom can there be to choose, what continence to forbear, without the knowledge of evil? He that can apprehend and consider vice with all her baits and seeming pleasures, and yet abstain, and yet distinguish, and yet prefer that which is truly better, he is the true warfaring Christian. I cannot praise a fugitive and cloistered virtue unexercised and unbreathed, that never sallies out and seeks her adversary, but slinks out of the race, where that immortal garland is to be run for, not without dust and heat. Assuredly we bring not innocence into the world—we bring impurity much rather; that which purifies us is trial, and trial is by what is contrary. That virtue, therefore, which is but a youngling in the contemplation of evil, and knows not the utmost that vice promises to her followers, and rejects it, is but a blank virtue, not a pure; her whiteness is but an excremental whiteness, which was the reason why our sage and serious poet Spencer (whom I dare be known to think a better teacher than Scotus or Aquinas), describing true temperance under the person of Guion, brings him in with his palmer through the cave of Mammon, and the bower of earthly bliss, that he might see and know, and yet abstain.

"Since therefore the knowledge and survey of vice

is in this world so necessary to the constituting of human virtue, and the scanning of error to the confirmation of truth, how can we more safely, and with less danger, scout into the regions of sin and falsity, than by reading all manner of tractates, and hearing all manner of reason ?   And this is the benefit which may be had of books promiscuously read.   But or the harm that may result hence, three kinds are usually reckoned.   First is feared the infection that may spread ; but then, all human learning and controversy in religious points must remove out of the world, yea, the Bible itself ; for that ofttimes relates blasphemy not nicely ; it describes the carnal sense of wicked men not elegantly, it brings in holiest men passionately murmuring against Providence through all the arguments of Epicurus : in other great disputes it answers dubiously and darkly to the common reader ; and ask a Talmudist what ails the modesty of his marginal Keri, that Moses and all the prophets cannot persuade him to pronounce the textual Chetiv.   For these causes we all know the Bible itself put by the papist into the first rank of prohibited books.   The ancientest fathers must be next removed, as Clement of Alexandria, and that Eusebian book of evangelic preparation, transmitting our ears through a hoard of heathenish obscenities to receive the gospel.   Who finds not that Irenæus, Epiphanius, Jerome, and others discover more heresies than they well confute, and that oft for heresy which is the truer opinion?

" Nor boots it to say for these, and all the heathen writers of greatest infection, if it must be thought so, with whom is bound up the life of human learning, that they wrote in an unknown tongue, so long as we are sure those languages are known as well to the worst of men, who are both most able and most diligent to instil the poison they suck, first into the courts of princes, acquainting them with the choicest delights and criticisms of sin. As perhaps did that Petronius, whom Nero called his arbiter, the master of his revels ; and that notorious ribald of Arezzo, dreaded and yet dear to the Italian courtiers. I name not him, for posterity's sake, whom Henry the Eighth named in merriment his vicar of hell. By which compendious way all the contagion that foreign books can infuse will find a passage to the people far easier and shorter than an Indian voyage, though it could be sailed either by the north of Cataio eastward, or of Canada westward, while our Spanish licensing gags the English press never so severely.

" But, on the other side, that infection which is from books of controversy in religion is more doubtful and dangerous to the learned than to the ignorant ; and yet those books must be permitted untouched by the licenser. It will be hard to instance where any ignorant man hath been ever seduced by any papistical book in English, unless it were commended and expounded to him by some of that clergy ; and indeed all such tractates, whether false or true, are as the prophecy of Isaiah was to the eunuch, not to be "understood without a guide." But of our priests and doctors, how many have been corrupted by studying the comments of Jesuits and Sorbonists, and how fast they could transfuse that corruption into the people, our experience is both late and sad. It is not forgot, since the acute and distinct Arminius was perverted merely by the perusing of a nameless discourse written at Delft, which at first he took in hand to confute.

"Seeing therefore that those books, and those in great abundance, which are likeliest to taint both life and doctrine, cannot be suppressed without the fall of learning, and of all ability in disputation, and that these books of either sort are most and soonest catching to the learned (from whom to the common people whatever is heretical or dissolute may quickly be conveyed), and that evil manners are as perfectly learnt without books a thousand other ways which cannot be stopped, and evil doctrine not with books can propagate, except a teacher guide, which he might also do without writing, and so beyond prohibiting ; I am not unable to unfold how this cautelous enterprise of licensing can be exempted from the number of vain and impossible attempts. And he who were pleasantly disposed could not well avoid to liken it to the exploit of that gallant man, who thought to pound up the crows by shutting his park gate.

" Besides another inconvenience, if learned men be the first receivers out of books, and dispreaders both of vice and error, how shall the licensers themselves be confided in, unless we can confer upon them, or they assume to themselves, above all others in the land, the grace of infallibility and uncorruptedness ? And again, if it be true that a wise man, like a good refiner, can gather gold out of the drossiest volume, and that a fool will be a fool with the best book, yea, or without a book ; there is no reason that we should deprive a wise man of any advantage to his wisdom, while we seek to restrain from a fool that which, being restrained, will be no hinderance to his folly. For if there should be so much exactness always used to keep that from him which is unfit for his reading, we should in the judgment of Aristotle not only, but of Solomon, and of our Saviour, not vouchsafe him good precepts, and by consequence not willingly admit him to good books ; as being certain that a wise man will make better use of an idle pamphlet than a fool will do of sacred Scripture.

" It is next alleged, we must not expose ourselves to temptations without necessity, and next to that, not employ our time in vain things. To both these objections one answer will serve, out of the grounds already laid, that to all men such books are not temptations nor vanities; but useful drugs and materials where-with to temper and compose effective and strong medicines, which man's life cannot want (dispense with). The rest, as children and childish men, who have not the art to qualify and prepare these working minerals, well may be exhorted to forbear; but hindered forcibly they cannot be, by all the licencing that sainted inquisition could ever yet contrive; which is what I promised to deliver next: that this order of licencing conduces nothing to the end for which it was framed; and hath almost prevented me by being clear already while thus much hath been explaining. See the ingenuity of truth, who, when she gets a free and willing hand, opens herself faster than the pace of method and discourse can overtake her. It was the task which I began with, to show, that no nation, or well instituted state, if they valued books at all, did ever use this way of licencing; and it might be answered, that this is a piece of prudence lately discovered.

"To which I return, that as it was a thing slight and obvious to think on, so if it had been difficult to to find out, there wanted not among them long since who suggested such a course; which they not following, leave us a pattern of their judgment that it was not the not knowing, but the not approving, which was the cause of their not using it. Plato, a man of high authority indeed, but least of all for his Commonwealth, in the book of his laws, which no city ever yet received, fed his fancy with making many edicts to his airy burgomasters, which they who otherwise admire him, wish had been rather buried and excused in the genial cups of an academic night-sitting. By which laws he seems to tolerate no kind of learning, but by unalterable decree, consisting most of practical traditions, to the attainment whereof a library of smaller bulk than his own dialogues would be abundant. And there also enacts, that no poet should so much as read to any private man what he had written, until the judges and law-keepers had seen it, and allowed it; but that Plato meant this law peculiarly to that commonwealth which he had imagined, and to no other, is evident. Why was he not else a lawgiver to himself, but a transgressor, and to be expelled by his own magistrates, both for the wanton epigrams and dialogues which he made, and his perpetual reading of Sophron Mimus and Aristophanes, books of grossest infamy; and also for commending the latter of them, though he were the malicious libeller of his chief friends, to be read by the tyrant Dionysius, who had little need of such trash to spend his time on? But that he knew this licencing of poems had reference and dependence to many other provisoes there set down in his fancied republic, which in this world could have no place; and so neither he himself, nor any magistrate or city, ever imitated that course, which, taken apart from those other collateral injunctions, must needs be vain and fruitless.

" For if they fell upon one kind of strictness, unless their care were equal to regulate all other things of like aptness to corrupt the mind, that single endeavour they knew would be but a fond labour; to shut and fortify one gate against corruption, and be necessitated to leave others round about wide open. If we think to regulate printing, thereby to rectify manners, we must regulate all recreations and pastimes, all that is delightful to man. No music must be heard, no song be set or sung, but what is grave and doric. There must be licensing dancers, that no gesture, motion, or deportment be taught our youth, but what by their allowance shall be thought honest; for such Plato was provided of. It will ask more than the work of twenty licensers to examine all the lutes, the violins, and the guitars in every house; they must not be suffered to prattle as they do, but must be licensed what they may say. And who shall silence all the airs and madrigals that whisper softness in chambers? The windows also, and the balconies, must be thought on; these are shrewd books, with dangerous frontispieces, set to sale: who shall prohibit them, shall twenty licensers? The villages also must have their visitors to inquire what lectures the bagpipe and the rebec reads, even to the ballatry and the gamut of every municipal fiddler; for these are the countryman's Arcadias, and his Monte Mayors.

"Next, what more national corruption, for which England hears ill abroad, than household gluttony? Who shall be the rectors of our daily rioting? And what shall be done to inhibit the multitudes that frequent those houses where drunkenness is sold and harboured? Our garments also should be referred to the licensing of some more sober workmaster, to see them cut into a less wanton garb. Who shall regulate all the mixed conversation of our youth, male and female together, as is the fashion of this country? Who shall still appoint what shall be discoursed, what presumed, and no further? Lastly, who shall forbid and separate all idle resort, all evil company? These things will be, and must be: but how they shall be least hurtful, how least enticing, herein consists the grave and governing wisdom of a state.

"To sequester out of the world into Atlantic and Utopian politics, which never can be drawn into use, will not mend our condition; but to ordain wisely as in this world of evil, in the midst whereof God hath placed us unavoidably. Nor is it Plato's licensing of books will do this, which necessarily pulls along with it so many other kinds of licensing, as will make us all both ridiculous and weary, and yet frustrate; but those unwritten, or at least unconstraining laws of virtuous education, religious and civil nurture, which Plato there mentions, as the bonds and ligaments of the commonwealth, the pillars and the sustainers of every written statute; these they be, which will bear chief sway in such matters as these, when all licensing will be easily eluded. Impunity and remissness for certain are the bane of a commonwealth; but here the great art lies, to discern in what the law is to bid restraint and punishment, and in what things persuasion only is to work. If every action which is good or evil in man at ripe years were to be under pittance, prescription, and compulsion, what were virtue but a name, what praise could be then due to well-doing, what gramercy to be sober, just or continent?

"Many there be that complain of divine Providence for suffering Adam to transgress. Foolish tongues! when God gave him reason, He gave him freedom to choose, for reason is but choosing; he had been else a mere artificial Adam, such an Adam as he is in the motions. We ourselves esteem not of that obedience, or love, or gift, which is of force; God therefore left him free, set before him a provoking object ever almost in his eyes; herein consisted his merit, herein the right of his reward, the praise of his abstinence. Wherefore did he create passions within us, pleasures round about us, but that these rightly tempered are the very ingredients of virtue? They are not skilful considerers of human things, who imagine to remove sin, by removing the matter of sin; for, besides that it is a huge heap increasing under the very act of diminishing, though some part of it may for a time be withdrawn from some persons, it cannot from all, in such a universal thing as books are ; and when this is done, yet the sin remains entire. Though ye take from a covetous man all his treasure, he has yet one jewel left, ye cannot bereave him of his covetousness. Banish all objects of lust, shut up all youth into the severest discipline that can be exercised in any hermitage, ye cannot make them chaste, that came not thither so : such great care and wisdom is required to the right managing of this point.

"Suppose we could expel sin by this means ; look how much we thus expel of sin, so much we expel of virtue : for the matter of them both is the same : remove that, and ye remove them both alike. This justifies the high providence of God, who, though He commands us temperance, justice, continence, yet pours out before us even to a profuseness all desirable things, and gives us minds that can wander beyond all limit and satiety. Why should we then affect a vigour contrary to the manner of God and of nature, by abridging or scanting those means, which books freely permitted, are both to the trial of virtue, and the exercise of truth ?

"It would be better done, to learn that the law must needs be frivolous, which goes to restrain things, uncertainly and yet equally working to good and to evil. And were I the chooser, a dram of well-doing should be preferred before many times as much the forcible hindrance of evil doing. For God sure esteems the growth and completing of one virtuous person, more than the restraint of ten vicious. And albeit, whatever thing we hear or see, sitting, walking, travel- ling, or conversing, may be fitly called our book, and is of the same effect that writings are ; yet grant the thing to be prohibited were only books, it appears that this order hitherto is far insufficient to the end which it intends. Do we not see, not once or oftener, but weekly, that continued court libel against the par- liament and city, printed, as the wet sheets can wit- ness, and dispersed among us for all that licensing can do ? Yet this is the prime service a man would think wherein this order should give proof of itself. If it were executed, you will say. But certain, if exe- cution be remiss or blindfold now, and in this par- ticular, what will it be hereafter, and in other books?

" If then the order shall not be vain and frustrate, behold a new labour, lords and commons, ye must re- peal and proscribe all scandalous and unlicensed books already printed and divulged; after ye have drawn them up into a list, that all may know which are con- demned, and which not ; and ordain that no foreign books be delivered out of custody, till they have been read over. This office will require the whole time of not a few overseers, and those no vulgar men. There be also books which are partly useful and excellent, partly culpable and pernicious ; this work will ask as many more officials, to make expurgations and expunctions, that the commonwealth of learning be not damnified. In fine, when the multitude of books increase upon their hands, he must fain to catalogue all those printers who are found frequently offending, and forbid the importation of their whole suspected typography. In a word, that this your order may be exact, and not deficient, ye must reform it perfectly, according to the model of Trent and Sevil, which I know ye abhor to do.

" Yet though ye should condescend to this, which God forbid, the order still would be but fruitless and defective to that end, whereto ye meant it. If to prevent sects and schisms, who is so unread or uncatechised in story, that hath not heard of many sects refusing books as a hinderance, and preserving their doctrine unmixed for many ages, only by unwritten traditions ? The Christian faith (for that was once a schism !) is not unknown to have spread all over Asia, ere any gospel or epistle was seen in writing. If the amendment of manners be aimed at, look into Italy and Spain, whether those places be one scruple the better, the honester, the wiser, the chaster, since all the inquisitional rigour that hath been executed upon books.

" Another reason, whereby to make it plain that

this order will miss the end it seeks, consider by the quality which ought to be in every licenser. It cannot be denied, but that he who is made judge to sit upon the birth or death of books, whether they may be wafted into this world or not, had need to be a man above the common measure, both studious, learned, and judicious; there may be also no mean mistakes in the censure of what is passable or not; which is also no mean injury. If he be of such worth as behoves him, there cannot be a more tedious and unpleasing journey-work, a greater loss of time levied upon his head, than to be made the perpetual reader of unchosen books and pamphlets, oftimes huge volumes. There is no book that is acceptable, unless at certain seasons; but to be enjoined the reading of that at all times, and in a hand scarce legible, whereof three pages would not down at any time in the fairest print, is an imposition I cannot believe how he that values time, and his own studies, or is but of a sensible nostril, should be able to endure. In this one thing I crave leave of the present licensers to be pardoned for so thinking: who doubtless took this office up, looking on it through their obedience to the parliament, whose command perhaps made all things seem easy and un-laborious to them; but that this short trial hath wearied them out already, their own expressions and excuses to them who make so many journeys to solicit their license, are testimony enough. Seeing therefore those, who now possess the employment, by all evident signs wish themselves well rid of it, and that no man of worth, none that is not a plain unthrift of his own hours, is ever likely to succeed them, except he mean to put himself to the salary of a press corrector, we may easily foresee what kind of licensers we are to expect hereafter, either ignorant, imperious, and remiss, or basely pecuniary. This is what I had to show, wherein this order cannot conduce to that end whereof it bears the intention.

" I lastly proceed from the no good it can do, to the manifest hurt it causes, in being first the greatest discouragement and affront that can be offered to learning and to learned men. It was the complaint and lamentation of prelates, upon every least breath of a motion to remove pluralities, and to distribute more equally church revenues, that then all learning would be for ever dashed and discouraged. But as for that opinion, I never found cause to think that the tenth part of learning stood or fell with the clergy : nor could I ever but hold it for a sordid and unworthy speech of any churchman, who had a competency left him. If therefore ye be loath to dishearten utterly and discontent, not the mercenary crew of false pretenders to learning, but the free ingenuous sort of such as evidently were born to study and love learning for itself, not for lucre, or any other end, but the service of God and of truth, and perhaps that lasting

o

fame and perpetuity of praise, which God and good men have consented shall be the reward of those whose published labours advance the good of mankind : then know, that so far to distrust the judgment and the honesty of one who hath but a common repute in learning, and never yet offended, as not to count him fit to print his mind without a tutor and examiner, lest he should drop a schism, or something of corruption, is the greatest displeasure and indignity to a free and knowing spirit that can be put upon him.

" What advantage is it to be a man, over it is to be a boy at school, if we have only escaped the ferule, to come under the fescue of an imprimatur ? if serious and elaborate writings, as if they were no more than the theme of a grammar-lad under his pedagogue, must not be uttered without the cursory eyes of a temporizing and extemporizing licenser ? He who is not trusted with his own actions, his drift not being known to be evil, and standing to the hazard of the law and penalty, has no great argument to think himself reputed in the commonwealth wherein he was born for other than a fool or a foreigner. When a man writes to the world, he summons up all his reason and deliberation to assist him ; he searches, meditates, is industrious, and likely consults and confers with his judicious friends ; after all which done, he takes himself to be informed in what he writes, as

well as any that wrote before him, if in this, the most
consummate act of his fidelity and ripeness, no years,
no industry, no former proof of his abilities, can bring
him to that state of maturity, as not to be still mis-
trusted and suspected, unless he carry all his considerate diligence, all his midnight watchings, and expense
of Palladian oil, to the hasty view of an unleisured
licenser, perhaps much his younger, perhaps far his
inferior in judgment, perhaps one who never knew
the labour of book-writing; and if he be not repulsed,
or slighted, must appear in print like a puny with his
guardian, and his censor's hand on the back of his
title to be his bail and surety, that he is no idiot or
seducer; it cannot be but a dishonour, and deroga-
tion to the author, to the book, to the privilege and
dignity of learning.

"And what if the author shall be one so copious of
fancy, as to have many things well worth the adding,
come into his mind after licensing, while the book is
yet under the press, which not seldom happens to the
best and diligent writers; and that perhaps a dozen
times in one book. The printer dares not go beyond
his licensed copy; so often then must the author
trudge to his leave-giver, that those his new insertions
may be viewed; and many a jaunt will be made, ere
that licenser, for it must be the same man, can either
be found, or found at leisure; meanwhile either the
press must stand still, which is no small damage, or

the author lose his accuratest thoughts, and send the book forth worse than he had made it, which to a diligent writer is the greatest melancholy and vexation than can befall.

"And how can a man teach with authority, which is the life of teaching; how can he be a doctor in his book, as he ought to be, or else had better be silent, whenas all he teaches, all he delivers, is but under the tuition, under the correction of his patriarchal licenser, to blot or alter what precisely accords not with the hide-bound humour which he calls his judgment? When every acute reader, upon the first sight of a pedantic licence will be ready with these like words to ding the book a quoit's distance from him:—"I hate a pupil teacher; I endure not an instructor that comes to me under the wardship of an over-seeing fist. I know nothing of the licenser, but that I have his own hand here for his arrogance; who shall warrant me his judgment?" "The state, sir," replies the stationer: but has a quick return:—"The state shall be my governors, but not my critics; they may be mistaken in the choice of a licenser, as easily as this licenser may be mistaken in an author. This is some common stuff:" and we might add from Sir Francis Bacon, that "such authorised books are but the language of the times." For though a licenser should happen to be judicious more than ordinary, which will be a great jeopardy of the next succession, yet his very office and his commission enjoins him to let pass nothing but what is vulgarly received already.

"Nay, which is more lamentable, if the work of any deceased author, though never so famous in his lifetime, and even to this day, comes to their hands for licence to be printed, or reprinted, if there be found in his book, one sentence of a venturous edge, uttered in the height of zeal (and who knows whether it might not be the dictate of a divine spirit?), yet, not suiting with every low decrepit humour of their own, though it were Knox himself, the reformer of a king-dom, that spake it, they will not pardon him their dash; the sense of that great man shall to all pos-terity be lost, for the fearfulness, or the presumptuous rashness of a perfunctory licenser. And to what an author this violence hath been lately done, and in what book, of greatest consequence to be faithfully published, I could now instance, but shall forbear till a more convenient season. Yet if these things be not resented seriously and timely by them who have the remedy in their power, but that such ironmoulds as these thall have authority to gnaw out the choicest periods of exquisitest books, and to commit such a treacherous fraud against the often remainders of worthiest men after death, the more sorrow will belong to that hapless race of men, whose misfortune it is to have understanding. Henceforth let no man care to learn, or care to be more than worldly wise;

for certainly in higher matters to be ignorant and slothful, to be a common steadfast dunce, will be the only pleasant life and only in request.

" And as it is a particular disesteem of every knowing person alive, and most injurious to the written labours and monuments of the dead, so to me it seems an undervaluing and vilifying of the whole nation. I cannot set so light by all the invention, the art, the wit, the grave and solid judgment which is in England, as that it can be comprehended in any twenty capacities, how good soever ; much less that it should not pass except their superintendence be over it, except it be sifted and strained with their strainers, that it should be uncurrent without their manual stamp. Truth and understanding are not such wares as to be monopolized and traded in by tickets, and statutes, and standards.   We must not think to make a staple commodity of all the knowledge in the land, to mark and license it like our broadcloth and our woolpacks. What is it but a servitude like that imposed by the Philistines, not to be allowed the sharpening of our own axes and coulters, but we must repair from all quarters to twenty licensing forges ?

" Had any one written and divulged erroneous things and scandalous to honest life, misusing and forfeiting the esteem had of his reason among men, if after conviction this only censure were adjudged him, that he should never henceforth write but what were first examined by an appointed officer, whose hand should be annexed to pass his credit for him, that now he might be safely read; it could not be apprehended less than a disgraceful punishment. Whence to include the whole nation, and those that never yet thus offended, under such a diffident and suspectful prohibition, may plainly be understood what a disparagement it is. So much the more whenas debtors and delinquents may walk abroad without a keeper, but unoffensive books must not stir forth without a visible jailor in their title. Nor is it to the common people less than a reproach; for if we be so jealous over them as that we dare not trust them with an English pamphlet, what do we but censure them for a giddy, vicious, and ungrounded people; in such a sick and weak state of faith and discretion, as to be able to take nothing down but through the pipe of a licenser? That this is care or love of them, we cannot pretend, whenas in those popish places, where the laity are most hated and despised, the same strictness is used over them. Wisdom we cannot call it, because it stops but one breach of licence, nor that neither: whenas those corruptions, which it seeks to prevent, break in faster at other doors, which cannot be shut.

" And in conclusion it reflects to the disrepute of our ministers also, of whose labours we should hope better, and of their proficiency which their flock reaps by them, than that after all this light of the gospel which is, and is to be, and all this continual preaching, they should be still frequented with such an unprincipled, unedified, and laic rabble, as that the whiff of every new pamphlet should stagger them out of their catechism and Christian walking. This may have much reason to discourage the ministers, when such a low conceit is had of all their exhortations, and the benefiting of their hearers, as that they are not thought fit to be turned loose to three sheets of paper without a licenser; that all the sermons, all the lectures preached, printed, vended in such numbers, and such volumes, as have now well-nigh made all other books unsaleable, should not be armour enough against one single Euchiridion, without the castle of St. Angelo of an imprimatur.

"And lest some should persuade ye, lords and commons, that these arguments of learned men's discouragement at this your order are mere flourishes, and not real, I could recount what I have seen and heard in other countries, where this kind of inquisition tyrannizes; when I have sat among their learned men (for that honour I had), and been counted happy to be born in such a place of philosohpic freedom, as they supposed England was, while themselves did nothing but bemoan the servile condition into which learning amongst them was brought; that this was it which had damped the glory of Italian wits;

that nothing had been there written now these many years but flattery and fustian. There it was that I found and visited the famous Galileo, grown old, a prisoner to the inquisition, for thinking in astronomy otherwise than the Franciscan and Dominican licensers thought. And though I knew that England then was groaning loudest under the prelatical yoke, nevertheless I look it as a pledge of future happiness, that other nations were so persuaded of her liberty.

" Yet was it beyond my hope, that those worthies were then breathing in her air, who should be her leaders to such a deliverance, as shall never be forgotten by any revolution of time that this world hath to finish. When that was once begun, it was as little in my fear, that what words of complaint I heard among learned men of other parts uttered against the inquisition, the same I should hear, by as learned men at home, uttered in time of parliament against an order of licensing ; and that so generally, that when I had disclosed myself a companion of their discontent, I might say, if without envy, that he whom an honest quæstorship had endeared to the Sicilians was not more by them importuned against Verres, than the favourable opinion which I had among many who honour ye, and are known and respected by ye, loaded me with entreaties and persuasions, that I would not despair to lay together that which just reason should bring into my mind, towards the removal of an undeserved thraldom of learning.

"That this is not therefore the disburdening of a particular fancy, but the common grievance of all those who had prepared their minds and studies above the vulgar pitch, to advance truth in others, and from others to entertain it, thus much may satisfy. And in their name I shall for neither friend nor foe conceal what the general murmur is; that if it come to inquisitioning again, and licensing, and that we are so timorous of ourselves, and suspicious of all men, as to fear each book, and the shaking of each leaf, before we know what the contents are; if some who but of late were little better than silenced from preaching, shall come now to silence us from reading, except what they please, it cannot be guessed what is intended by some but a second tyranny over learning: and will soon put it out of controversy, that bishops and presbyters are the same to us, both name and thing.

"That those evils of prelaty which before from five or six and twenty sees were distributively charged upon the whole people will now light wholly on learning, is not obscure to us: whenas now the pastor of a small unlearned parish, on the sudden shall be exalted archbishop over a large diocess of books and yet not remove, but keep his other cure too, a mystical pluralist. He who but of late cried down the sole ordination of every novice bachelor of

MILTON'S PROSE WORKS. 203

art, and denied sole jurisdiction over the simplest parishioner, shall now, at home in his private chair, assume both these over worthiest and excellentest books, and ablest authors that write them. This is not the covenants and protestations that we have made! This is not to put down prelacy; this is but to chop an episcopacy; this is but to translate the palace metropolitan from one kind of dominion into another; this is but an old canonical sleight of commuting our penance. To startle thus betimes at a mere unlicensed pamphlet, will, after awhile, be afraid of every conventicle, and a while after will make a conventicle of every Christian meeting.

"But I am certain, that a state governed by the rules of justice and fortitude, or a church built and founded upon the rock of faith and true knowledge, cannot be so pusillanimous. While things are yet not constituted in religion, that freedom of writing should be restrained by a discipline initiated from the prelates, and learned by them from the inquisition to shut us up all again into the breast of a licenser, must needs give cause of doubt and discouragement to all learned and religious men; who cannot but discern the fineness of this politic drift, and who are the contrivers; that while bishops were to be bated down, then all presses might be open; it was the people's birthright and privilege in time of parliament, it was the breaking forth of light.

" But now the bishops abrogated and voided out of
the church, as if our reformation sought no more, but
to make room for others into their seats under another
name ; the episcopal arts begin to bud again ; the
cruse of truth must run no more oil ; liberty of printing must be enthralled again, under a prelatical commission of twenty; the privilege of the people nullified;
and, which is worse, the freedom of learning must
groan again, and to her old fetters : all this, the parliament yet sitting. Although their own late arguments and
defences against the prelates might remember them,
that this obstructing violence meets for the most part
with an event utterly opposite to the end which it
drives at : instead of suppressing sects and schisms, it
raises them and invests them with a reputation : " the
punishing of wits enhances their authority," saith the
Viscount St. Albans ; " and a forbidden writing is
thought to be a certain spark of truth, that flys up in
the faces of them who seek to tread it out." This
order, therefore, may prove a nursing mother to sects,
but I shall easily show how it will be a step-dame to
truth : and first, by disenabling us to the maintenance
of what is known already.

" Well knows he who uses to consider, that our
faith and knowledge thrives by exercise, as well as
our limbs and complexion. Truth is compared in
scripture to a streaming fountain ; if her waters flow
not in a perpetual progression, they sicken into a

muddy pool of conformity and tradition. A man may be a heretic in the truth ; and if he believe things only because his pastor says so, or the assembly so determines, without knowing other reason, though his belief be true, yet the very truth he holds becomes his heresy. There is not any burden that some would gladlier post off to another, than the charge and care of their religion. There be, who knows not that there be ? of protestants and professors, who live and die in as errant and implicit faith, as any lay papist of Loretto.

"A wealthy man, addicted to his pleasure and to his profits, finds religion to be a traffic so entangled, and of so many fiddling accounts, that of all mysteries he cannot skill to keep a stock going upon that trade. What should he do ? Fain he would have the name to be religious, fain he would bear up with his neighbours in that. What does he therefore, but resolves to give over toiling, and to find himself out some factor, to whose care and credit he may commit the whole managing of his religious affairs ; some divine of note and estimation that must be. To him he adheres, resigns the whole warehouse of his religion, with all the locks and keys, into his custody ; and indeed makes the very person of that man his religion; esteems his associating with him a sufficient evidence and commendatory of his own piety. So that a man may say his religion is now no more within himself, but is become a dividual moveable, and goes and comes near him, according as that good man frequents the house. He entertains him, gives him gifts, feasts him, lodges him; his religion comes home at night, prays, is liberally supped, and sumptuously laid to sleep; rises, is saluted, and after the malmsey, or some well-spiced bruage, and better breakfasted, than he whose morning appetite would have gladly fed on green figs between Bethany and Jerusalem, his religion walks abroad at eight, and leaves his kind entertainer in the shop trading all day without his religion.

"Another sort there be, who when they hear that all things shall be ordered, all things regulated and settled; nothing written but what passes through the custom-house of certain publicans that have the tonnaging and poundaging of all free-spoken truth, will straight give themselves up into your hands, make them and cut them out what religion ye please: there be delights, there be recreations and jolly pastimes, that will fetch the day about from sun to sun, and rock the tedious year as in a delightful dream. What need they torture their heads with that which others have taken so strictly, and so unalterably into their own purveying? These are the fruits which a dull ease and cessation of our knowledge will bring forth among the people. How goodly, and how to be wished were such an obedient unanimity as this! What a fine conformity would it starch us all into!

Doubtless a staunch and solid piece of framework, as any January could freeze together.

"Nor much better will be the consequence even among the clergy themselves: it is no new thing never heard of before, for a parochial minister, who has his reward and is at his Hercules' pillars in a warm benefice, to be easily inclinable, if he have nothing else that may rouse up his studies, to finish his circuit in an English Concordance and a topic folio, the gatherings and savings of a sober graduateship, a Harmony and a Catena, treading the constant round of certain common doctrinal heads, attended with their uses, motives, marks, and means; out of which, as out of an alphabet or sol-fa, by forming and transforming, joining and disjoining variously, a little book-craft, and two hours' meditation, might furnish him unspeakably to the performance of more than a weekly charge of sermoning: not to reckon up the infinite helps of interliniaries, breviaries, synopses, and other loitering gear. But as for the multitude of sermons ready printed and piled up, on every text that is not difficult, our London trading St. Thomas in his vestry, and add to boot St. Martin and St. Hugh, have not within their hallowed limits more vendible ware of all sorts ready made: so that penury he never need fear of pulpit provision, having where so plenteously to refresh his magazine. But if his rear and flanks be not impaled, if his back-door be not secured by the rigid licenser, but that a

bold book may now and then issue forth, and give the
assault to some of his old collections in their trenches,
it will concern him then to keep waking, to stand in
watch, to set good guards and sentinels about his received opinions, to walk the round and counter-round
with his fellow-inspectors, fearing lest any of his flock
be seduced who also then would be better instructed,
better exercised, and disciplined.   And God send that
the fear of this diligence, which must then be used, do
not make us affect the laziness of a licensing church!

" For if we be sure we are in the right, and do not
hold the truth guiltily, which becomes not, if we ourselves condemn not our own weak and frivolous teaching, and the people for an untaught and irreligious
gadding rout; what can be more fair, than when a
man judicious, learned, and of a conscience, for aught
we know, as good as theirs that taught us what we
know, shall not privily from house to house, which is
more dangerous, but openly by writing, publish to
the world what his opinion is, what his reasons, and
wherefore that which is now thought cannot be sound?
Christ urged it as wherewith to justify Himself, that
He preached in public; yet writing is more public
than preaching; and more easy to refutation it need
be, there being so many whose business and profession
merely it is to be the champions of truth; which if
they neglect, what can be imputed but their sloth or
inability ?

"Thus much we are hindered and disinured by this course of licensing towards the true knowledge of what we seem to know. For how much it hurts and hinders the licensers themselves in the calling of their ministry, more than any secular employment, if they will discharge that office as they ought, so that of necessity they must neglect either the one duty or the other, I insist not, because it is a particular, but leave it to their own conscience, how they will decide it there.

"There is yet behind of what I purposed to lay open, the incredible loss and detriment that this plot of licensing puts us to, more than if some enemy at sea should stop up all our havens, and ports, and creeks: it hinders and retards the importation of our richest merchandise,—truth: nay, it was first established and put in practice by anti-Christian malice and mystery, or set purpose to extinguish, if it were possible, the light of reformation, and to settle falsehood; little differing from that policy wherewith the Turk upholds his Alcoran, by the prohibiting of printing. It is not denied, but gladly confessed, we are to send our thanks and vows to heaven, louder than most of nations, for that great measure of truth which we enjoy, especially in those main points between us and the Pope, with his appurtenances the prelates: but he who thinks we are to pitch our tent here, and have attained the utmost prospect of reformation that the mortal glass wherein we contemplate can show us, till we come to beatific vision, that man by this very opinion declares that he is yet far short of truth.

"Truth indeed came once into the world with her divine Master, and was a perfect shape most glorious to look on: but when He ascended, and His apostles after Him were laid asleep, then straight arose a wicked race of deceivers, who, as that story goes of the Egyptian Typhon with his conspirators, how they dealt with the good Osiris, took the virgin Truth, hewed her lovely form into a thousand pieces, and scattered them to the four winds. From that time ever since, the sad friends of Truth, such as durst appear, imitating the careful search that Isis made for the mangled body of Osiris, went up and down gathering up limb by limb still as they could find them. We have not yet found them all, lords and commons, nor ever shall do, till her Master's second coming. He shall bring together every joint and member, and shall mould them into an immortal feature of loveliness and perfection. Suffer not these licensing prohibitions to stand at every place of opportunity forbidding and disturbing them that continue seeking, that continue to do our obsequies to the torn body of our martyred saint.

"We boast our light; but if we look not wisely on the sun itself, it smites us into darkness. Who can discern those planets that are oft combust, and those stars of brightest magnitude that rise and set with the sun, until the opposite motion of their orbs bring them to such a place in the firmament, where they may be seen evening or morning? The light which we have gained was given us, not to be ever staring on, but by it to discover onward things more remote from our knowledge. It is not the unfrocking of a priest, the unmitring of a bishop, and the removing him from off the presbyterian shoulders, that will make us a happy nation: no; if other things as great in the church, and in the rule of life both œconomical and political, be not looked into and reformed, we have looked so long upon the blaze that Zuinglius and Calvin have beaconed up to us, that we are stark blind.

"There be who perpetually complain of schisms and sects, and make it such a calamity that any man dissents from their maxims. It is their own pride and ignorance which causes the disturbing, who neither will hear with meekness, nor can convince, yet all must be suppressed which is not found in their syntagma. They are the troublers, they are the dividers of unity, who neglect and permit not others to unite those dissevered pieces, which are yet wanting to the body of truth. To be still searching what we know not, by what we know, still closing up truth to truth as we find it (for all her body is homogeneal, and proportionable), this is the golden rule in theology as well as in arithmetic, and makes up the best harmony in a church; not the forced and outward union of cold, and neutral, and inwardly divided mind.

"Lords and Commons of England! consider what nation it is whereof ye are, and whereof ye are the governors: a nation not slow and dull, but of a quick, ingenious, and piercing spirit; acute to invent, subtle and sinewy to discourse, not beneath the reach of any point the highest that human capacity can soar to. Therefore the studies of learning in her deepest sciences have been so ancient, and so eminent among us, that writers of good antiquity and able judgment have been persuaded, that even the school of Pythagoras, and the Persian wisdom, took beginning from the old philosophy of this island. And that wise and civil Roman, Julius Agricola, who governed once here for Cæsar, preferred the natural wits of Britain before the laboured studies of the French.

"Nor is it for nothing that the grave and frugal Transylvanian sends out yearly from as far as the mountainous borders of Russia, and beyond the Hercynian wilderness, not their youth, but their staid men, to learn our language and our theological arts. Yet that which is above all this, the favour and the love of Heaven, we have great argument to think in a peculiar manner propitious and propending towards us. Why else was this nation chosen before any other, that out of her, as out of Sion, should be proclaimed and sounded forth the first tidings and trumpet of reformation to all Europe? And had it not been the obstinate perverseness of our prelates against the divine and admirable spirit of Wickliffe, to suppress him as a schismatic and innovator, perhaps neither the Bohemian Husse and Jerome, no, nor the name of Luther or of Calvin, had been ever known : the glory of reforming all our neighbours had been completely ours. But now, as our obdurate clergy have with violence demeaned the matter, we are become hitherto the latest and the backwardest scholars, of whom God offered to have made us the teachers.

"Now once again by all concurrence of signs, and by the general instinct of holy and devout men, as they daily and solemnly express their thoughts, God is decreeing to begin some new and great period in His church, even to the reforming of reformation itself; what does He then but reveal Himself to His servants, and as His manner is, first to His Englishmen? I say, as His manner is, first to us, though we mark not the method of His counsels, and are unworthy. Behold now this vast city, a city of refuge, the mansion-house of liberty, encompassed and surrounded with His protection; the shop of war hath not there more anvils and hammers working, to fashion out the plates and instruments of armed justice in defence of beleagured truth, than there be

pens and heads there, sitting by their studious lamps,
musing, searching, revolving new notions and ideas
wherewith to present, as with their homage and their
fealty, the approaching reformation: others as fast
reading, trying all things, assenting to the force of
reason and convincement.

"What could a man require more from a nation so
pliant and so prone to seek after knowledge? What
wants there to such a towardly and pregnant soil, but
wise and faithful labourers, to make a knowing people,
a nation of prophets, of sages, and of worthies? We
reckon more than five months yet to harvest; there
need not be five weeks, had we but eyes to lift up,
the fields are white already. Where there is much
desire to learn, there of necessity will be much
arguing, much writing, many opinions; for opinion in
good men is but knowledge in the making. Under
these fantastic terrors of sect and schism, we wrong
the earnest and zealous thirst after knowledge and
understanding, which God has stirred up in this city.
What some lament of we rather should rejoice at,
should rather praise this pious forwardness among
men, to re-assume the ill-deputed care of their
religion into their own hands again. A little generous prudence, a little forbearance of one another,
and some grain of charity might win all these dili-
gences to join and unite into one general and brotherly
search after truth; could we but forego this prelatical

tradition of crowding free consciences and Christian liberties into canons and precepts of men. I doubt not, if some great and worthy stranger should come among us, wise to discern the mould and temper of a people, and how to govern it, observing the high hopes and aims, the diligent alacrity of our extended thoughts and reasonings in the pursuance of truth and freedom, but that he would cry out, as Pyrrhus did, admiring the Roman docility and courage, " If such were my Epirots, I would not despair the greatest design that could be attempted to make a church or kingdom happy."

" Yet these are the men cried out against for schismatics and sectaries, as if, while the temple of the Lord was building, some cutting, some squaring the marble, others hewing the cedars, there should be a sort of irrational men, who could not consider there must be many schisms and many dissections made in the quarry and in the timber ere the house of God can be built. And when every stone is laid artfully together, it cannot be united into a continuity, it can but be contiguous in this world: neither can every piece of the building be of one form; nay, rather the perfection consists in this, that out of many moderate varieties and brotherly dissimilitudes that are not vastly disproportional, arises the goodly and the graceful symmetry that commends the whole pile and structure.

"Let us therefore be more considerate builders, more wise in spiritual architecture, when great reformation is expected. For now the time seems come, wherein Moses, the great prophet, may sit in heaven rejoicing to see that memorable and glorious wish of his fulfilled, when not only our seventy elders, but all the Lord's people, are become prophets. No marvel then though some men, and some good men too perhaps, but young in goodness, as Joshua then was, envy them. They fret, and out of their own weakness are in agony, lest these divisions and subdivisions will undo us. The adversary again applauds, and waits the hour : when they have branched themselves out, saith he, small enough into parties and partitions, then will be our time. Fool! he sees not the firm root, out of which we all grow, though into branches; nor will beware, until he see our small divided maniples cutting through at every angle of his ill-united and unwieldy brigade. And that we are to hope better of all these supposed sects and schisms, and that we shall not need that solicitude, honest perhaps, though overtimorous, of them that vex in this behalf, but shall laugh in the end at those malicious applauders of our differences, I have these reasons to persuade me.

" First, when a city shall be as it were besieged and blocked about, her navigable river infested, inroads and incursions round, defiance and battle oft rumoured to be marching up, even to her walls and suburb trenches; that then the people, or the greater part, more than at other times, wholly taken up with the study of highest and most important matters to be reformed, should be disputing, reasoning, reading, inventing, discoursing, even to a rarity and admiration, things not before discoursed or written of, argues first a singular good will, contentedness, and confidence in your prudent foresight, and safe government, lords and commons; and from thence derives itself to a gallant bravery and well-grounded contempt of their enemies, as if there were no small number of as great spirits among us, as his was who, when Rome was nigh besieged by Hannibal, being in the city, bought that piece of ground at no cheap rate whereon Hannibal himself encamped his own regiment.

"Next, it is a lively and cheerful presage of our happy success and victory. For as in a body when the blood is fresh, the spirits pure and vigorous, not only to vital, but to rational faculties, and those in the acutest and the pertest operations of wit and subtlety, it argues in what good plight and constitution the body is; so when the cheerfulness of the people is so sprightly up, as that it has not only wherewith to guard well its own freedom and safety, but to spare, and to bestow upon the solidest and sublimest points of controversy and new invention, it betokens us not degenerated, nor drooping to a fatal decay, by casting

off the old and wrinkled skin of corruption to outlive
these pangs, and wax young again, entering the glorious ways of truth and prosperous virtue, destined to
become great and honourable in these latter ages.
Methinks I see in my mind a noble and puissant
nation rousing herself like a strong man after sleep,
and shaking her invincible locks: methinks I see her
as an eagle mewing her mighty youth, and. kindling
her undazzled eyes at the full midday beam ; purging
and unscaling her long-abused sight at the fountain
itself of heavenly radiance ; while the whole noise of
timorous and flocking birds, with those also that love
the twilight, flutter about, amazed at what she means,
and in their envious gabble would prognosticate a
year of sects and schisms.

"What should ye do then, should ye suppress all
this flowery crop of knowledge and new light sprung
up and yet springing daily in this city ?   Should ye
set an oligarchy of twenty engrossers over it, to bring
a famine upon our minds again, when we shall know
nothing but what is measured to us by their bushel?
Believe it, lords and commons ! they who counsel ye
to such a suppressing, do as good bid ye suppress yourselves ; and I will soon show how.   If it be desired
to know the immediate cause of all this free writing
and free speaking, there cannot be assigned a truer
than your own mild, and free, and humane government; it is the liberty, lords and commons, which

your own valorous and happy counsels have purchased us ; liberty which is the nurse of all great wits : this is that which hath rarefied and enlightened our spirits like the influence of heaven ; this is that which hath enfranchised, enlarged, and lifted up our apprehensions degrees above ourselves. Ye cannot make us now less capable, less knowing, less eagerly pursuing of the truth, unless ye first make yourselves, that made us so, less the lovers, less the founders of our true liberty. We can grow ignorant again, brutish, formal, and slavish, as ye found us ; but you then must first become that which ye cannot be, oppressive, arbitrary, and tyrannous, as they were from whom ye have freed us. That our hearts are now more capacious, our thoughts more erected to the search and expectation of greatest and exactest things, is the issue of your own virtue propagated in us ; ye cannot suppress that, unless ye reinforce an abrogated and merciless law, that fathers may dispatch at will their own children. And who shall then stick closest to ye and excite others? Not he who takes up arms for coat and conduct, and his four nobles of Danegelt. Although I dispraise not the defence of just immunities, yet love my peace better, if that were all. Give me the liberty to know, to utter, and to argue freely according to conscience, above all liberties.

"What would be best advised then, if it be found so hurtful and so unequal to suppress opinions for the

newness or the unsuitableness to a customary acceptance, will not be my task to say; I shall only repeat
what I have learned from one of your own honourable
number, a right noble and pious lord, who had he
not sacrificed his life and fortunes to the church and
commonwealth, we had not now missed and bewailed
a worthy and undoubted patron of this argument. Ye
know him, I am sure; yet I for honour's sake, and
may it be eternal to him, shall name him, the Lord
Brook. He writing of episcopacy, and by the way
treating of sects and schisms, left ye his vote, or rather
now the last words of his dying charge, which I know
will ever be of dear and honoured regard with ye, so
full of meekness and breathing charity, that next to
His last testament, who bequeathed love and peace to
His disciples, I cannot call to mind where I have read
or heard words more mild and peaceful. He there
exhorts us to hear with patience and humility those,
however they be miscalled, that desire to live
purely, in such a use of God's ordinances, as the best
guidance of their conscience gives them, and to tolerate
them, though in some disconformity to ourselves. The
book itself will tell us more at large, being published
to the world, and dedicated to the parliament by him,
who both for his life and for his death deserves, that
what advice he left be not laid by without perusal.

"And now the time in special is, by privilege to
write and speak what may help to the further dis-

cussing of matters in agitation. The temple of Janus, with his two controversial faces, might now not insignificantly be set open. And though all the winds of doctrine were let loose to play upon the earth, so truth be in the field, we do injuriously by licensing and prohibiting to misdoubt her strength. Let her and falsehood grapple; who ever knew truth put to the worse, in a free and open encounter? Her confuting is the best and surest suppressing. He who hears what praying there is for light and clear knowledge to be sent down among us, would think of other matters to be constituted beyond the discipline of Geneva, framed and fabricated already to our hands.

" Yet when the new light which we beg for shines in upon us, there be who envy and oppose, if it come not first in at their casements. What a collusion is this, whenas we are exhorted by the wise man to use diligence, " to seek for wisdom as for hidden treasures," early and late, that another order shall enjoin us, to know nothing but by statute? When a man hath been labouring the hardest labour in the deep mines of knowledge, hath furnished out his findings in all their equipage, drawn forth his reasons as it were a battle ranged, scattered and defeated all objections in his way, calls out his adversary into the plain, offers him the advantage of wind and sun, if he please, only that he may try the matter by dint of argument; for his opponents then to skulk, to lay ambushments, to keep a narrow bridge of licensing where the challenger should pass, though it be valour enough in soldiership, is but weakness and cowardice in the wars of truth. For who knows not that truth is strong, next to the Almighty; she needs no policies, nor stratagems, nor licensings to make her victorious, those are the shifts and the defences that error uses against her power: give her but room, and do not bind her when she sleeps, for then she speaks not true, as the old Protends did, who spake oracles only when he was caught and bound, but then rather she turns herself into all shapes except her own, and perhaps tunes her voice according to the time, as Micaiah did before Ahab, until she be adjured into her own likeness.

"Yet is it not impossible that she may have more shapes than one? What else is all that rank of things indifferent, wherein truth may be on this side, or on the other, without being unlike herself? What but a vain shadow else is the abolition of "those ordinances, that handwriting nailed to the cross"? What great purchase is this Christian liberty which Paul so often boasts of? His doctrine is that he who eats or eats not, regards a day or regards it not, may do either to the Lord. How many other things might be tolerated in peace, and left to conscience, had we but charity, and were it not the chief stronghold of our hypocrisy to be ever judging one another? I fear yet this iron yoke of outward conformity hath left a slavish print upon our necks: the ghost of a linen decency yet haunts us. We stumble, and are impatient at the least dividing of one visible congregation from another, though it be not in fundamentals; and through our forwardness to suppress, and our backwardness to recover, any enthralled piece of truth out of the gripe of custom, we care not to keep truth separated from truth, which is the fiercest rent and disunion of all. We do not see that while we still affect by all means a rigid external formality, we may as soon fall again into a gross conforming stupidity, a stark and dead congealment of " wood and hay and stubble " forced and frozen together, which is more to the sudden degenerating of a church than many subdichotomies of petty schisms.

" Not that I can think well of every light separation; or that all in a church is to be expected " gold and silver, and precious stones ": it is not possible for man to sever the wheat from the tares, the good fish from the other fry; that must be the angels' ministry at the end of mortal things. Yet if all cannot be of one mind, as who looks they should be? this doubtless is more wholesome, more prudent, and more Christian, that many be tolerated rather than all compelled. I mean not tolerated popery, and open superstition, which as it extirpates all religious and civil supremacies, so itself should be extirpate, provided first that all charitable and compassionate means be used to win and regain the weak and the misled: that also which is impious or evil absolutely either against faith or manners, no law can possibly permit that intends not to unlaw itself: but those neighbouring differences, or rather indifferences, are what I speak of, whether in some point of doctrine or of discipline, which though they may be many, yet need not interrupt the unity of spirit, if we could but find among us the bond of peace.

"In the meanwhile, if any one would write, and bring his helpful hand to the slow-moving reformation which we labour under, if truth have spoken to him before others, or but seemed at least to speak, who hath so bejesuited us, that we should trouble that man with asking licence to do so worthy a deed; and not consider this, that if it come to prohibiting, there is not aught more likely to be prohibited than truth itself: whose first appearance to our eyes, bleared and dimmed with prejudice and custom, is more unsightly and unplausible than many errors; even as the person is of many a great man slight and contemptible to see. And what do they tell us vainly of new opinions, when this very opinion of theirs, that none must be heard but whom they like, is the worst and newest opinion of all others; and is the chief cause why sect and schisms do so much abound, and true knowledge is kept at distance from us; besides yet a greater danger which is in it. For when God shakes a kingdom, with strong and healthful commotions, to a general reforming, it is not untrue that many sectaries and false teachers are then busiest in seducing.

" But yet more true it is, that God then raises to His own work men of rare abilities, and more than common industry, not only to look back and revive what hath been taught heretofore, but to gain further, and to go on some new enlightened steps in the discovery of truth. For such is the order of God's enlightening His church, to dispense and deal out by degrees His beams, so as our earthly eyes may best sustain it. Neither is God appointed and confined, where and out of what place these His chosen shall be first heard to speak ; for He sees not as man sees, chooses not as man chooses, lest we should devote ourselves again to set places and assemblies, and outward callings of men ; planting our faith one while in the old convocation house ; and another while in the chapel at Westminster ; when all the faith and religion that shall be there canonized, is not sufficient without plain convincement, and the charity of patient instruction, to supple the least bruise of conscience, to edify the meanest Christian, who desires to walk in the spirit, and not in the letter of human trust, for all the number of voices that can be there made ; no, though Harry the Seventh himself there, with all his liege tombs about him, should lend them voices from the dead to swell their number.

" And if the men be erroneous who appear to be
the leading schismatics, what withholds us but our
sloth, our self-will, and distrust in the right cause,
that we do not give them gentle meetings and gentle
dismissions, that we debate not and examine the
matter thoroughly with liberal and frequent audience;
if not for their sakes yet for our own? Seeing no
man who hath tasted learning, but will confess the
many ways of profiting by those who, not contented
with stale receipts, are able to manage and set forth
new positions to the world. And were they but as
the dust and cinders of our feet, so long as in that
notion they may yet serve to polish and brighten the
armoury of truth, even for that respect they were not
utterly to be cast away. But if they be of those
whom God hath fitted for the special use of these
times with eminent and ample gifts, and those perhaps neither among the priests, nor among the pharisees, and we, in the haste of a precipitant zeal, shall
make no distinction, but resolve to stop their mouths,
because we fear they come with new and dangerous
opinions, as we commonly forejudge them ere we
understand them; no less than woe to us, while,
thinking thus to defend the gospel, we are found the
persecutors!

" There have been not a few since the beginning of
this parliament, both of the presbytery and others,
who by their unlicensed books to the contempt of an

imprimatur first broke that triple ice clung about our hearts, and taught the people to see day; I hope that none of those were the persuaders to renew upon us this bondage, which they themselves have wrought so much good by contemning. But if neither the check that Moses gave to young Joshua, nor the countermand which our Saviour gave to young John, who was so ready to prohibit those whom he thought unlicensed, be not enough to admonish our elders how unacceptable to God their testy mood of prohibiting is; if neither their own remembrance what evil hath abounded in the church by this lett of licensing, and what good they themselves have begun by transgressing it, be not enough, but that they will persuade and execute the most Dominican part of the inquisition over us, and are already with one foot in the stirrup so active at suppressing, it would be no unequal distribution in the first place to suppress the suppressors themselves; whom the change of their condition hath puffed up, more than their late experience of harder times hath made wise.

"And as for regulating the press, let no man think to have the honour of advising ye better than yourselves have done in that order published next before this, "That no book be printed, unless the printer's and the author's name, or at least the printer's, be registered." Those which otherwise come forth, if they be found mischievous and libellous, the fire and

the executioner will be the timeliest and the most
effectual remedy that man's prevention can use.   For
this authentic Spanish policy of licensing books, if I
have said aught, will prove the most unlicensed book
itself within a short while ; and was the immediate
image of a star-chamber decree to that purpose made
in those times when that court did the rest of those
her pious works, for which she is now fallen from the
stars with Lucifer.   Whereby ye may guess what
kind of state prudence, what love of the people, what
care of religion or good manners there was at the
contriving, although with singular hypocrisy it pretended to bind books to their good behaviour.   And
how it got the upper hand of your precedent order so
well constituted before, if we may believe those men
whose profession gives them cause to inquire most, it
may be doubted there was in it the fraud of some old
patentees and monopolizers in the trade of booksell-
ing ; who, under the pretence of the poor in their
company not to be defrauded, and the just retaining
of each man his several copy (which God forbid should
be gainsaid !), brought divers glossing colours to the
house, which were indeed but colours, and serving to
no end except it be to exercise a superiority over
their neighbours ; men who do not therefore labour
in an honest profession, to which learning is indebted,
that they should be made other men's vassals.   Another end is thought was aimed at by some of them

in procuring by petition this order, that having power in their hands, malignant books might . the easier escape abroad, as the event shows. But these sophisms and elenchs of merchandise I skill not : this I know, that errors in a good government and in a bad are equally almost incident ; for what magistrate may not be misinformed, and much the sooner, if liberty of printing be reduced into the power of a few? But to redress willingly and speedily what hath been erred, and in highest authority to esteem a plain advertisement more than others have done a sumptuous bride, is a virtue (honoured lords and commons !) answerable to your highest actions, and whereof none can participate but greatest and wisest men."

THE TENURE OF KINGS AND MAGISTRATES:

PROVING

THAT IT IS LAWFUL, AND HATH BEEN HELD SO THROUGH ALL
AGES, FOR ANY, WHO HAVE THE POWER, TO CALL TO AC-
COUNT A TYRANT, OR WICKED KING, AND AFTER DUE CON-
VICTION, TO DEPOSE, AND PUT HIM TO DEATH, IF THE OR-
DINARY MAGISTRATE HAVE NEGLECTED, OR DENIED TO DO
IT. AND THAT THEY WHO OF LATE SO MUCH BLAME DE-
POSING, ARE THE MEN THAT DID IT THEMSELVES.

THE enunciation of this elaborate and wicked title
is quite enough to deter any from wasting their
time in the perusal of the Treatise itself. We pronounce this, published in 1650, the year following
the murder and execution of Charles I., and his once
celebrated work, EICONOCLASTES, written at the request of Parliament, in 1651, in answer to a book
entitled "Eikon Basilikè, the portraiture of his sacred
Majesty in his solitudes and sufferings," to be the drossiest of all Milton's prose works, from which we are
unable to extract any single grain of gold. In the
Second Defence of the People of England, we shall
come to a most interesting account of the circumstances under which both of these were written, which
we shall quote in its place. From that passage we

learn that the first four books of his History of England were composed at this period—that is, in 1650; but the remainder did not appear till a considerable time afterwards. He now kept himself secluded at home, and thought he was about to enjoy an interval of uninterrupted literary ease, or, rather, of political ease and literary labour, for his active mind could not long be idle. To his surprise, the Council of State requested him to reply to the King's book, of which, in a short time, forty-seven editions had been sold, comprising forty-eight thousand five hundred copies. He opposed, accordingly, the Iconoclast to his Icon. " I did not," says he, " insult over fallen majesty, as is pretended; I only preferred Queen Truth to King Charles." Reginam Veritatem regi Carolo anteponendam arbitratus. Almost immediately afterwards he was appointed by the Council to reply to Salmasius, which he does in his Defensio pro populo Anglicano, to which we shall presently proceed. We do not intend to enter into a defence of Charles himself, though our own inclinations and sympathies would certainly lead us to do this, nor into the authenticity of his celebrated book. We agree with Southey, that, ' in any other age, Charles I. would have been the best and the most popular of kings. His unambitious and conscientious spirit would have preserved the kingdom in peace; his private life would have set an example of dignified virtue, such as had rarely been seen in courts; and his love of arts and letters would have conferred permanent splendour upon his age, and secured for himself the grateful applause of after generations.' Under more favourable circumstances, we can even imagine that such a king as he might have been would have become the friend and patron of such a man as Milton would then have been, and in spite of untoward circumstances was, the fosterer of his genius, the admirer of his learning, the rewarder of his merit.

One word more on the authenticity of the Eikon Basilikè; judging from external evidence it may be doubtful whether Charles or Bishop Gauden were the author, but the internal evidence is wholly in favour of the former. Southey says 'there is very little testimony on Gauden's side (strictly speaking, perhaps, none at all), except his own. There is a mass of testimony which shows that the king had the book continually in his hand, revised it much, and had many transcripts of it. Had it been the work of Gauden, or of any person writing to support the royal cause, a higher tone concerning episcopacy and prerogative would have been taken; there would have been more effort at justification; and there would not have been that inefficient but conscientious defence of fatal concessions; that penitent confession of sin where weakness had been sinful; that piety without alloy; that character of mild and even magnanimity; and that

heavenly-mindedness, which render the Eikon Basilikè
one of the most interesting books in our language.'
—*Southey's Life of Cromwell.* We may just remark that
the editor of Bohn's edition of Milton's Prose Works,
pronounces the Eikon Basilikè to be 'a volume too
dull to be now read with patience'; and consistently
with his republican principles and predilections he ad-
mires and extols the Eiconoclastes. We leave it to
others to decide which opinion is the correct one, only
ourselves avowing our inability to detect in Milton's
answer to the Eikon any of his usual sentences of a
venturous edge, uttered in the height of zeal, and possibly at the dictate of a divine spirit. Alas, his good
genius seems to have forsaken him, and we cannot
wonder at it. His diction here corresponds with his
theme; and never rises to a higher level. No angel
held the pen while he wrote.

There is, however, one celebrated passage in the
first chapter of the Eiconoclastes, which we must not
omit, though it has often been misunderstood. It is
this :

"Andronicus Comnenus, the Byzantine emperor,
though a most cruel tyrant, is reported by Nicetas to
have been a constant reader of St. Paul's Epistles; and
by continual study had so incorporated the phrase and
style of that transcendant Apostle into all his familiar
letters, that the imitation seemed to vie with the
original. Yet this availed not to deceive the people
of that empire, who, notwithstanding his saint's vizard,

tore him to pieces for his tyranny. From stories of this nature both ancient and modern which abound, the poets also, and some English, have been in this point so mindful of decorum, as to put never more pious words in the mouth of any person, than of a tyrant. I shall not instance an abstruse author, wherein the king might be less conversant, but one whom we well know was the closet companion of these his solitudes, William Shakespeare; who introduces the person of Richard the Third, speaking in as high a strain of piety and mortification as is uttered in any passage of this book, and sometimes to the same sense and purpose with some words in this place: 'I intended,' saith he, 'not only to oblige my friends, but my enemies.' The like saith Richard, ii. 1.

> 'I do not know that Englishman alive
> With whom my soul is any jot at odds,
> More than the infant that is born to-night;
> I thank my God for my humility.'

Other stuff of this sort may be read throughout the whole tragedy, wherein the poet used not much licence in departing from the truth of history, which delivers him a deep dissembler, not of his affections only, but of religion."

Warton and others have supposed that Milton is here reproaching Charles with being familiar with Shakespeare. Nothing can be farther from the fact, as well might we say that he censures Comnenus for studying St. Paul's Epistles. Milton himself was familiar with and greatly admired the bard of Avon.

To prove this assertion we need only quote his beautiful "Epitaph on the admirable Dramatic Poet, William Shakespeare," written in his twenty-first year, in
1630, and a passage from the L'Allegro, written a few
years afterwards.

> " What needs my Shakespeare for his honour'd bones,
> The labour of an age in piled stones ?
> Or that his hallow'd relics should be hid
> Under a star-ypointing pyramid ?
> Dear son of memory, great heir of fame,
> What need'st thou such weak witness of thy name?
> Thou, in our wonder and astonishment,
> Hast built thyself a live-long monument.
> For whilst, to the shame of slow-endeavouring art,
> Thy easy numbers flow ; and that each heart
> Hath, from the leaves of thy unvalued book,
> Those Delphic lines with deep impression took ;
> Then thou, our fancy of itself bereaving,
> Dost make us marble with too much conceiving;
> And so sepulchred, in such pomp dost lie,
> That kings, for such a tomb, would wish to die."

> " Then to the well-trod stage anon,
> If Jonson's learned sock be on,
> Or sweetest Shakespeare, Fancy's child,
> Warble his native wood-notes wild."

There can be no doubt that Milton both admired
and appreciated Shakespeare. The word "stuff" is
not used in a disparaging sense, but simply means that
this and similar passages prove that tyrants have often
counterfeited a religious character. Shakespeare frequently uses it in the sense of material, matter, or
essence of anything; thus in Othello, 'stuff o' the conscience,' in Macbeth, 'that perilous stuff that weighs
upon the heart,' and in Julius Cæsar, 'ambition should
be made of sterner stuff.'

A DEFENCE OF THE PEOPLE OF ENGLAND,

IN ANSWER TO

SALMASIUS'S DEFENCE OF THE KING.—DEFENSIO PRO POPULO ANGLICANO, CONTRA CLAUDII SALMASII DEFENSIONEM REGIAM.

THE First Defence was probably published in the same year as the Iconoclastes, and the Second Defence in 1654. Both were undertaken at the request of Parliament; the one in reply to Salmasius, the other to an anonymous writer, who appears to have been Alexander More. Both were written in Latin, and therefore in a translation can afford no just criterion of Milton's real and unique style. We must here be 'delighted with ideas rather than words;' and indeed they are mainly interesting from the personal details of his own life, habits, and travels, the references to his blindness and personal appearance, and the motives and occasions of his various works, which they contain. The autobiography of any great man or notoriety must ever be invaluable, and we should treasure up any chance sentence in which he may speak of himself, and be thankful for the egotism in which circumstances may have caused him to indulge.

From his Second Defence, the Apology for Smectymnuus, and his Familiar Letters, an Apologia pro vitâ
suâ might easily be constructed in Milton's own words,
as interesting as that of the great heresiarch Newman ;
and must always afford valuable material to any one
who undertakes to write the life, or illustrate the
works, or who would really understand the grand and
colossal character and genius of our immortal Poet.

From this time we notice that Milton begins to indulge in coarse and intemperate language, and in
acrimonious vituperations against his opponents. We
shall here cite, as a fitting introduction to this Treatise
and some that followed, the observations of Isaac
Disraeli on the acrimony which the most eminent
scholars have infused frequently in their controversial
writings.

'The celebrated controversy of *Salmasius* continued
by Morus with *Milton*—the first the pleader of King
Charles, the latter the advocate of the people—was of
that magnitude, that all Europe took a part in the
paper-war of these two great men. The answer of
Milton, who perfectly massacred Salmasius, is now
read but by the few. Whatever is addressed to the
times, however great may be its merit, is doomed to
perish with the times ; yet on these pages the philosopher will not contemplate in vain.

' It will form no uninteresting article to gather a few
of the rhetorical *weeds*, for *flowers* we cannot well call

them, with which they mutually presented each other.
Their rancour was at least equal to their erudition,
the two most learned antagonists of a learned age!
Salmasius was a man of vast erudition, but no taste.
His writings are learned; but sometimes ridiculous.
He called his work *Defensio Regia*, Defence of Kings.
The opening of this work provokes a laugh. "Eng-
lishmen! who toss the heads of kings as so many
tennis-balls; who play with crowns as if they were
bowls; who look upon sceptres as so many crooks."

'That the deformity of the body is an idea we attach to the deformity of the mind, the vulgar must
acknowledge; but surely it is unpardonable in the
enlightened philosopher thus to compare the crookedness of corporeal matter with the rectitude of the intellect. Salmasius seems also to have entertained this
idea, though his spies in England gave him wrong
information; or, possibly, he only drew the figure
of his own distempered imagination.

'Salmasius sometimes reproaches Milton as being
but a puny piece of man; an homunculous, a dwarf
deprived of the human figure, a bloodless being, composed of nothing but skin and bone; a contemptible
pedagogue, fit only to flog his boys; and sometimes
elevating the ardour of his mind into a poetic
frenzy, he applies to him the words of Virgil, "*Mon-
strum horrendum, informe, ingens, cui lumen ademp-
tum.*" Our great poet thought this senseless declama-

tion merited a serious refutation ; perhaps he did not wish to appear despicable in the eyes of the ladies ; and he would not be silent on the subject, he says, lest any one should consider him as the credulous Spaniards are made to believe by their priests, that a heretic is a kind of rhinoceros, or a dog-headed monster. Milton says, that he does not think any one ever considered him as unbeautiful; that his size rather approaches mediocrity than the diminutive ; that he still felt the same courage and the same strength which he possessed when young, when, with his sword, he felt no difficulty to combat with men more robust than himself; that his face, far from being pale, emaciated, and wrinkled, was sufficiently creditable to him; for though he had passed his fortieth year, he was in all other respects ten years younger. And very pathetically he adds, " that even his eyes, blind as they are, are unblemished in their appearance ; in this instance alone, and much against my inclination, I am a deceiver."

' Morus, in his epistle dedicatory of his *Regii Sanguinis Clamor*, compares Milton to a hangman ; his disordered vision to the blindness of his soul, and vomits forth his venom.

' When Salmasius found that his strictures on the person of Milton were false, and that, on the contrary, it was uncommonly beautiful, he then turned his battery against those graces with which nature had so liberally adorned his adversary. And it is now that he seems to have laid no restrictions on his pen ; but raging with the irritation of Milton's success, he throws out the blackest calumnies, and the most infamous aspersions.

'It must be observed, when Milton first proposed to answer Salmasius he had lost the use of one of his eyes : and his physicians declared, that if he applied himself to the controversy, the other would likewise close for ever ! His patriotism was not to be baffled but with life itself. Unhappily, the prediction of his physicians took place. Thus a learned man in the occupations of study falls blind : a circumstance even now not read without sympathy. Salmasius considers it as one from which he may draw caustic ridicule and satiric severity.

'Salmasius glories that Milton lost his health and his eyes in answering this apology for King Charles ! He does not now reproach him with natural deformities; but he malignantly sympathises with him, that he now no more is in possession of that beauty which rendered him so amiable during his residence in *Italy*. He speaks more plainly in a following page; and in a word, would blacken the austere virtue of Milton with a crime too infamous to name.

'Impartiality of criticism obliges us to confess that Milton was not destitute of rancour. When he was told that his adversary boasted he had occasioned the loss of his eyes, he answered, with the ferocity of irritated passion—"*And I shall cost him his life!*" A prediction which was soon after verified : for Christina, queen of Sweden, withdrew her patronage from Salmasius, and sided with Milton. The universal neglect the proud scholar felt hastened his death in the course of a twelvemonth.

'How the greatness of Milton's mind was degraded! He actually condescended to enter into a correspondence in Holland to obtain little scandalous anecdotes of his miserable adversary Morus, and deigned to adulate the unworthy Christina of Sweden, because she had expressed herself favourably on his "Defence." Of late years we have had but too many instances of this worst of passions, the antipathies of politics!'

One more quotation from Disraeli's Curiosities of Literature, and we have done.

'Salmasius' wife was a termagant; and Christina said she admired his patience more than his erudition, married to such a shrew. Mrs. Salmasius indeed considered herself as the queen of science, because her husband was acknowledged as sovereign among the critics. She boasted that she had for her husband the most learned of all the nobles, and the most noble of all the learned. Our good lady always joined the learned conferences which he held in his study. She spoke loud, and decided with a tone of majesty. Salmasius was mild in conversation, but the

R

reverse in his writings, for our proud Xantippe considered him as acting beneath himself if he did not
magisterially call every one names !'

The translation we shall make use of is ascribed by
Toland to Mr. Washington, a member of the Temple ;
that of the Second Defence to Robert Fellowes, M.A.,
Oxon.   In the first we find only one passage worthy
transcribing, and that a very interesting one, occurring
in the Preface.

" I am about to discourse of matters neither inconsiderable nor common, but how a most potent king, after
he had trampled upon the laws of the nation, and began
to rule at his own will and pleasure, was at last subdued in the field by his own subjects, who had undergone a long slavery under him ; how afterwards he
was cast into prison, and when he gave no ground,
either by words or actions, to hope better things of
him, was finally by the supreme council of the kingdom condemned to die, and beheaded before the very
gates of the royal palace.   I shall likewise relate by
what right this judgment was given, and all these
matters transacted ; and shall easily defend my countrymen from the most wicked calumnies both of domestic and foreign railers.   Which things, if I should
so much as hope by any diligence or ability of mine,
such as it is, to discourse of as I ought to do, and to
commit them so to writing, as that perhaps all nations
and all ages may read them, it would be a very vain

thing in me. For what style can be august and magnificent enough ? Since we find by experience that in so many ages as are gone over the world, there has been but here and there a man found, who has been able worthily to recount the actions of great heroes, and potent states ; can any man have so good an opinion of his own talents, as to think himself capable of reaching these glorious and wonderful works of Almighty God, by any language, by any style of his? Which enterprise, though some of the most eminent persons in our commonwealth have prevailed upon me by their authority to undertake (whose opinion I consider as a very great honour, that they should pitch upon me before others to be serviceable in this kind ; and true it is that from my very youth, I have been bent exremely upon such sort of studies, as inclined me, if not to do great things myself, at least to celebrate those that did) ; yet as having no confidence in any such advantages, I have recourse to the divine assistance; and invoke the great and holy God, the giver of all good gifts, that I may as substantially, and as truly, discourse and refute the sauciness and lies of this foreign declaimer, as our noble generals piously and successfully by force of arms broke the king's pride, · and his unruly domineering, and afterwards put an end to both by inflicting a memorable punishment upon himself, and as thoroughly as a single person" (meaning himself in his Iconoclastes) " did with ease but of late confute and confound the king himself, rising as it were from the grave, and recommending himself to the people in a book published after his death, with new artifices and allurements of words and expressions.

"If it be asked, why we did not attack him sooner? why we suffered him to triumph so long, and pride himself in our silence? For others I am not to answer; for myself I can boldly say, that I had neither words nor arguments long to seek for the defence of so good a cause, if I had enjoyed such a measure of health, as would have endured the fatigue of writing. And being but weak in body, I am forced to write by piecemeal, and break off almost every hour, though the subject be such as requires an uninterrupted study and intenseness of mind. But though this bodily indisposition may be a hinderance to me in setting forth the just praises of my most worthy countrymen; yet I hope it will be no difficult matter for me to defend them from the insolence of this silly little scholar."

THE SECOND DEFENCE OF THE PEOPLE OF ENGLAND:

AGAINST AN ANONYMOUS LIBEL, ENTITLED, "THE ROYAL BLOOD CRYING TO HEAVEN FOR VENGEANCE ON THE ENGLISH PARRICIDES."

" A GRATEFUL recollection of the divine goodness is the first of human obligations; and extraordinary favours demand more solemn and devout acknowledgments: with such acknowledgments I feel it my duty to begin this work. First, because I was born at a time when the virtue of my fellow-citizens, far exceeding that of their progenitors in greatness of soul and vigour of enterprise, having invoked Heaven to witness the justice of their cause, has succeeded in delivering the commonwealth from the most grievous tyranny, and religion from the most ignominious degradation. And next, because when there suddenly arose many who basely calumniated the most illustrious achievements, and when one eminent above the rest (Salmasius), inflated with literary pride, had in a scandalous publication, which was particularly levelled against me, nefariously undertaken to plead the cause of despotism, I, who was neither deemed unequal to so renowned an adversary, nor to so great a subject, was particularly selected by the deliverers of our country, and by the general suffrage of the public, openly to vindicate the rights of the English nation, and consequently of liberty itself. Lastly, because in a matter of so much moment, I did not disappoint the hopes nor the opinions of my fellow-citizens; while men of learning and eminence abroad honoured me with unmingled approbation; while I obtained such a victory over my opponent, that he was obliged to quit the field with his courage broken and his reputation lost; and for the three years which he lived afterwards he gave me no further trouble.

"Though I did not participate in the toils or dangers of the war, yet I was at the same time engaged in a service not less hazardous. For since from my youth I was devoted to the pursuits of literature, and my mind had always been stronger than my body, I did not court the labours of a camp, but resorted to that employment in which my exertions were likely to be of most avail. Thus, with the better part of my frame I contributed as much as possible to the good of my country, and to the success of the glorious cause in which we were engaged; and I thought that if God willed the success of such glorious achievements, it was equally agreeable to His will that there should be others by whom those achievements should be recorded with dignity and elegance; and that the truth, which had been defended by arms, should also be defended by reason; which is the best and only legitimate means of defending it. Hence, while I applaud those who were victorious in the field, I will not complain of the providence which was assigned me; but rather thank the Author of all good for having placed me in a station which may be an object of envy to others rather than of regret to myself. I am far from wishing to speak ostentatiously of myself; but in a cause so great and glorious I can hardly refrain from assuming a more lofty and swelling tone than the simplicity of an exordium may seem to justify. The subject of which I treat has excited such general and such ardent expectation, that I imagine myself not in the forum or on the rostra, surrounded only by the people of Athens or of Rome, but about to address in this, as I did in my former Defence, the whole collective body of people, through the wide expanse of anxious and listening Europe. I seem to survey, as from a towering height, the far-extended tracts of sea and land, and innumerable crowds of spectators, betraying in their looks the liveliest interest, and sensations the most congenial with my own. Here I behold the stout and manly prowess of the Germans disdaining servitude; there the generous and lively impetuosity of the French; on this side, the calm and stately valour of the Spaniard; on that,

the composed and wary magnanimity of the Italian.
Of all the lovers of liberty and virtue, the magnani-
mous and the wise, in whatever quarter they may be
found, some secretly favour, others openly approve;
some greet me with congratulations and applause,
others, who had long been proof against conviction,
at last yield themselves captive to the force of truth.
Surrounded by congregated multitudes, I now imagine
that, from the columns of Hercules to the Indian
Ocean, I behold the nations of the earth recovering
that liberty which they had so long lost. Nor shall I
approach unknown, nor perhaps unloved, if it be told
that I am the same person who engaged in single
combat that fierce advocate of despotism; till then
reputed invincible in the opinion of many, and in his
own conceit; whom I silenced with his own weapons;
and over whom I gained a complete and glorious
victory. That this is the plain unvarnished fact
appears from this : that after the most noble Queen of
Sweden had invited Salmasius or Salmatia (for to
which sex he belonged is a matter of uncertainty) to
her court, where he was received with great distinction, my Defence suddenly surprised him in the midst
of his security. It was generally read, and by the
queen among the rest, who, attentive to the dignity
of her station, let the stranger experience no diminution of her former kindness and munificence. But
with respect to the rest, such a change was instantly

effected in the public sentiment, that he, who but yesterday flourished in the highest degree of favour, seemed to-day to wither in neglect; and soon after receiving permission to depart, he left it doubtful among many whether he were more honoured when he came, or more disgraced when he went away. And all this I have mentioned that I might clearly show what reasons I had for commencing this work with an effusion of gratitude to the Father of the universe. Such a preface was most appropriate, in which I might prove, by an enumeration of particulars, that I had not been without my share of human misery; but that I had, at the same time, experienced singular marks of the divine regard; and I again invoke the same Almighty Being, that I may still be able with the same integrity, the same diligence, and the same success to defend the dearest interests, not merely of one people, but of the whole human race, against the enemies of human liberty.

" But the conflict between me and Salmasius is now finally terminated by his death; and I will not write against the dead; nor will I reproach him with the loss of life as he did me with the loss of sight; though there are some who impute his death to the penetrating severity of my strictures, which he rendered only the more sharp by his endeavours to resist. And he was destroyed, after three years of grief, rather by the force of depression than disease."

He then passes to his present anonymous opponent, whom, however, he well knows, and after severely handling him, mentions by name. We are thankful to meet with the following passage :—" If I inveigh against tyrants, what is this to kings ? whom I am far from associating with' tyrants (quos ego a tyrannis longissime sejungo). As much as an honest man differs from a rogue, so much I contend that a king differs from a tyrant. Whence it is clear that a tyrant is so far from being a king, that he is always in direct opposition to a king. And he who peruses the records of history will find that more kings have been subverted by tyrants than by their subjects. He therefore who would authorize the destruction of tyrants, does not authorize the destruction of kings, but of the most inveterate enemies to kings. But that right which you concede to kings, the right of doing what they please, is not justice, but injustice, ruin, and despair (non est jus, sed injuria, sed scelus, sed ipsa pernicies)."

" Let us now come to the charges which were brought against myself. Is there anything reprehensible in my manners or my conduct? Surely nothing. What no one, not totally divested of all generous sensibility, would have done, Salmasius reproaches me with want of beauty and loss of sight.

" A monster huge and hideous, void of sight."

I certainly never supposed that I should have been

obliged to enter into a competition for beauty with
the Cyclops; but he immediately corrects himself,
and says, "though not indeed huge, for there cannot
be a more spare, shrivelled, and bloodless form." It
is of no moment to say anything of personal appearance, yet lest (as the Spanish vulgar, implicitly con-
fiding in the relations of their priests, believe of heretics) anyone, from the representations of my enemies,
should be led to imagine that I have either the head
of a dog, or the horn of a rhinoceros, I will say something on the subject, that I may have an opportunity
of paying my grateful acknowledgments to the Deity,
and of refuting the most shameless lies. I do not believe that I was ever noted for deformity by anyone
who ever saw me; but the praise of beauty I am not
anxious to obtain. My stature certainly is not tall,
but it rather approaches the middle than the diminutive. Yet what if it were diminutive, when so many
men, illustrious both in peace and war, have been the
same? And how can that be called diminutive,
which is great enough for every virtuous achieve-
ment? Nor, though very thin, was I ever deficient
in courage or in strength; and I was wont constantly
to exercise myself in the use of the broadsword, as
long as it comported with my habit and my years.
Armed with this weapon, as I usually was, I should
have thought myself quite a match for anyone, though
much stronger than myself; and I felt perfectly secure

against the assault of any open enemy. At this moment I have the same courage, the same strength, though not the same eyes; yet so little do they betray any external appearance of injury, that they are as unclouded and bright as the eyes of those who most distinctly see. In this instance alone I am a dissembler against my will. My face, which is said to indicate a total privation of blood, is of a complexion entirely opposite to the pale and the cadaverous; so that, though I am more than forty years old, there is scarcely anyone to whom I do not appear ten years younger than I am; and the smoothness of my skin is not, in the least, affected by the wrinkles of age. If there be one particle of falsehood in this relation, I should deservedly incur the ridicule of many thousands of my countrymen, and even many foreigners to whom I am personally known. Thus much necessity compelled me to assert concerning my personal appearance. I wish that I could with equal facility refute what this barbarous opponent has said of my blindness; but I cannot do it; and I must submit to the affliction. It is not so wretched to be blind, as it is not to be capable of enduring blindness. But why should I not endure a misfortune which it behoves every one to be prepared to endure, if it should happen; which may, in the common course of things, happen to any man; and which has been known to happen to the most distinguished and vir-

tuous persons in history. Shall I mention those wise
and ancient bards, whose misfortunes the gods are
said to have compensated by superior endowments?
But God Himself is truth; in propagating which, as
men display a greater integrity and zeal, they approach
nearer to the similitude of God, and possess a greater
portion of His love. We cannot suppose the Deity
envious of truth, or unwilling that it should be freely
communicated to mankind. The loss of sight, therefore, which these inspired sages, who were so eager
in promoting knowledge among men, sustained,
cannot be considered as a judicial punishment. Or
shall I mention those worthies who were as distinguished for wisdom in the cabinet, as for valour in
the field? And first, Timoleon of Corinth, who
delivered his city and all Sicily from the yoke of
slavery; than whom there never lived in any age,
a more virtuous man, or a more incorrupt statesman: next Appius Claudius, whose discreet counsels
in the senate, though they could not restore sight to
his eyes, saved Italy from the formidable inroads of
Pyrrhus: then Cæcilius Metellus the high-priest, who
lost his sight, while he saved, not only the city, but
the palladium, the protection of the city, and the most
sacred relics, from the destruction of the flames.
On other occasions Providence has indeed given
conspicuous proofs of its regard for such singular exertions of patriotism and virtue; what, therefore, hap-

pened to so great and so good men, I can hardly place in the catalogue of misfortunes.   Why should
I mention others of later time, as Dandolo of Venice,
the incomparable Doge ; or Boemar Zisca, the bravest
of generals, and the champion of the cross ; or Jerome
Zanchius, and some other theologians of the highest
reputation ?   For it is evident that the patriarch
Isaac, than whom no man ever enjoyed more of the
divine regard, lived blind for many years ; and perhaps also his son Jacob, who was equally an object of
the divine benevolence.   And in short, did not our
Saviour Himself clearly declare that the poor man
whom He restored to sight had not been born blind,
either on account of his own sins, or those of his progenitors ?   And with respect to myself, though I have
accurately examined my conduct, and scrutinized my
soul, I call Thee, O God, the searcher of hearts, to
witness, that I am not conscious, either in the more
early, or in the later periods of my life, of having
committed any enormity, which might deservedly have
marked me out as a a fit object for such a calamitous
visitation.   But since my enemies boast that this affliction is only a retribution for the transgressions of
my pen, I again invoke the Almighty to witness, that
I never, at any time, wrote anything which I did not
think agreeable to truth, to justice, and to piety. This
was my persuasion then, and I feel the same persuasion now.   Nor was I ever prompted to such exer-

tions by the influence of ambition; by the lust of lucre or of praise; it was only by the conviction of duty, and the feeling of patriotism, a disinterested passion for the extension of civil and religious liberty. Thus, therefore, when I was publicly solicited to write a reply to the Defence of the royal cause, when I had to contend with the pressure of sickness, and with the apprehension of soon losing the sight of my remaining eye, and when my medical attendants clearly announced, that if I did engage in the work, it would be irreparably lost, their premonitions caused no hesitation and inspired no dismay.   I would not have listened to the voice even of Esculapius himself from the shrine of Epidauris, in preference to the suggestions of the heavenly monitor within my breast; my resolution was unshaken, though the alternative was either the loss of my sight, or the desertion of my duty.   I considered that many had purchased a less good by a greater evil, the meed of glory by the loss of life; but that I might procure great good by little suffering; that though I am blind, I might still discharge the most honourable duties, the performance of which, as it is something more durable than glory, ought to be an object of superior admiration and esteem; I resolved, therefore, to make the short interval of sight, which was left me to enjoy, as beneficial as possible to the public interest.   Thus it is clear by what motives I was governed in the measures which

I took, and the losses which I sustained. Let, then, the calumniators of the divine goodness cease to revile, or to make me the object of their superstitious imaginations. Let them consider, that my situation, such as it is, is neither an object of my shame or my regret, that my resolutions are too firm to be shaken, that I am not depressed by any sense of the divine displeasure; that, on the other hand, in the most momentous periods, I have had full experience of the divine favour and protection; and that, in the solace and the strength which have been infused into me from above, I have been enabled to do the will of God; that I may oftener think on what he has bestowed, than on what He has withheld; that, in short, I am unwilling to exchange my consciousness of rectitude with that of any other person; and that I feel the recollection a treasured store of tranquillity and delight. But if the choice were necessary, I would, sir, prefer my blindness to yours; yours is a cloud spread over the mind, which darkens both the light of reason and of conscience; mine keeps from my view only the coloured surfaces of things, while it leaves me at liberty to contemplate the beauty and stability of virtue and of truth. How many things are there besides which I would not willingly see; how many things which I must see against my will; and how few which I feel any anxiety to see! There is, as the Apostle has remarked (rather, exemplified, the Latin is, præeunte Apostolo), a way to strength through weakness. Let me then be the most feeble creature alive, as long as that feebleness serves to invigorate the energies of my rational and immortal spirit; as long as in that obscurity, in which I am enveloped, the light of the divine presence more clearly shines, then, in proportion, as I am weak, I shall be invincibly strong; and in proportion as I am blind, I shall more clearly see. Oh! that I may thus be perfected by feebleness, and irradiated by obscurity! And indeed, in my blindness, I enjoy in no inconsiderable degree the favour of the Deity, who regards me with more tenderness and compassion in proportion as I am able to behold nothing but Himself. Alas! for him who insults me, who maligns and merits public execration! For the divine law not only shields me from injury, but almost renders me too sacred to attack; not indeed so much from the privation of my sight, as from the overshadowing of those heavenly wings which seem to have occasioned this obscurity; and which, when occasioned, he is wont to illuminate with an interior light, more precious and more pure."

Nothing can surpass the beauty, the pathos, and the piety of the original in this splendid passage, which the very free translation of Mr. Fellowes, in Bohn's edition, fails altogether to convey. One sentence he has entirely omitted, by a lapsus plumæ, we suppose.

s

That our readers may judge for themselves we will
here set down the Latin which Milton actually wrote;
which will also serve as a sample of his elegant and
pure style of writing in that language.

" Ad cæcitatem denique quod attinet, malle me, si
necesse est, meam, quam vel suam, More, vel tuam.
Vestra imis sensibus immersa, ne quid sani videatis aut
solidi, mentem obcæcat : mea, quam objicitis, colorem
tantummodo rebus et superficiem demit; quod verum
ac stabile in iis est contemplationi mentis non adimit.
Quam multa deinde sunt quæ videre nollem, quam
multa quæ possem libens non videre, quam panca re-
liqua sunt quæ videre cupiam.   Sed neque ego cæcis,
afflictis, mœrentibus, imbecillis, tametsi vos id miserum
ducitis, aggregari me discrutior; quandoquidem spes
est eo me propius ad misericordiam summi Patris
atque tutelam pertinere.   Est quoddam per imbecilli-
tatem, præeunte Apostolo, ad maximas vires iter: sin
ego debilissimus, dummodo in meâ debilitate immor-
talis ille et melior vigor eo se efficacius exerat; dummodo in meis tenebris divini vultûs lumen eo clarius
eluceat; tum enim infirmissimus ero simul et vali-
dissimus, cæcus eodem tempore et perspicacissimus; hac
possim ego infirmitate consummari, hac perfici, possim
in hâc obscuritate sic ego irradiari.   Et sane haud
ultima Dei cura cæci sumus ; qui nos, quo minus quic-
quam aliud præter ipsum cernere valemus, eo cle-
mentius atque benignius respicere diguatur.   Væ qui

illudit nos, væ qui lædit, exsecratione publicâ devo-
vendo; nos ab injuriis homnium non modo incolumes
sed pene sacros, divina lex reddidit, divinus favor; nec
tam oculorum hebetudine, quam celestium alarum
umbrâ ras nobis fecisse tenebras videtur, factas illus-
trare rursus interiore ac longe præstabiliore lumine
haud raro solet."

"To this I ascribe the more tender assiduities of my
friends, their soothing attentions, their kind visits, their
reverential observances. (Huc refero, quod et amici
officiosius nunc etiam quam solebant, colunt, obser-
vant, adsunt.) This extraordinary kindness, which I
experience, cannot be any fortuitous combination; and
friends, such as mine, do not suppose that all the
virtues of a man are contained in his eyes. Nor do
the persons of principal distinction in the commonwealth suffer me to be bereaved of comfort, when they
see me bereaved of sight, amid the exertions which I
made, the zeal which I showed, and the dangers which
I run for the liberty which I love. But, soberly reflecting on the casualties of human life, they show me
favour and indulgence, as to a soldier who has served
his time, and kindly concede to me an exemption from
care and toil. They do not strip me of the badges of
honour which I have once worn; they do not deprive
me of the places of public trust to which I have
been appointed: they do not abridge my salary or
emoluments; (si quid est ornamenti, non detrahunt;

si quid publici numeris, non adimunt ; si quid ex eâ re commodi, non minuunt;) which, though I may not do so much to deserve as I did formerly, they are too considerate and too kind to take away; and, in short, they honour me as much as the Athenians did those whom they determined to support at the public expense in the Prytaneum. Thus, while both God and man unite in solacing·me under the weight of my affliction, let no one lament my loss of sight in so honourable a cause. And let me not indulge in unavailing grief, or want the courage either to despise the revilers of my blindness, or the forbearance easily to pardon the offence. I return to you, whoever you may be, who, with a remarkable inconsistency, seem to consider me at one time as a giant, and at another as a dwarf. (Nunc pumilionem me, nunc Antæum vis esse.)"

We now pass on to the interesting episode of his autobiography.

"I will now mention who and whence I am. I was born at London, of an honest family; my father was distinguished by the undeviating integrity of his life ; my mother, by the esteem in which she was held, and the alms which she bestowed. My father destined me from a child to the pursuits of literature; and my appetite for knowledge was so voracious, that, from twelve years of age, I hardly ever left my studies, or went to bed before midnight.   This primarily led to my loss of sight.   My eyes were naturally weak, and I was subject to frequent headaches; which, however, could not chill the ardour of my curiosity, or retard the progress of my improvement.   My father had me daily instructed in the grammar-school, and by other masters at home.   He then, after I had acquired a proficiency in various languages, and had made a considerable progress in philosophy, sent me to the University of Cambridge.   Here I passed seven years in the usual course of instruction and study, with the approbation of the good, and without any stain upon my character, till I took the degree of Master of Arts. After this I did not, as this miscreant feigns, run away into Italy, but of my own accord retired to my father's house (at Horton, in Buckinghamshire), whither I was accompanied by the regrets of most of the fellows of the college, who showed me no common marks of friendship and esteem.   On my father's estate, where he had determined to pass the remainder of his days, I enjoyed an interval of uninterrupted leisure which I entirely devoted to the perusal of the Greek and Latin classics; though I occasionally visited the metropolis, either for the sake of purchasing books, or of learning something new in mathematics or in music, in which I, at that time, found a source of pleasure and amusement.   In this manner I spent five years till my mother's death.   I then became anxious to visit foreign parts, and particularly Italy. My father gave me his permission, and I left home with one servant. On my departure, the celebrated Henry Wootton, who had long been King James's ambassador at Venice, gave me a signal proof of his regard, in an elegant letter which he wrote, breathing not only the warmest friendship, but containing some maxims of conduct which I found very useful in my travels. The noble Thomas Scudamore, King Charles's ambassador, to whom I carried letters of recommendation, received me most courteously at Paris. His lordship gave me a card of introduction to the learned Hugo Grotius, at that time ambassador from the Queen of Sweden to the French court; whose acquaintance I anxiously desired, and to whose house I was accompanied by some of his lordship's friends. A few days after, when I set out for Italy, he gave me letters to the English merchants on my route, that they might show me any civilities in their power. Taking ship at Nice, I arrived at Genoa, and afterwards visited Leghorn, Pisa, and Florence. In the latter city, which I have always more particularly esteemed for the elegance of its dialect, its genius, and its taste, I stopped about two months; when I contracted an intimacy with many persons of rank and learning; and was a constant attendant at their literary parties; a practice which prevails there, and tends so much to the diffusion of knowledge, and the preservation of friendship. No time will ever abolish the agreeable recollections which I cherish of Jacob Gaddi, Carolo Dati, Frescobaldo, Cultellero, Bonomatthai, Clementillo, Francisco, and many others. From Florence I went to Siena, thence to Rome, where, after I had spent about two months in viewing the antiquities of that renowned city, where I experienced the most friendly attentions from Lucas Holstein, and other learned and ingenious men, I continued my route to Naples. There I was introduced by a certain recluse, with whom I had travelled from Rome, to John Baptista Manso, marquis of Villa, a nobleman of distinguished rank and authority, to whom Torquato Tasso, the illustrious poet, inscribed his book on friendship. During my stay, he gave me singular proofs of his regard; he himself conducted me round the city, and to the palace of the viceroy; and more than once paid me a visit at my lodgings. On my departure he gravely apologised for not having shewn me more civility, which he said he had been restrained from doing, because I had spoken with so little reserve on matters of religion. When I was preparing to pass over into Sicily and Greece, the melancholy intelligence which I received of the civil commotions in England made me alter my purpose; for I thought it base to be travelling for amusement abroad, while my fellow-citizens were fighting for liberty at home. While I was on my way back to Rome, some merchants informed me that the English Jesuits had formed a plot

against me if I returned to Rome, because I had
spoken too freely on religion ; for it was a rule which
I laid down to myself in those places, never to be the
first to begin any conversation on religion ; but if any
questions were put to me concerning my faith, to declare it without any reserve or fear.   I, nevertheless,
returned to Rome.   I took no steps to conceal either
my person or my character ; and for about the space of
two months I again openly defended, as I had done
before, the reformed religion in the very metropolis of
popery.   By the favour of God, I got safe back to
Florence, where I was received with as much affection
as if I had returned to my native country.   There I
stopped as many months as I had done before, except
that I made an excursion for a few days to Lucca ;
and, crossing the Apennines, passed through Bologna
and Ferrara to Venice.   After I had spent a month
in surveying the curiosities of this city, and had put on
board a ship the books which I had collected in Italy,
I proceeded through Verona and Milan, and along the
Leman Lake to Geneva.   The mention of this city
brings to my recollection the slandering More, and
makes me again call the Deity to witness, that in all
those places in which vice meets with so little discouragement, and is practised with so little shame, I never
once deviated from the paths of integrity and virtue, and
perpetually reflected that, though my conduct might
escape the notice of men, it could not elude the in-

spection of God. At Geneva I held daily conferences with John Deodati, the learned professor of Theology. Then pursuing my former route through France, I returned to my native country, after an absence of one year and about three months; at the time when Charles, having broken the peace, was renewing what is called the episcopal war with the Scots, in which the royalists being routed in the first encounter, and the English being universally and justly disaffected, the necessity of his affairs at last obliged him to convene a Parliament. As soon as I was able, I hired a spacious house in the city for myself and my books; where I again with rapture renewed my literary pusuits and where I calmly awaited the issue of the contest, which I trusted to the wise conduct of Providence, and to the courage of the people. The vigour of the Parliament had begun to humble the pride of the bishops. They said that it was unjust that they alone should differ from the model of other reformed churches; that the government of the church should be according to the pattern of other churches, and particularly the word of God. This awakened all my attention and my zeal. I saw that a way was opening for the establishment of real liberty; that the foundation was laying for the deliverance of man from the yoke of slavery and superstition; that the principles of religion, which were the first objects of our care, would exert a salutary influence on the manners and constitution of the republic; and as I had from my youth studied the distinctions between religious and civil rights, I perceived that if I ever wished to be of use, I ought at least not to be wanting to my country, to the church, and to so many of my fellow-Christians, in a crisis of so much danger. I therefore determined to relinquish the other pursuits in which I was engaged, and to transfer the whole force of my talents and my industry to this one important object. I accordingly wrote two books to a friend concerning the Reformation of the Church of England. Afterwards, when two bishops of superior distinction (Bishop Hall and Archbishop Usher) vindicated their privileges against some principal ministers (the five whose initials form the word Smectymnuus), I thought that on those topics, to the consideration of which I was led solely by my love of truth, and my reverence for Christianity, I should not probably write worse than those who were contending only for their own emoluments and usurpations. I therefore answered the one in two books, of which the first is inscribed, Concerning Prelatical Episcopacy, and the other Concerning the mode of Ecclesiastical Government; and I replied to the other in some Animadversions, and soon after in an Apology. On this occasion it was supposed that I brought a timely succour to the ministers, who were hardly a match for the eloquence of their opponents;

and from that time I was actively employed in refuting any answers that appeared. When the bishops could no longer resist the multitude of their assailants, I had leisure to turn my thoughts to other subjects; to the promotion of real and substantial liberty; which is rather to be sought from within than from without; and whose existence depends, not so much on the terror of the sword, as on sobriety of conduct and integrity of life. When, therefore, I perceived that there were three species of liberty which are essential to the happiness of social life—religious, domestic, and civil; and as I had already written concerning the first, and the magistrates were strenuously active in obtaining the third, I determined to turn my attention to the second, or the domestic species. As this seemed to involve three material questions, the conditions of the conjugal tie, the education of the children, and the free publication of the thoughts, I made them objects of distinct consideration. I explained my sentiments, not only concerning the solemnization of the marriage, but the dissolution, if circumstances rendered it necessary; and I drew my arguments from the divine law, which Christ did not abolish, or publish another more grievous than that of Moses. I stated my own opinions, and those of others, concerning the exclusive exception of fornication, which our illustrious Selden has since, in his Hebrew Wife, more copiously discussed; for he in vain makes a vaunt of liberty in the senate or in the forum, who languishes under the vilest servitude, to an inferior at home. On this subject, therefore, I published some books which were more particularly necessary at that time, when man and wife were often the most inveterate foes, when the man often staid to take care of his children at home, while the mother of the family was seen in the camp of the enemy, threatening death and destruction to her husband. I then discussed the principles of Education in a summary manner, but sufficiently copious for those who attend seriously to the subject; than which nothing can be more necessary to principle the minds of men in virtue, the only genuine source of political and individual liberty, the only true safeguard of states, the bulwark of their prosperity and renown. Lastly, I wrote my Areopagitica, in order to deliver the press from the restraints with which it was encumbered; that the power of determining what was true and what was false, what ought to be published and what to be suppressed, might no longer be entrusted to a few illiterate and illiberal individuals, who refused their sanction to any work which contained views or sentiments at all above the level of the vulgar superstition. On the last species of civil liberty, I said nothing, because I saw that sufficient attention was paid to it by the magistrates; nor did I write anything on the prerogative of the crown, till the king, voted an enemy by the Parliament, and vanquished in the field, was summoned before the tribunal which condemned him to lose his head. But when, at length, some Presbyterian ministers, who had formerly been the most bitter enemies to Charles, became jealous of the growth of the Independents, and of their ascendancy in the Parliament, most tumultuously clamoured against the sentence, and did all in their power to prevent the execution, though they were not angry so much on the account of the act itself, as because it was not the act of their party; and when they dared to affirm that the doctrine of the Protestants, and of all the reformed churches, was abhorrent to such an atrocious proceeding against kings, I thought that it became me to oppose such a glaring falsehood; and accordingly, without any immediate or personal application to Charles, I showed, in an abstract consideration of the question, what might be lawfully done against tyrants; and in support of what I advanced, produced the opinions of the most celebrated divines; while I vehemently inveighed against the egregious ignorance or effrontery of men, who professed better things, and from whom better things might have been expected. That book (the Tenure of Kings and Magistrates, 1650) did not make its appearance till after the death of Charles, and was written rather to reconcile the minds of the people to the event, than to discuss the legitimacy of that particular sentence which concerned the magistrates, and which was already executed. Such were the fruits of my private studies which I gratuitously presented to the church and to the state, and for which I was recompensed by nothing but impunity; though the actions themselves procured me peace of conscience, and the approbation of the good; while I exercised that freedom of of discussion which I loved. Others, without labour or desert, got possession of honours and emoluments; but no one ever knew me either soliciting anything myself, or, through the medium of my friends, ever beheld me in a supplicating posture at the doors of the senate, or the levees of the great. I usually kept myself secluded at home, where my own property, part of which had been withheld during the civil commotions, and part of which had been absorbed in the oppressive contributions which I had to sustain, afforded me a scanty subsistence. When I was released from these engagements, and thought that I was about to enjoy an interval of uninterrupted ease, I turned my thoughts to a continued history of my country, from the earliest times to the present period. I had already finished four books, when, after the subversion of the monarchy, and the establishment of a republic, I was surprised by an invitation from the Council of State, who desired my services in the office for foreign affairs. A book appeared soon after, which was ascribed to the King, and contained the most invidious charges against the Parliament. I was ordered to answer it; and opposed the Iconoclast to his Icon. I did not insult over fallen majesty, as is pretended; I only preferred queen Truth to king Charles. The charge of insult, which I saw that the malevolent would urge, I was at some pains to remove in the beginning of the work; and as often as possible in other places. Salmasius then appeared, to whom they were not, as More says, long in looking about for an opponent, but immediately appointed me, who happened at the time to be present at the council. I have thus given some account of myself, in order to stop your mouth, and to remove any prejudices which your falsehoods and misrepresentations might cause even good men to entertain against me."

We must not omit the characters which he here draws of the Regicides, or, as they would prefer to be called, the Tyrannicides, the leading and master spirits of the Commonwealth, such as Cromwell, Bradshaw, Fairfax, Fleetwood, and others.

CHARACTER OF BRADSHAW.

" John Bradshaw (a name which will be repeated with applause wherever liberty is cherished or is

known) was sprung from a noble family. All his
early life he sedulously employed in making himself
acquainted with the laws of his country; he then
practised with singular success and reputation at the
bar; he showed himself an intrepid and unwearied
advocate for the liberties of the people: he took an
active part in the most momentous affairs of the state,
and occasionally discharged the functions of a judge
with the most inviolable integrity. At last, when he
was entreated by the Parliament to preside in the
trial of the king, he did not refuse the dangerous
office. To a profound knowledge of the law, he added the most comprehensive views, the most generous
sentiments, manners the most obliging and the most
pure. Hence he discharged that office with a pro-
priety almost without a parallel; he inspired both
respect and awe; and, though menaced by the dag-
gers of so many assassins, he conducted himself with
so much consistency and gravity, with so much presence of mind and so much dignity of demeanour,
that he seems to have been purposely destined by
Providence for that part which he so nobly acted on
the theatre of the world. And his glory is as much
exalted above that of all other tyrannicides, as it is
both more humane, more just, and more strikingly
grand, judicially to condemn a tyrant, than to put
him to death without a trial. In other respects,
there was no forbidding austerity, no moroseness, in

his manner ; he was courteous and benign ; but the great character which he then sustained, he with perfect consistency still sustains, so that you would suppose that not only then, but in every future period of his life, he was sitting in judgment upon the king. In the public business his activity is unwearied ; and he alone is equal to a host. At home his hospitality is as splendid as his fortune will permit: in his friendships there is the most inflexible fidelity ; and no one more readily discerns merit, or more liberally rewards it. Men of piety and learning, ingenious persons in all professions, those who have been distinguished by their courage or their misfortunes, are free to participate his bounty; they are sure to share his friendship and esteem. He never ceases to extol the merits of others, or to conceal his own ; and no one was ever more ready to accept the excuses, or to pardon the hostility, of his political opponents. If he undertake to plead the cause of the oppressed, to solicit the favour or deprecate the resentment of the powerful, to reprove the public ingratitude towards any particular individual, his address and his perseverance are beyond all praise. On such occasions no one could desire a patron or a friend more able, more zealous, or more eloquent. No menace could divert him from his purpose ; no intimidation on the one hand, and no promise of emolument or promotion on the other, could alter the serenity of his countenance, or shake

T

the firmness of his soul. By these virtues which endeared him to his friends and commanded the respect even of his enemies, he has acquired a name which will flourish in every age and in every country of the world."

We subjoin the Latin, though both this and the too brief autobiography are, on the whole, very faithfully rendered; but no translation can ever equal the original.

"Est Joannes Bradscianus (quod nomen libertas ipsa, quacunque gentium colitur, memoriæ sempiternæ celebrandum commendavit), nobili familia, ut satis notum est, ortus; unde patriis legibus addiscendis, primam omnem ætatem sedulo impendit; dein consultissimus cansarum ac dissertissimus patronus, libertatis et populi vindex acerrimus, et magnis rei-publicæ negotiis est adhibitus, et incorrupti Judicis munere aliquoties perfunctus: tandem uti Regis judicio præsidere vellet, à senatu rogatus, provinciam sane periculosissimam non recusavit. Attulerat enim ad legum scientiam ingenium liberale, animum excelsum, mores integros ac nemini obnoxios; unde illud munus omni prope exemplo majus ac formidabilius, tot Sicariorum pugionibus ac minis petitus, ita constanter, ita graviter, tanta animi cum præsentia ac dignitate gessit atque implevit, ut ad hoc ipsum opus, quod jam olim Deus edendum in hoc populo mirabili providentia decre-

verat, ab ipso Numine designatus atque factus videretur;
et Tyrannicidarum omnium gloriam tantum superaverit,
quanto est humanius, quanto justius, ac majestate ple-
nius, Tyrannum judicare, quam injudicatum occidere.
Alioqui nec tristis, nec severus, sed comis ac placidus,
personam tamen quam suscepit tantam, æqualis ubique
sibi, ac veluti consul non unius anni, pari gravitate
sustinet : ut non de tribunali tantum, sed per omnem
vitam judicare Regem diceres.   In consiliis ac labori-
bus publicis maxime omnium indefesssus, multisque
par unus; domi, si quis alius, pro suis facultatibus hos-
pitalis ac splendidus, amicus longe fidelissimus, atque
in omni fortuna certissimus, bene merentes quoscunque
nemo citius aut libentius agnoscit, neque majore benevo-
lentia prosequitur ; nunc pios, nunc doctos, aut quavis
ingenii laude cognitos, nunc militares etiam et fortes
viros ad inopiam redactos suis opibus sublevat; iis si
non indigent, colit tamen libens atque amplectitur ;
alienas laudes perpetuo prædicare, suas tacere solitus ;
hostium quoque civilium, si quis ad sanitatem rediit,
quod experti sunt plurimi, nemo ignoscentior.   Quod
si causa oppressi cujuspiam defendenda palam, si gratia
aut vis potentiorum oppuganda, si in quenquam bene
meritum, ingratitudo publica objurganda sit, tum
quidem in illo viro, vel facundiam vel constantiam
nemo desideret, non patronum, non amicum, vel ido-
neum magis et intrepidum, vel disertiorem alium quis-
quam sibi optet; habet, quem non minæ dimovere

recto, non metus aut munera proposito bono atque officio, vultusque ac mentis firmissimo statu dejicere valeant. Quibus virtutibus, et plerisque merito charus, et inimicissimis non contemnendus, gestarum egregie rerum in republica laudem, apud omnes tum exteros tum posteros, in omne ævum propagabit."

CHARACTER OF CROMWELL.

"OLIVER CROMWELL was sprung from a line of illustrious ancestors, who were distinguished for the civil functions which they sustained under the monarchy, and still more for the part which they took in restoring and establishing true religion in this country. In the vigour and maturity of his life, which he passed in retirement, he was conspicuous for nothing more than for the strictness of his religious habits, and the innocence of his life; and he had tacitly cherished in his breast that flame of piety which was afterwards to stand him in so much stead on the greatest occasions, and in the most critical exigencies. In the last Parliament which was called by the King, he was elected to represent his native town, when he soon became distinguished by the justness of his opinions, and the vigour and decision of his counsels. When the sword was drawn, he offered his services, and was appointed to a troop of horse, whose numbers were soon increased by the pious and the good, who flocked from all quarters to his standard; and in a short time he almost surpassed the greatest generals in the magnitude and the rapidity of his achievements. Nor is this surprising; for he was a soldier disciplined to perfection in the knowledge of himself. He had either extinguished, or by habit had learnt to subdue, the whole host of vain hopes, fears, and passions, which infest the soul. He first acquired the government of himself, and over himself acquired the most signal victories; so that on the first day he took the field against the external enemy, he was a veteran in arms consummately practised in the toils and exigencies of war. It is not possible for me in the narrow limits in which I circumscribe myself on this occasion, to ennumerate the many towns which he has taken, the many battles which he has won. The whole surface of the British Empire has been the scene of his exploits, and the theatre of his triumphs; which alone would furnish ample materials for a history, and want a copiousness of narration not inferior to the magnitude and diversity of the transactions. This alone seems to be a sufficient proof of his extraordinary and almost supernatural virtue, that by the vigour of his genius, or the excellence of his discipline, adapted, not more to the necessities of war than to the precepts of Christianity, the good and the brave were from all quarters attracted to his camp, not only as to the best school of military talents, but of piety and virtue; and

that during the whole war, and the occasional inter-
vals of peace, amid so many vicissitudes of faction and
of events, he retained and still retains the obedience
of his troops, not by largesses or indulgence, but by
his sole authority, and the regularity of his pay.   In
this instance his fame may rival that of Cyrus, of
Epaminondas, or of any of the great generals of antiquity. Hence he collected an army as numerous and as
well equipped as any one ever did in so short a time ;
which was uniformly obedient to his orders, and dear
to the affections of the citizens ; which was formidable to the enemy in the field, but never cruel to
those who laid down their arms; which committed no
lawless ravages on the persons or the property of the
inhabitants ; who, when they compared their conduct
with the turbulence, the intemperance, the impiety,
and the debauchery of the royalists, were wont to
salute them as friends, and to consider them as guests.
They were a stay to the good, a terror to the evil,
and the warmest advocates for every exertion of piety
and virtue."

CHARACTER OF FAIRFAX.

"Nor would it be right to pass over the name of
Fairfax, who united the utmost fortitude with the utmost courage, and the spotless innocence of whose life
seemed to point him out as the peculiar favourite of

Heaven. Justly, indeed, may you be excited to receive this wreath of praise ; though you have retired
as much as possible from the world, and seek those
shades of privacy which were the delight of Scipio.
Nor was it only the enemy whom you subdued, but
you have triumphed over that flame of ambition, and
that lust of glory which are wont to make the best
and the greatest of men their slaves. The purity of
your virtues, and the splendour of your actions, con-
secrate those sweets of ease which you enjoy, and
which constitute the wished-for haven of the toils of
man. Such was the ease which, when the heroes of
antiquity possessed, after a life of exertion and glory
not greater than yours, the poets, in despair of finding ideas or expressions better suited to the subject,
feigned that they were received into heaven, and invited to recline at the tables of the gods. But whether it were your health, which I principally believe,
or any other motive which caused you to retire, of
this I am convinced, that nothing could have induced
you to relinquish the service of your country, if you
had not known that in your successor liberty would
meet with a protector, and England with a stay to its
safety, and a pillar to its glory. For while you, O
Cromwell, are left among us, he hardly shows a proper
confidence in the Supreme, who distrusts the security
of England ; when he sees that you are in so special a
manner the favoured object of the divine regard."

COMMEMORATION OF FLEETWOOD, LAMBERT AND OTHERS.

"I now feel myself irresistibly compelled to commemorate the names of some of those who have most conspicuously signalized themselves in these times: and first, thee, O Fleetwood, whom I have known from a boy to the present blooming maturity of your military fame, to have been inferior to none in humanity, in gentleness, in benignity of disposition, whose intrepidity in the combat, and whose clemency in victory, have been acknowledged even by the enemy: next thee, O Lambert, who, with a mere handful of men, checked the progress, and sustained the attack of the Duke of Hamilton, who was attended by the whole flower and vigour of the Scottish youth: next thee, O Desborough, and thee, O Hawley, who wast always conspicuous in the heat of the combat, and the thickest of the fight: thee, O Overton, who hast been most endeared to me now for so many years by the similitude of our studies, the suavity of your manners, and the more than fraternal sympathy of our hearts; you, who, in the memorable battle of Marston Moor, when our left wing was put to the rout, were beheld with admiration, making head against the enemy with your infantry, and repelling his attack, amid the thickest of the carnage; and lastly you, who, in the Scotch war, when under the auspices of Cromwell, occupied the coast of Fife, opened a passage beyond Stirling, and made the Scotch of the west, and of the north, and even the remotest Orkneys, confess your humanity, and submit to your power. Besides these, I will mention some as celebrated for their political wisdom and their civil virtues, who are known to me by friendship or by fame. Whitlocke, Pickering, Strickland, Sydenham, Sydney, (a name indissolubly attached to the interests of liberty,) Montacute, Laurence, both of highly cultivated minds and polished taste; besides many other citizens of singular merit, some of whom were distinguished by their exertions in the senate, and others in the field."

The last few sentences of the peroration are all that appear to us worth preserving.

" With respect to myself, whatever turn things may take, I thought that my exertions on the present occasion would be serviceable to my country; and as they have been cheerfully bestowed, I hope that they have not been bestowed in vain. And I have not circumscribed my defence of liberty within any petty circle around me, but have made it so general and comprehensive, that the justice and the reasonableness of such uncommon occurrences explained and defended, both among my countrymen and among foreigners, and which all good men cannot but approve, may serve to exalt the glory of my country, and to excite the imitation of posterity. If the conclusion do not answer to the beginning, that is their concern; I have delivered my testimony, I would almost say, have erected a monument that will not readily be destroyed, to the reality of those singular and mighty achievements which were above all praise. As the epic poet, who adheres at all to the rules of that species of composition, does not profess to describe the whole life of the hero whom he celebrates, but only some particular action of his life, as the resentment of Achilles at Troy, the return of Ulysses, or the coming of Æneas into Italy; so it will be sufficient, either for my justification or apology, that I have heroically celebrated at least one exploit of my countrymen; I pass by the rest, for who could recite the achievements of a whole people? If after such a display of courage and vigour, you basely relinquish the path of virtue, if you do anything unworthy of yourselves, posterity will sit in judgment on your conduct. They will see that the foundations were well laid; that the beginning (nay, it was more than a beginning) was glorious; but with deep emotions of concern will they regret, that those were wanting who might have completed the structure. They will lament that perseverance was not conjoined with such exertions and such virtues. They will see that there was a rich harvest of glory, and an opportunity afforded for the greatest achievements, but that men only were wanting for the execution; while they were not wanting who could rightly counsel, exhort, inspire, and bind an unfading wreath of praise round the brows of the illustrious actors in so glorious a scene."

We here insert that beautiful sonnet, addressed to his pupil and friend, Cyriack Skinner, which Milton wrote on the total loss of his sight, occasioned, as he has already told us, by his writing these Treatises in Defence of the People.

> " Cyriack, this three years' day these eyes, though clear,
>   To outward view, of blemish or of spot,
>   Bereft of light, their seeing have forgot ;
> Nor to their idle orbs doth sight appear
> Of sun, or moon, or star, throughout the year,
>   Or man, or woman.   Yet I argue not
>   Against Heaven's hand or will, nor bate a jot
> Of heart or hope ; but still bear up and steer
>   Right onward.   What supports me, dost thou ask ?
> The conscience, friend, to have lost them overplied
>   In liberty's defence, my noble task,
> Of which all Europe rings from side to side.
>   This thought might lead me through the world's vain mask
> Content, though blind, had I no better guide."

AUTHORIS PRO SE DEFENSIO.

THIS Third Defence is omitted in Bohn's edition
of the Prose Works of Milton, and the reason I
presume to be, because no translation into English of
this work exists. Its full title is, "The Author's
Defence of himself, against Alexander More, Ecclesi-
astic, that he is rightly said to be the author of an
infamous libel, entitled, 'The Cry of the Royal Blood
to Heaven for vengeance on the English Parricides.'"
In this he vindicates himself, as in the First and
Second Defence he had vindicated the people and the
Republic. "Quando hoc necessario tollendum mihi
onus est, dabit quisque veniam, uti spero, si populo
qui non defui pridem et Reipublicæ, mihimet nunc
non defuero." It consists of two parts, in the first he
proves that he had correctly assumed in his Second
Defence that More was the author of the pamphlet in
question ; and in the second he replies to a rejoinder
which his 'miserable adversary' had put forth.
This Milton entitles, "Authoris ad Alexandri Mori
Supplementum Responsio." No doubt it is to this
"Authoris pro se Defensio" that the elder Disraeli
especially alludes when he descants on the acrimony

of Milton. How ridiculous the attitudes in which great men appear, when they sink 'the dignity of the author in the malignity of the man,' and 'employ the style of the fish-market.' We have too much reverence for Milton to follow him in his, in some respects, still magnificent, torrent of abuse in which he well-nigh annihilates his opponent; nor shall we retail that mutual recrimination of infamous and scurrilous charges of which perhaps both were innocent; certainly the one, who had obtained his information by hearsay, and by, I regret to write it, a mean and dishonourable correspondence with friends abroad where More resided. Besides our design is to reproduce whatever is of intrinsic worth and interest in the prose of Milton, and in this performance we meet with no sentence of a venturous edge; on the contrary, all is uttered in the height of malice and irritation. Consequently there is nothing to transcribe—nothing to rescue from that oblivion in which it has so long lain buried in a learned language. We must except the incidental allusions to some personal details of his history, as, for instance, the state of his health and of his eyesight, and the domestic affliction under which he was suffering when he wrote the Second Defence; and now, two years after, he writes this Treatise, his great adversary, Salmasius, dead, his eyesight irrecoverably gone, and his health partially despaired of, and partially restored. The "domestic 'grief of two funerals," mentioned in the passage we shall quote, we conceive—for the chronological arrangement of the events of Milton's life is by no means very clear—refers to the death of his second wife in childbed, Catharine Woodcock, whom he lost the year after their marriage; that his grief was most poignant appears from his exquisite sonnet on his deceased wife, beginning—

> "Methought I saw my late espoused saint
> Brought to me, like Alcestis, from the grave."

It is remarkable that he lost his first wife, Mary Powell, the mother of his three daughters, on a similar melancholy occasion. "Verum me, tum maxime, et infirma simul valetudo, et *duorum funerum luctus domesticus*, et defectum jam penitus oculorum lumen diversâ longe sollicitudine urgebat: foris quoque adversarius ille prior (Salmasius), isti (More) longe præferendus, impendebat; jamjamque se totis viribus incursurum indies minatabitur; quo derepente mortuo, levatum me parte aliquâ laboris ratus, et valetudine partim desperatâ partim restitutâ, utcunque confirmatus, ne omnino vel summorum hominum expectationi deesse, vel omnem inter tot mala abjecisse curam existimationis viderer, ut primum de isto Clamatore anonymo certum aliquid comperiendi facultas data est, hominem aggredior. De te, More, dictum hoc volo; quem ego nefandi illius clamoris vel esse authorem, vel esse pro authore haud injuria habendum statuo."

We are now approaching the conclusion of our task, or the one book of Familiar Letters is all that remains for examination and selection. We find nothing further which will serve our purpose either in this "Authoris pro se Defensio," or in those smaller works of which we have given the dates, or in the History of England, which, though written by a schoolmaster, has never become a school-book, or in the Latin Grammar, which no one has ever used, or in the Treatise on Logic, which has never displaced Aldrich or Huyshe, or, lastly, in his posthumous Treatise on Christian Doctrine. We confess to a little disappointment, notwithstanding the considerable amount of genuine gold we have succeeded in extracting even from some of the most unpromising and drossiest of his works. We thought, unreasonably perhaps, that " the precious life-blood of a master spirit, embalmed and treasured up on purpose to a life beyond life," would prove the vitality, and be found somewhere latent in every single work he had published. We thought that it might be said of him, ' nihil tetigit quod non ornavit '—that such a mind could not write long on any subject without some scintillation of transcendant genius sparkling on the page sooner or later ; with this conviction we set out, but we now close our labours with this sanguine feeling considerably modified. We do not just see that he who enchants and enchains us in his poetry must necessarily do the same in his prose; that he who could write the Paradise Lost, and Comus, and Lycidas, must be the same 'thing to worship and to wonder at,' when, with passions roused and self-love wounded, he takes up his pen and parable against some wretched and contemptible libeller like Salmasius or Alexander More.   Passion and prejudice can throw a dark and impenetrable cloud over the brightest intellect—even over such a mind as Milton's; and the Divine Spirit which dictated to him the whole of Paradise Lost, and most certainly some parts of the Areopagitica, forsook him when he took the field against such miserable antagonists, and in so bad and unrighteous a quarrel.

The fact is, our mind has so long dwelt upon Milton, that we fear it has contracted an almost morbid over-activity—what the Greeks express by the one word περίνοια, but which has no equivalent in our own language. This expressive word, translated by Liddell and Scott, 'over-wiseness,' occurs in Thucydides (iii. 43,) in the speech of Diodotus, and denotes that over-suspiciousness of the motives of their public men, into which fault the Athenians were so apt to fall. Thus the word is used in a good and bad sense, but in both signifies the excess of an active mind, which not only sees all that is really to be seen in a subject, but fancies something more. We were amused to read Arnold's note, explanatory of this word, as it exactly expresses what some reviewer might possibly say of us, charging us with the Athenian failing of περίνοια. His words are these, ' It is the fault into which men are apt to fall in commenting upon works which they highly admire ; because from an attentive study of them they discover beauties which general readers do not notice, they are tempted to think that still deeper study will bring to light still greater treasures ; and attribute to every word of their author some deep meaning, or some particular beauty.' We plead guilty to the impeachment in some slight degree, but with very large reservations ; on no subject would περίνοια be more pardonable, than when exhibited in commenting on the prose works of our great national Poet ; and we only hope, that, if it be our failing, it may be the failing also of every one who condescends to criticise our labours.

But we must not forget that our labour of love, for such it has in truth been to us, is not quite ended ; but at once proceed to our author's Familiar Letters, originally written in Latin, and translated in Bohn's edition, by Mr. Fellowes, of Oxford, whose translation of the Second Defence we were not altogether pleased with. They extend over a period of about forty years, the date of the first being 1625, and of the last 1666. And we cannot better express our own views and feelings than by adopting, and cordially subscribing to those expressed by the Editor of the above named edition in his introductory remarks.

'For nobleness of sentiment, and lofty dignity of thought, no letters with which I am acquainted surpass these. They commence in youth, and, few, alas, as they are, carry us forward to a period not far removed from the writer's death. It seems to me impossible to peruse them without the deepest interest. They open to us, though doubtless much too little, a view into the every-day frame of mind, and household habits, of our great poet; and few, perhaps, will read these valued fragments of his inner life, without experiencing the sincerest regret that there should be no more of them, without perceiving with sorrow the number of the leaves decrease, and the end approaching, of what, to all who love, as I do, the memory of this good and great man, must be an enjoyment of the most perfect and exalted nature.'

These letters were published by Milton himself, in 1674, the last year of his life, to which he added some Academical Exercises to complete the volume. The title in Latin is "Authoris Epistolarum Familiarum Liber Unus: Quibus accesserunt ejusdem, jam olim in Collegio Adolescentis Prolusiones quædam Oratoriæ." These latter are seven in number, and though highly lauded by Masson, in his Life of Milton, as distinguished by peculiar characteristics, and full of biographical light, and each described and translated by him in part, they are, in the opinion of the editor, uninteresting and unreadable. Masson states, 'though they have been in print since 1674, I really have found no evidence that as many as ten persons have read them through before me.' At all events, there is another who has read them through, of whom the biographer has never heard. We shall, therefore, pass them by, only remarking that Masson has restored to its proper connexion the sixth with the first piece in his " Miscellaneous Poems," commencing, " Hail native language," &c., and which is thus headed, " Anno ætatis xix. At a Vacation Exercise in in the College, part Latin, part English. The Latin speeches ended, the English thus began." The Latin is in prose, that of this sixth Prolusion, and the English is in verse. The above-named writer says, ' the sixth exercise stands by itself, as a voluntary discourse delivered by appointment in the summer vacation, 1628, at a meeting of the youths of the University, held for the purpose of fun and frolic. The essay consists of two parts—the first being a dissertation on the compatibility of occasional frolic with philosophical studies ; and the second a frolicsome harangue, expressly comic and even coarse, introductory to the other sports of the day. We have the interesting fact, handed down to us by Aubrey and after him by Wood, here authenticated for us by Milton himself, that, at Christ's College, he used to go by the nickname of 'the Lady?' "An denique ego à Deo aliquo vitiatus * * * ut sic repente ἐκ θηλείας εἰς ἄρρενά ἀλλαχθείην ἄν? A quibusdam audivi nuper Domina. At cur videor illis parum masculus? verum utinam illi possint tam facile exuere asinos, quam ego quicquid est faminæ."

FAMILIAR LETTERS.

1.—*To his Tutor, Thomas Young.*

"THOUGH I had determined, my excellent tutor, to write you an epistle in verse, yet I could not satisfy myself without sending also another in prose, for the emotions of my gratitude, which your services so justly inspire, are too expansive and too warm to be expressed in the confined limits of poetical metre; they demand the unrestrained freedom of prose, or rather the exuberant richness of Asiatic phraseology: though it would far exceed my power accurately to describe how much I am obliged to you, even if I could drain dry all the sources of eloquence, or exhaust all the topics of discourse which Aristotle or the famed Parisian Logician has collected. You complain with truth that my letters have been very few and very short; but I do not grieve at the omission of so pleasurable a duty, so much as I rejoice at having such a place in your regard as makes you anxious often to hear from me. I beseech you not to take it amiss, that I have not now written to you for more than three years; but with your usual benignity impute it rather to circumstances than to inclination. For heaven knows, that I regard you as a Parent (te instar Patris colam), that I have always treated you with the utmost respect, and that I was unwilling to tease you with my compositions. And I was anxious that if my letters had nothing else to recommend them, they might be recommended by their rarity. And lastly, since the ardour of my regard makes me imagine that you are always present, that I hear your voice and contemplate your looks; and as thus (which is usually the case with lovers) I charm away my grief by the illusion of your presence, I was afraid when I wrote to you the idea of your distant separation should forcibly rush upon my mind; and that the pain of your absence, which was almost soothed into quiescence, should revive and disperse the pleasurable dream. I long since received your desirable present of the Hebrew Bible. I wrote this at my lodgings in the city, not, as usual, surrounded by my books. If, therefore, there be any thing in this letter which either fails to give pleasure, or which frustrates expectation, it shall be compensated by a more elaborate composition as soon as I return to the dwelling of the Muses."

London, March 26, 1625.

———

II.—*To Alexander Gill.*

" I RECEIVED your letters and your poem, with which

I was highly delighted, and in which I discover the majesty of a poet, and the style of Virgil. I knew how impossible it would be for a person of your genius entirely to divert his mind from the culture of the muses, and to extinguish those heavenly emotions, and that sacred and ethereal fire which is kindled in your heart. For what Claudian said of himself may be said of you, your " whole soul is instinct with the fire of Apollo." If, therefore, on this occasion, you have broken your own promises, I here commend the want of constancy which you mention ; I commend the want of virtue, if any want of virtue there be. But in referring the merits of your poem to my judgment, you confer on me as great an honour as the gods would if the contending musical immortals had called me in to adjudge the palm of victory ; as poets babble that it formerly fell to the lot of Tmolus, the guardian of the Lydian mount. I know not whether I ought to congratulate Henry Nassau more on the capture of the city, or the composition of your poems. For I think that this victory produced nothing more entitled to distinction and to fame than your poem. But since you celebrate the successes of our allies in lays so harmonious and energetic, what may we not expect when our own successes call for the congratulations of your muse ? Adieu, learned sir, and believe me greatly obliged by the favour of your verses."

London, May 26, 1628.

III.—*To the Same.*

" IN my former letter I did not so much answer yours
as deprecate the obligation of then answering it; and
therefore at the time I tacitly promised that you should
soon receive another, in which I would reply at length
to your friendly challenge. But, though I had not
promised this, it would most justly be your due, since
one of your letters is full worth two of mine, or
rather, on an accurate computation, worth a hundred.
When your letter arrived I was strenuously engaged
in that work concerning which I had given you some
obscure hints, and the execution of which could not be
delayed." [Probably the Ode on Christ's Nativity,
which seems to have been intended as part of a
larger work, which the author, finding above his years,
abandoned.] " One of the fellows of our college, who
was to be the respondent in a philosophical disputation
for his degree, engaged me to furnish him with some
verses which are annually required on this occasion;
since he himself had long neglected such frivolous pursuits, and was then intent on more serious
studies. Of these verses" [the fourth in his Sylvarum
Liber, headed " Naturam non pati senium,"] " I sent
you a printed copy, since I knew both your dis-
criminating taste in poetry, and your candid allow-
ances for poetry like mine. If you will in your
turn deign to communicate to me any of your productions, you will, I can assure you, find no one to

whom they will give more delight, or who will more impartially endeavour to estimate their worth. For as often as I recollect the topics of your conversation, the loss of which I regret even in this seminary of erudition, (vel ipsis Athenis, ipsâ in Academiâ,) I cannot help painfully reflecting on what advantages I am deprived by your absence, since I never left your company without an increase of knowledge, and always had recourse to your mind as an emporium of literature. Among us, as far as I know, there are only two or three, who, without any acquaintance with philology or philosophy, do not unfledged betake themselves to theology ; and of this they acquire only a slender smattering, not more than sufficient to enable them to patch together a sermon with scraps pilfered, with little discrimination, from this author and from that."

There is a very curious passage from an old book, entitled ' Microcosmographie, or a Piece of the World Discovered,' published in 1628 by John Earle, who was made a Bishop at the Restoration, cited in a note to the Areopagitica in Bohn's edition of Milton's Prose Works, which we will here transcribe. It is the picture of ' a young raw preacher, who is a bird not yet fledged, that hath hopped out of his nest to be chirping on a hedge, and will be straggling abroad at what peril soever. His collections of study are the notes of sermons, which, taken up at St. Mary's, he utters in

the country. And if he writes Brachigraphy, his stock
is so much the better. His prayer is conceited, and
no man remembers his college more at large. The
pace of his sermon is a full career, and he runs wildly
over hill and dale until the clock stop him. The
labours of it is chiefly in his lungs; and the only thing
he has made of it himself is the faces. He takes on
against the Pope without mercy, and has a jest still in
lavender for Bellarmine. His action is all passion, and
his speech interjections : he has an excellent faculty
in bemoaning the people, and spits with a very good
grace. He will not draw his handkerchief out of its
place, nor blow his nose without discretion. He
preaches but once a year, though twice on Sunday :
for the stuff is still the same, only the dressing a little
altered. He has more tricks with a sermon, than a
tailor with an old cloak, to turn it, and piece it, and
at last quite disguise it with a new preface. His
fashion and demure habit get him in with some town-
precision, and make him a guest on Friday nights.
You shall know him by his narrow velvet cape, and
serge facing, and his ruff, next his hair, the shortest
thing about him. The companion of his walks is some
zealous tradesman, whom he astonisheth with strange
points, which they both understand alike. His friends,
and much painfulness, may prefer him to thirty pounds
a year ; and this means, to a chambermaid : with

whom we leave him now in the bonds of wedlock.
Next Sunday you shall have him again.'

" Hence I fear lest our clergy should relapse into
the sacerdotal ignorance of a former age. Since I find
so few associates in study here I should instantly direct
my steps to London, if I had not determined to spend
the summer vacation in the depths of literary solitude,
and, as it were, hide myself in the chamber of the
muses. (Claustris Musarum.) As you do this every
day, it would be injustice in me any longer to divert
your attention or engross your time. Adieu."

Cambridge, July 2, 1628.

IV.—*To Thomas Young.*

" On reading your letter, I find only one superfluous
passage, an apology for not writing to me sooner ; for
though nothing gives me more pleasure than to hear
from you, how can I or ought I to expect that you
should always have leisure enough from more serious
and more sacred engagements to write to me ; particularly when it is kindness, and not duty, which
prompts you to write ? Your many recent services
must prevent me from entertaining any suspicion of
your forgetfulness or neglect. Nor do I see how you
could possibly forget one on whom you had conferred
so many favours. Having an invitation into your part
of the country in the spring, I shall readily accept it,

that I may enjoy the deliciousness of the season, as well as that of your conversation; and that I may withdraw myself for a short time from the tumult of the city to your rural mansion, as to the renowned portico of Zeno, or Tusculan of Cicero, where you live on your little farm, with a moderate fortune, but a princely mind; and where you practise the contempt and triumph over the temptations of ambition, pomp, luxury, and all that attracts the gaze and admiration of the multitude. I hope that you who deprecated the blame of delay, will pardon me for my precipitance; for after deferring this letter to the last, I chose rather to write a few lines, however deficient in elegance, than to say nothing at all. Adieu, Reverend Sir."

Cambridge, July 21, 1628.

V.—*To Alexander Gill.*

" If you had made me a present of a piece of plate, or any other valuable which excites the admiration of mankind, I should not be ashamed in my turn to remunerate you, as far as my circumstances would permit. But since you, the day before yesterday, presented me with an elegant and beautiful poem in Hendecasyllabic verse, which far exceeds the worth of gold, you have increased my solicitude to discover in what manner I may requite the favour of so

acceptable a gift. I had by me at the time no compositions in a like style which I thought fit to come in
competition with the excellence of your performance.
I send you therefore a composition which is not
entirely my own," a Greek translation of Ps. cxiv.,
"but the production of a truly inspired bard, from
whom I last week rendered this ode into Greek
heroic verse, as I was lying in bed before the day
dawned, without any previous deliberation, but with
a certain impelling faculty, for which I know not how
to account. By his help who does not less surpass
you in his subject than you do me in the execution, I
have sent something which may serve to restore the
equilibrium between us. If you see reason to find
fault with any particular passage, I must inform you
that, from the time I left your school, this is the first
and the last piece I have ever composed in Greek;
since, as you know, I have attended more to Latin
and to English composition. He who at this time
employs his labour and his time in writing Greek, is
in danger of writing what will never be read. Adieu,
and expect to see me, God willing, at London on
Monday, among the booksellers. In the meantime,
if you have interest enough with that Doctor who is
the master of the college, to promote my business, I
beseech you to see him as soon as possible, and to act
as your friendship for me may prompt."

From my Villa, Dec. 4, 1634.

VI.—*To Charles Deodati.*

CHARLES DEODATI was educated with Milton at St. Paul's School in London, of which Alexander Gill, celebrated for his Latin poetry, was master. His admirable character, and intimacy with our author, are evident from these letters, from the first and sixth Elegies, the fourth Sonnet, and the Epitaphium Damonis, to which we refer our readers.

" I clearly see that you are determined not to be overcome in silence ; if this be so, you shall have the palm of victory, for I will write first. Though if the reasons which make each of us so long in writing to the other should ever be judicially examined, it will appear that I have many more excuses for not writing than you. For it is well known, and you well know, that I am naturally slow in writing, and averse to write ; while you, either from disposition or from habit, seem to have little reluctance in engaging in these literary allocutions. It is also in my favour, that your method of study is such as to admit of frequent interruptions, in which you visit your friends, write letters, or go abroad ; but it is my way to suffer no impediment, no love of ease, no avocation whatever to chill the ardour, to break the continuity, or divert the completion of my literary pursuits. From this and no other reason it often happens that I do not readily employ my pen in any gratuitous exertions; but I am not nevertheless a very sluggish correspondent; nor has it at any time happened that I ever left any letters of yours unanswered till another came. So I hear that you write to the bookseller, and often to your brother, either of whom, from their nearness, would readily have forwarded any communication from you to me. But what I blame you for is, the not keeping your promise of paying me a visit when you left the city; a promise which, if it had once occurred to your thoughts, would certainly have forcibly suggested the necessity of writing. These are my reasons for expostulation and censure. You will look to your own defence. But what can occasion your silence? Is it ill health? Are there in those parts any literati with whom you may play and prattle as we used to do? When do you return? How long do you mean to stay among the Hyperboreans? I wish you would give me an answer to each of these questions; and that you may not suppose I am quite unconcerned about what relates to you, I must inform you that in the beginning of the autumn I went out of my way to see your brother, in order to learn how you did. And lately when I was accidentally informed in London that you were in town, I instantly hastened to your lodgings; but it was only the shadow of a dream, for you were nowhere to be found. Wherefore as soon as you can do it without inconvenience to yourself, I beseech you to take up your quar-

ters where we may at least be able occasionally to
visit one another; for I hope you would not be a
different neighbour to us in the country than you are
in town. But this is as it pleases God. I have much
to say to you concerning myself and my studies, but I
would rather do it when we meet; and as to-morrow
I am about to return into the country, and am busy in
making preparations for my journey, I have but just
time to scribble this. Adieu."

London, Sep. 7, 1637.

VII.—*To the Same.*

"MOST of my other friends think it enough to give
me one farewell in their letters, but I see why you do
it so often; for you give me to understand that your
medical authority (he was a physician in Cheshire) is
now added to the potency, and subservient to the
completion of those general expressions of goodwill
which are nothing but words and air. You wish me
my health six hundred times, in as great a quantity
as I can wish, as I am able to bear, or even more
than this. Truly, you should be appointed butler to
the house of health, whose stores you so lavishly bestow; or at least Health should become your parasite,
since you so lord it over her, and command her at
your pleasure. I send you therefore my congratulations and my thanks, both on account of your friend-

ship and your skill. I was long kept waiting in expectation of a letter from you, which you had engaged
to write; but when no letter came, my old regard for
you suffered not, I can assure you, the smallest diminution, for I had supposed that the same apology for
remissness, which you had employed in the beginning
of our correspondence, you would again employ.
This was a supposition agreeable to truth and to the
intimacy between us. For I do not think that true
friendship consists in the frequency of letters or in
professions of regard, which may be counterfeited;
but it is so deeply rooted in the heart and affections,
as to support itself against the rudest blast; and when
it originates in sincerity and virtue, it may remain
through life without suspicion and without blame,
even when there is no longer any reciprocal inter-
change of kindnesses. For the cherishing aliment of
a friendship such as this, there is not so much need of
letters as of a lively recollection of each other's virtues. And though you have not written, you have
something that may supply the omission; your pro-
bity writes to me in your stead; it is a letter ready
written on the innermost membrane of the heart; the
simplicity of your manners, and the rectitude of your
principles, serve as correspondents in your place: your
genius, which is above the common level, writes, and
serves in a still greater degree to endear you to me.
But now you have got possession of this despotic

x

citadel of medicine, do not alarm me with the menace
of being obliged to repay those six hundred healths
which you have bestowed, if I should, which God forbid, ever forfeit your friendship. Remove that formidable battery which you seem to have placed upon
my breast to keep off all sickness, but what comes by
your permission. But that you may indulge any excess of menace, I must inform you that I cannot help
loving such as you are; for whatever the Deity may
have bestowed upon me in other respets, He has certainly inspired me, if any ever were inspired, with a
passion for the good and beautiful. Nor did Ceres,
according to the fable, ever seek her daughter Proser-
pine with such unceasing solicitude as I have sought
this τοῦ καλοῦ ἰδέαν, this perfect model of the beautiful
in all the forms and appearances of things (πολλαὶγμὰρ
μορφαὶ τῶν Δαιμόνιων, many are the forms of the Divini-
ties). I am wont day and night to continue my
search; and I follow in the way in which you go
before. Hence, I feel an irresistible impulse to culti-
vate the friendship of him who, despising the prejudices and false conceptions of the vulgar, dares to
think, to speak, and to be that which the highest
wisdom has in every age taught to be the best. But
if my disposition or my destiny were such that I could
without any conflict or any toil emerge to the highest
pitch of distinction and of praise, there would nevethe-
less be no prohibition, either human or divine, against

my constantly cherishing and revering those who have either obtained the same degree of glory, or are successfully labouring to obtain it. But now I am sure that you wish me to gratify your curiosity, and to let you know what I have been doing, or am meditating to do. Hear me, my Deodati, and suffer me for a moment to speak without blushing in a more lofty strain. Do you ask what I am meditating? By the help of heaven, an immortality of fame. But what am I doing? πτεροφυῶ, I am letting my wings grow and preparing to fly; but my Pegasus has not yet feathers enough to soar aloft in the fields of air. I will now tell you seriously what I design; to take chambers in one of the inns of court, where I may have the benefit of a pleasant and shady walk; and where with a few associates I may enjoy more comfort when I choose to stay at home, and have a more elegant society when I choose to go abroad. In my present situation, you know in what obscurity I am buried, and to what inconveniences I am exposed. You shall likewise have some information respecting my studies. I went through the perusal of the Greek authors to the time when they ceased to be Greeks; I was long employed in unravelling the obscure history of the Italians under the Lombards, the Franks, and Germans, to the time when they received their liberty from Rodolphus, king of Germany. From that time it will be better to read separately the particular

x 2

transactions of each state. But how are you employed? How long will you attend to your domestic ties and forget your city connexions? But unless this novercal hostility be more inveterate than that of the Dacian or Sarmatian, you will feel it a duty to visit me in my winter quarters. In the meantime, if you can do it without inconvenience, I will thank you to send me Guistiniani, the historian of Venice. I will either keep it carefully till your arrival, or, if you had rather, will soon send it back again. Adieu."

London, Sept. 23, 1637.

VIII.—*To Benedetto Buonmattai, a Florentine.*

HITHERTO we have transcribed these letters entire, but some of those which remain may with advantage be abridged, which is especially the case with the one before us.

"Among foreigners, there is no one at all conspicuous for genius or for elegance, who does not make the Tuscan language his delight, and indeed consider it as an essential part of education, particularly if he be only slightly tinctured with the literature of Greece or of Rome. I, who certainly have not merely wetted the tip of my lips in the stream of those languages, but, in proportion to my years, have swallowed the most copious draughts, can yet sometimes retire with avidity and delight to feast on Dante, Petrarch, and many others; nor has Athens itself been able to confine me to the transparent wave of its Ilissus, nor ancient Rome to the banks of its Tiber, so as to prevent my visiting with delight the stream of the Arno and the hills of Fæsolæ. A stranger from the shores of the farthest ocean, I have now spent some days among you, and am become quite enamoured of your nation. * * * On this occasion I have employed the Latin rather than your own language, that I might in Latin confess my imperfect acquaintance with that language which I wish you by your precepts to embellish and adorn. And I hoped that if I invoked the venerable Latian mother, hoary with years, and crowned with the respect of ages, to plead the cause of her daughter, I should give to my request a force and authority which nothing could resist."

Florence, Sept. 10, 1638.

———

IX.—*To Luke Holstein, in the Vatican at Rome.*

" Though in my passage through Italy, many persons have honoured me with singular and memorable proofs of their civility and friendship, yet on so short an acquaintance I know not whether I can truly say that any one ever gave me stronger marks of his regard than yourself. For, when I went to visit you in the Vatican, though I was not at all known to you, you

received me with the utmost kindness. You afterwards obligingly admitted me into the Museum, you
permitted me to see the precious repository of literature, and many Greek MSS. adorned with your own
observations. Some of which you have already published, which are greedily received by the learned.
You presented me with copies of these on my departure. And I cannot but impute it to your kind
mention of me to the noble Cardinal Francisco Barbe-
rino, that at a grand musical entertainment which he
gave, he waited for me at the door, sought me out
among the crowd, took me by the hand, and introduced me into the palace with every mark of the
most flattering distinction. I strenuously urged my
friends, according to your instructions, to inspect the
Codex Mediceus; though they have at present but
little hope of being able to do it. For in that Library
nothing can be transcribed, nor even a pen put to
paper, without permission been previously obtained.
* * * I add that you will lay me under new obligations, if you will express my warmest acknowledgments, and my most respectful compliments to the
most noble Cardinal, whose great virtues, and whose
honest zeal, so favourable to the encouragement of all
the liberal arts, are the constant objects of my admiration. Nor can I look without reverence on that
mild and, if I may so speak, that lowly loftiness of
mind, which is exalted by its own humiliation."

X.—*To Charles Deodati, a Florentine Noble.*

WE must distinguish this Charles Deodati from Milton's schoolfellow and most intimate friend, whose death nine years before the date of this letter is alluded to here in such pathetic terms. He is called Damon, as under the name of Lycidas he laments the death of his friend, Edward King. In the argument of his poem entitled "Epitaphium Damonis," we read, "Damonis autem sub personâ hic intelligitur CAROLUS DEODATUS ex urbe Hetruriæ Luca paterno genere oriundus cætera Anglus."

"I derived from the unexpected receipt of your letter a pleasure greater than I can express; but of which you may have some notion from the pain with which it was attended; and without a mixture of which hardly any great pleasure is conceded to mankind. For as soon as I came to that passage in which you tell me you had previously sent me three letters which must have been lost, the simplicity of my joy began to be imbued with grief and agitated with regret. I would not conceal from you that my departure from Florence excited in me the most poignant sensations of uneasiness; that city was and is to me most dear. I appeal to the tomb of Damon, which I shall ever cherish and revere; his death occasioned the most bitter sorrow and regret, which I could find no more easy way to mitigate than by recalling the

memory of those times, when, with so many kind
friends, and particularly with you, I tasted bliss without alloy. This you would have known long since,
if you received my poem on that occasion. I had it
carefully sent, that whatever poetical merit it might
possess, the few verses which are included in the
manner of an emblem might afford no doubtful proof
of my love for you. * * * I confess that I found
other reasons for silence in these convulsions which
my country has experienced since my return home,
which necessarily diverted my attention from the
prosecution of my studies to the preservation of my
property and my life. For can you imagine that I
could have leisure to taste the sweets of literary ease
while so many battles were fought, so much blood
shed, and while so much ravage prevailed among my
fellow-citizens? But even in the midst of this tem-
pestuous period, I have published several works in my
native language, which if they had not been written
in English, I should have pleasure in sending to you.
My Latin poems I will soon send as you desire; and
this I should have done long ago without being
desired, if I had not suspected that some rather harsh
expressions which they contained against the Roman
Pontiff would have rendered them less pleasing to
your ears. Now I request, whenever I mention the
rites of your religion in my own way, that you will
prevail on your friends (for I am under no apprehen-

sions from you) to show me the same indulgence not
only which they did to Algerius and to Petrarch on
a similar occasion, but which you did formerly with
such singular benevolence to the freedom of my conversation on topics of religion."

London, April 21, 1647.

XI.—*To Hermann Milles, Secretary to the Count of Oldenburgh.*

" FIRST, the delay of writing has been occasioned by
ill-health, whose hostilities I have now almost perpetually to combat, and which often keeps me from
the Council; next, by a cause of ill-health, a necessary
and sudden removal to another house, which had
accidentally begun to take place on the day that your
letter arrived; and lastly by shame that I had no intelligence concerning your business, which I thought
that it would be agreeable to communicate."

Westminster.

XII.—*To the renowned Leonard Philaras, the Athenian.*

" 1 WAS in some measure made acquainted with your
favourable opinion of my Defence of the People of
England by your letters to the Lord Auger. I then
received your compliments with your picture and an
eulogy worthy of your virtues. If Alexander the Great
declared that he encountered so many dangers of

warfare and trials for the sake of having his praises
celebrated by the Athenians, ought not I to congratulate myself on receiving the praises of a man in whom
alone the talents and virtues of the ancient Athenians
seem to recover their freshness and their strength after
so long an interval of corruption and decay. To the
writings of these illustrious men which your city has
produced, in the perusal of which I have been occupied from my youth, it is with pleasure I confess that
I am indebted for all my proficiency in literature.
Did I possess their command of language and their
force of persuasion, I should feel the highest satisfaction in employing them to excite our armies and our
fleets to deliver Greece, the parent of eloquence, from
the despotism of the Ottomans. Such is the enterprise
in which you seem to wish to implore my aid. And
what did formerly men of the greatest courage and
eloquence deem more noble or more glorious, than by
their orations or their valour to assert the liberty and
independence of the Greeks? But we ought besides
to attempt to inflame the present Greeks with an
ardent desire to emulate the virtue, the industry, the
patience of their ancient progenitors; and this we
cannot hope to see effected by any one but yourself,
and for which you seem adapted by the splendour of
your patriotism, combined with so much discretion, so
much skill in war, and such an unquenchable thirst
for the recovery of your ancient liberty. Nor do I

think that the Greeks would be wanting to themselves, nor that any other people would be wanting to the Greeks."

London, June, 1652.

———

XIV.—*To Henry Oldenburgh, Aulic Counsellor to the Senate of Bremen.*

" SOME unexpected engagements concurred to delay my answering your former letters, or I should not have sent you my Defence without any compliment or apology. I had more than once an intention of sub-stituting our English for your Latin, that you might lose no opportunity of writing it. With respect to the subject of your letter you are clearly of my opinion, that that cry to Heaven could not have been audible by any human being, which only serves the more palpably to show the effrontery of him who affirms with so much audacity that he heard it. Who he was you have caused a doubt; though long since, in some conversations which we had on the subject just after your return from Holland, you seemed to have no doubt but that More was the author to whom the composition was in those parts unanimously ascribed. If you have received any more authentic information on this subject, I wish that you would acquaint me with it. This unexpected contest with the enemies of liberty has involuntarily withdrawn my attention from very different and more pleasurable pursuits. What I have done I feel no reason to regret, and I am far from thinking, as you seem to suppose, that I have laboured in vain."

Westminster, July 6, 1654.

XV.—*To Leonard Philaras, the Athenian.*

" WHEN you unexpectedly came to London, and saw me who could no longer see, my affliction, which causes none to regard me with greater admiration, and perhaps many even with feelings of contempt, excited your tenderest sympathy and concern. You would not suffer me to abadon the hope of recovering my sight; and informed me that you had an intimate friend at Paris, Doctor Thevenot, who was particularly celebrated in disorders of the eyes, whom you would consult about mine, if I would enable you to lay before him the causes and symptoms of the complaint. I will do what you desire, lest I should seem to reject that aid which perhaps may be offered me by Heaven. It is now, I think, about ten years since I perceived my vision to grow weak and dull; and at the same time I was troubled with pain in my kidneys and bowels. In the morning, if I began to read, as was my custom, my eyes instantly ached intensely, but were refreshed after a little corporeal exercise. The candle which I looked at seemed as it were encircled with a rainbow. Not long after the sight in the left part of the left eye (which I lost some years before the other) became quite obscured; and prevented me from discerning any object on that side. The sight in my other eye has now been gradually and sensibly vanishing away for about three years; some months before it had entirely perished, though I stood motionless, everything which I looked at seemed in motion to and fro. A stiff cloudy vapour seemed to have settled on my forehead and temples, which usually occasions a sort of somnolent pressure upon my eyes, and particularly from dinner till the evening. I ought not to omit that while I had any sight left, as soon as I lay down on my bed and turned on either side, a flood of light used to gush from my closed eyelids. Then, as my sight became daily more impaired, the colours became more faint, and were emitted with a certain inward crackling sound; but at present, every species of illumination being, as it were, extinguished, there is diffused around me nothing but darkness, or darkness mingled and streaked with an ashy brown. Yet the darkness in which I am perpetually immersed; seems always, both by night and day, to approach nearer to white than black; and when the eye is rolling in its socket, it admits a little particle of light, as through a chink. And though your physician may kindle a small ray of hope, yet I make up my mind to the malady as quite incurable; and I often reflect, that as the wise man admonishes, days of darkness are destined to each of us, the darkness which I experience, less oppressive than that of the tomb, is, owing to the singular goodness of the Deity, passed amid the pursuits of literature, and the cheering salutations of friendship. But if, as it is written, " Man shall not live by bread alone, but by every word that proceedeth from the mouth of God," why may not anyone acquiesce in the privation of his sight, when God has so amply furnished his mind and his conscience with eyes? While he so tenderly provides for me, while He so graciously leads me by the hand, and conducts me on the way, I will, since it is His pleasure, rather rejoice than repine at being blind. And, my dear Philaras, whatever may be the event, I wish you farewell with no less courage and composure than if I had the eyes of a lynx."

Westminster, Sept. 28, 1654.

XVI.—To Leo, of Aizema.

" With respect to the book concerning Divorce, which you say you had engaged some one to turn it into Dutch, I would rather you had engaged him to turn it into Latin. For I have already experienced how the vulgar are wont to receive opinions which are not agreeable to vulgar prejudice. I formerly wrote three Treatises on this subject: one in two books, in which the Doctrine of Divorce is diffusely discussed : another entitled Tetrachordon, in which the four principal passages in Scripture relative to the doctrine are explained : a third, Colasterion, which contains an answer to some vulgar sciolist. I know not which of these works, or which edition, you have engaged him to translate. The first Treatise has been twice published, and the second edition has been much enlarged. If you have not already received this information, or wish me to send you the more correct edition, or the other Treatises, I shall do it immediately, and with pleasure. For I do not wish at present they should receive any alterations or additions. If you persist in your present purpose, I wish you a faithful translator and every success."

Westminster, Feb. 5, 1654.

XVII.—*To Ezekiel Spanheim, of Geneva.*

" It having been signified to you that it would be highly grateful to me if you would lend me your assistance against our common enemy, you have kindly done this in your present letter ; of which I have taken the liberty, without mentioning the Author's name, to insert a part in my Defence (pro testimonio inserere non dubitavi). This work I will send you as soon as possible after the publication."

Westminster, March 24, 1654.

XVIII.—*To Henry Oldenburgh.*

" THOSE ancient records of the Chinese from the period of the deluge, which you write are promised by the Jesuit Martinius, are no doubt on account of their novelty expected with avidity ; but I do not see. what authority or support they can add to the books of Moses," (verum auctoritatis, aut firmamenti, ad Mosaicos Libros adjungere quid possint non video.)

Westminster, June 25, 1656.

XX.—*To the accomplished youth, Peter Heimbach.*

" You have done all I desired respecting the Atlas, of which I wished to know the lowest price. You say it is a hundred and thirty florins, which I think is enough to purchase the mountain of that name. But such is the present rage for typographical luxury, that the sumptuous furniture of a Library costs less than that of a Villa. Paintings are of little use to me. While I roll my blind eyes about the world, I fear lest I should seem to lament the privation of sight in proportion to the exorbitance of the price for which I should have purchased the book. Do you endeavour to learn in how many volumes the entire work is contained ; and of the two editions whether that of Blaeu or Janson be the more accurate and complete."

Westminster, Nov. 8, 1656.

XXI.—*To the accomplished Emeric Bigot.*

" It gives me pleasure that you are convinced of the tranquillity which I possess under this afflicting privation of sight, as well as of the civility and kindness with which I receive those who visit me from other countries. And indeed why should I not submit with complacency to this loss of sight, which seems only withdrawn from the body without, to increase the sight of the mind within. (Orbitatem certe luminis quidni leniter feram, quod non tam amissum quam revocatum, intus atque retractum, ad acuendam potius mentis aciem quam ad hebetandam, sperem). Hence books have not incurred my resentment, nor do I intermit the study of books, though they have inflicted so heavy a penalty on me for my attachment; the example of Telephus, King of Mysia, who did not refuse to receive a cure from the same weapon by which he had been wounded, admonished me not to be so morose."

Westminster, March 24, 1658.

XXIII.—*To the illustrious Lord Henry De Bras.*

" I prefer Sallust to any of the Latin historians; which was also the general opinion of the ancients. Your favourite Tacitus deserves his meed of praise; but his highest praise, in my opinion, consists in his having imitated Sallust. In historical composition the style should correspond with the nature of the

Y

narrative. The historian should be able to say much in a few words, to unite copiousness with brevity. The decorations of style I do not greatly heed ; for I require an Historian, not a Rhetorician. I do not want frequent interspersions of sentiment, or prolix dissertations on transactions, which interrupt the series of events, and cause the Historian to entrench on the office of the Politician."

Westminster, July 15, 1657.

XXVI.—*To Lord Henry De Bras.*

" I CONGRATULATE myself on having been so fortunate in characterizing the merits of Sallust as to have excited you to the assiduous perusal of that author, who is so full of wisdom, and who may be read with so much advantage. Of him I will venture to assert what Quintilian said of Cicero, that he who loves Sallust is no mean proficient in historical composition. Polybius, Halicarnassus, Diodorus, and many others, whose works are interspersed with precepts on the subject, will better teach you what are the duties of an historian."

Westminster, Dec. 16, 1657.

XXIX.—*To Henry Oldenburgh.*

" I AM not willing, as you wish me, to compile a history of our troubles ; for they seem rather to require oblivion than commemoration; nor have we so much need of a person to compose a history of our troubles as happily to settle them. I fear with you lest our civil dissensions, or rather maniacal agitations, should expose us to the attack of the lately confederated enemies of religion and of liberty; but those enemies could not inflict a deeper wound upon religion than we ourselves have long since done by our follies and our crimes. But whatever disturbances kings and cardinals may meditate and contrive, I trust that God will not suffer the machinations and the violence of our enemies to succeed according to their expectations. I pray that the Protestant synod, which you say is soon to meet at Leyden, may have a happy termination, which has never yet happened to any synod that has ever met before. But the termination of this might be called happy, if it decreed nothing else but the expulsion of More. As soon as my posthumous adversary shall make his appearance, I request you to give me the earliest information."

Westminster, Dec. 20, 1659.

XXXI.—*To Peter Heimbach.*

WE will give Hayley's translation of this concluding letter:—

"If, among so many funerals of my countrymen, in a year so full of pestilence and sorrow, you were in-

Y 2

duced, as you say, by rumour, to believe that I also was snatched away, it is not surprising; and if such a rumour prevailed among those of your nation, as it seems to have done, because they were solicitous for my health, it is not unpleasing; for I must esteem it as a proof of their benevolence towards me. But by the graciousness of God, who had prepared for me a safe retreat in the country, I am still alive and well; and, I trust, not utterly an unprofitable servant, whatever duty in life there yet remains for me to fulfil. That you remember me after so long an interval in our correspondence, gratifies me exceedingly, though, by the politeness of your expression, you seem to afford me room to suspect that you have rather forgotten me, since, as you say, you admire in me so many different virtues wedded together. From so many weddings I should assuredly dread a family too numerous, were it not certain that in narrow circumstances, and under severity of fortune, virtues are most excellently reared, and most flourishing! Yet one of these said virtues has not very handsomely rewarded me for entertaining her; for that which you call my political virtue, and which I should rather wish you to call my devotion to my country (enchanting me with her captivating name), almost, if I may say so, expatriated me. Other virtues, however, join their voices to assure me that wherever we prosper in rectitude, there is our country. In ending my letter, let me ob-

tain from you this favour; that if you find any parts
of it incorrectly written, and without stops, you will
impute it to the boy who writes for me, who is utterly
ignorant of Latin, and to whom I am forced (wretch-
edly enough) to repeat every single letter of every
word that I dictate. I still rejoice that your merit
as an accomplished man, whom I knew as a youth of
the highest expectation, has advanced you so far in
the honourable favour of your Prince. For your prosperity in every other point you have both my wishes
and my hopes. Farewell."

London, Aug. 26, 1666.

Our task is now ended; but how pitiable and painful is the condition in which we here reluctantly leave
this great and good man, about eight years before his
death, obliged to employ, through stress of poverty
and the unkindness of his daughters, an ignorant lad
as his amanuensis, to whom he is compelled to dictate
not the Latin words only, but one by one the letters
of which they were composed. The question here
arises on what work in that language was he engaged
at this time, and why did he employ this wretched boy
and not his own daughters, to whom we know about
this period he dictated the Paradise Lost? Where
was Elwood? And was there no Macaulay, gladly to
sit at the feet of the immortal bard, for the sake of

his society and conversation, and write down the glorious sentences which flowed from his lips, not knowing whether they might not prove the dictate of a divine spirit ? It seems probable that he was now occupied with the composition of the latter part of his Treatise of Christian Doctrine, which is entitled "De Doctrinâ Christianâ, ex Sacris duntaxat Libris petitâ, Disquisitionum Libri duo posthumi." This work was discovered in 1823 by Mr. R. Lemon in the course of his researches in the State Paper Office, in one of the presses, together with a corrected copy of Milton's State Letters, the whole parcel being loosely wrapped in two or three sheets of newspaper and directed 'To Mr. Skinner, Mercht.' Here it had probably lain for nearly a century and a half. It was entrusted by the King into the hands of the late Bishop of Winchester, Dr. Sumner, to edit and translate, who thus writes. 'The manuscript itself consists of 735 pages, closely written on small quarto letter paper. The first part, as far as the 15th chapter of the first book, is in a small and beautiful Italian hand ; being evidently a corrected copy, prepared for the press, without interlineations of any kind. The character is evidently that of a female hand, and it is the opinion of Mr. Lemon, whose knowledge of the handwriting of that time is so ex- tensive that the greatest deference is due to his judg- ment, that Mary, the second daughter of Milton, was employed as amanuensis in this part of the volume.

The mistakes are of a nature to induce a suspicion that the transcriber was imperfectly acquainted with the learned languages. For instance, in quoting Heb. iv. 13, *patientia* is substituted for *patentia*. And we remember the charge, which, as Mr. Todd notices, has been brought against the paternal conduct of Milton; ' I mean his teaching his children to read and pronounce Greek and several other languages, *without understanding any but English.*' The remainder of the manuscript is in an entirely different hand, being a strong upright character, supposed by Mr. Lemon to be the handwriting of Edward Philipps, the nephew of Milton; but we believe it to be the handwriting of this very boy alluded to in this concluding letter, the date of which is 1666. The Bishop continues, ' This part of the volume is interspersed with numerous interlineations and corrections, differing from the body of the manuscript, but the greater part of them undoubtedly written by the same person who transcribed the first part of the volume. Hence it is probable that the latter part of the MS is a copy transcribed by Philips,' or, as we conjecture, by this boy, so given to make mistakes, ' and finally revised and corrected by Mary and Deborah Milton from the dictation of their father, as many of the alterations bear a strong resemblance to the reputed handwriting of Deborah, the youngest and favourite daughter of Milton, whom he trained up in Latin and Greek to make her his amanuensis.'

We however differ from the Bishop in this latter supposition, because there is evidence that all his daughters treated him unkindly and embittered the latter years of his life, at last deserting him altogether, probably upon his marrying his third wife, Elizabeth Minshull, in 1661. Their conduct necessitated his marriage, and at the same time necessitated the employment of this boy as amanuensis; whose copy of the latter part of this Treatise may have been revised by Philipps, or possibly, if the handwriting require it, by one or other of his 'pelican daughters' relenting. That this epithet is not too strong appears from the testimony of Milton's brother, Christopher Milton, and of his maidservant, Elizabeth Fisher, on the occasion of the trial of the validity of his nuncupative will in the Prerogative Court. The former proves that 'the said deceased was then ill of the goute; and what he then spoke touching his will was in a very calm manner; only (he) complained, but without passion, that his children had been unkind to him.' * * * 'That he knoweth not how the parties ministring these interrogatories frequent the church, or in what manner of behaviour of life and conversation they are of, they living apart from their father four or five years last past; and as touching his the deceased's displeasure with them, he only heard him say at the tyme of declaring of his will, that they were undutifull and unkind to him, not expressing any particulars;

but in former tymes he hath heard him complain that
they were careless of him being blind, and made
nothing of deserting him.'

The evidence of Elizabeth Fisher proves their mis-
conduct and inattention ' against that head so old and
white ' still more glaring. ' This respondent hath
heard the deceased declare his displeasure against the
parties ministrant his children ; and particularly the
deceased declared to this respondent that a little
before he was marryed to Elizabeth Milton, his own
relict, a former maid-servant of his, told Mary, one of
the deceased's daughter, and one of the ministrants,
that she heard the deceased was to be marryed, to
which the said Mary replied to the said maid-servant,
that that was no news to heare of his wedding, but if
shee could heare of his death that was something :
and further told this respondent, that all his said
children did combine together and counsel his maid-
servant to cheat him the deceased in her marketings,
and that his said children had made away some of his
bookes, and would have sold the rest of his books to
the dunghill women, or hee the deceased spoke words
to this respondent to the selfesame effect and purpose.' Again the picture rises before our eyes, not
such as Romney drew it, but such as this last epistle
depicts it. There is the same majestic form, seated in
the same elbow-chair, enshrouded in the same ample
cloak ; but the countenance is no longer lighted up

like the face of an angel, rapt into Paradise, and seeing its glories, and speaking its language. No sublime vision now lights up that calm and careworn face, and the words which fall from his lips are not inspired, breathing, living, burning words, but such as posterity cares not to read, mere antiquarian rubbish, words philosophical perhaps, but still naked, tame, prosaic. And to complete the sad picture, who are now his amanuenses? not loving, and partial, and wondering daughters, as Romney conceived them to be; not a Macaulay, who, we know, would gladly have filled that office, had he been Milton's contemporary; not Elwood, who often before formed one in this beautiful picture; not Heimbach, who surely after receiving this letter could scarcely help offering his services; not these, but a wretched hired blundering boy is sitting at that table in that temple of the muses, thinking of the bright fields instead of the task before him, as that blurred and well-nigh illegible manuscript plainly testifies. But it is well that it should be so; it is well that we should leave him thus, desolate indeed and neglected, but still self-collected, self-sustained, majestic and grand in his sorrows and in his ruins; for was he not the Martyr no less than the Champion of the Truth which he had always loved, but at times failed to find?

His own Muse shall answer the question :—

" God of our fathers ! what is man,
That Thou towards him with hand so various,
Or might I say contrarious,
Temper'st Thy providence through his short course,
Not evenly, as Thou rulest
The angelic orders, and inferior creatures mute,
Irrational and brute ?
Nor do I name of men the common rout,
That, wandering loose about,
Grow up and perish, as the summer fly,
Heads without name, no more remembered ;
But such as Thou hast solemnly elected,
With gifts and graces eminently adorn'd,
To some great work, Thy glory,
And people's safety, which in part they effect :
Yet toward these thus dignified, Thou oft,
Amidst their height of noon,
Changest Thy countenance, and Thy hand, with no regard
Of highest favours past
From Thee on them, or them to Thee of service.
   Nor only dost degrade them, or remit
To life obscured, which were a fair dismission,
But throw'st them lower than Thou didst exalt them high;
Unseemly falls in human eye,
Too grievous for the trespass or omission ;
Oft leavest them to the hostile sword
Of heathen and profane, their carcases
To dogs and fowls a prey, or else captived ;
Or to the unjust tribunals, under change of times,
And condemnation of the ingrateful multitude.
If these they 'scape, perhaps in poverty
With sickness and disease Thou bow'st them down,
Painful diseases and deform'd,
In crude old age ;
Though not disordinate, yet causeless suffering
The punishment of dissolute days : in fine,
Just or unjust, alike seem miserable,
For oft alike both come to evil end.
   So deal not with this once Thy glorious champion,
The image of Thy strength, and mighty minister.
What do I beg? how hast Thou dealt already?
Behold him in this state calamitous, and turn
His labours, for Thou canst, to peaceful end."

We can hardly even now tear ourselves away from the works and words of this great and good man, whose memory we so much revere and love. The last two lines of that magnificient chorus, which we have just cited from the Samson Agonistes, worthy of Æschylus, contain a prayer, applicable to himself, and answered in his own case. In the true words of his biographer Hayley, 'however various the opinions of men may be concerning the merits or demerits of Milton's political character, the integrity of his heart appears to have secured to him the favour of Providence; since it pleased the Giver of all good not only to turn his labour to a peaceful end, but to irradiate his declining life with the most abundant portion of those pure and sublime mental powers, for which he had constantly and fervently prayed, as the choicest bounty of Heaven.'

APPENDIX.

THERE is a poem on Milton, by Lord Lytton, which portrays our great patriot poet in his youth, manhood, and old age—youth of love, manhood of duty, age of suffering—the three words which sum up the history of his whole life. We propose, as a fitting conclusion to the work in which we have been so long engaged, translating it into humble prose, adopting as much as may be Lord Lytton's own phraseology. And we do so because we deeply feel that the prose we have been citing proceeded from a heart full of love, of duty, and of pain, and would repair any injustice we may have unwittingly done to the memory of so noble a man. The story is very likely to have been true, founded, as it is, on Milton's Italian sonnets, and on the well-known legend of an Italian lady, seeing the Poet lying asleep at the foot of a tree in his college gardens, and placing in his hand some verses. The same lady meets him on his tour in Italy, and the love which springs up between them is interrupted by his sudden determination to return to England, that he may wield his pen against the foes of Liberty.

It was in the merry month of June that young Milton lay dreaming under the shade of a beech-tree, on a violet bank, in the cloistered gardens of Christ's College, when lo! a beautiful stranger from Italian skies, passing by, bends over the unconscious dreamer, and silently gazes away her heart. Suddenly he starts from his sleep, and their eyes met one moment, and no more; in maiden shame she fled, and passed from his enamoured sight, perhaps for ever. No, not for ever. They met again by strange coincidence.

Time waned; the fair youth had grown into manhood, and now has left his father's hearth for foreign shores. He visits Galileo, and the sages and literati of Italy. One evening the glorious wanderer was invited to a banquet, perhaps at the house of his friend, the Marquis Manso. All admired—all yielded to that English guest. Ah! little dreamed those flatterers, as they gazed on his lofty brow, his locks of gold, and stately mien—the radiant cynosure of all—little dreamed they what that bright heart was destined to befall! Yes, the noblest heart is always the easiest wrung, and such was his. We know, how, returning to England, he bore the daily fever, and the midnight toil, in Liberty's defence, the hope defeated, and the name belied; and, worst of all, we know how sorrow coiled around his hearth, and on

his declining day neglect and obloquy wreaked their
spite. The bright eyes around him little dreamed of
all this, and still less of that rich flood of glorious
light, which yet should start through those clouds,
and gild that declining day.

But to our tale :—the festive rite was over, the
guests departed, and still our wanderer lingered on
the lovely scene. With folded arms and upward
brow, he leant against the pillar of a tree, when
hark! the still boughs rustle, and a light footstep
passed by the flowers. He turned;—what nymph is
there? 'Tis she, whose loveliness had, so long ago,
in his England's gardens, beamed on him as he slept
beneath the beech-tree. She fled not now, and they
became lovers. He knew not her name, nor would
she disclose it; so he found a name for her—" Zoe "
—stolen from the tuneful Greek, which means " life,"
when common lips do speak, and more on those that
love.

They met again in twilight and in stealth. Their
love made life one melody; for poetry lay deep within
the soul of each. Thus two months pass away; and
now Zoe waits her lover on the hill, where the ruins
of Cæsar's palace lay. He comes; and they sate them
on a fallen column. Then she, sighing, says, " O joy to
meet, but despair to part!" And he replies, " And
wherefore part? What, if my life be wrenched from
youth too soon to find in duty manhood's troubled

doom. As the star clings to the melancholy moon, so let thy soul to mine. I seek my England, canst thou leave thy Rome?" She, starting from his breast, faltered, "What dost thou ask? Must it all end in this? Rest here. England has toil—Italia happiness!" And thus the MAN replied, "Hear and approve me. In my father's land men are enslaved to Force and Tyranny; and Liberty now calls me with imperial voice homeward to her cause. And I am sworn by mine own free choice to serve her; and shall I be found recreant when she draws the sword?"

The lady yields, and consents to fly with him, and share his fate—when, suddenly her aged father stands a shadow in the shadow, and sternly moving his beckoning hand commands her, "Come!"

*   *   *   *   *   *   *   *

Years have flown by, and Civil Strife has raged and ceased. And on the doomed sight of the laborious student darkness has stolen. Yet he argues not against Heaven's hand or will, nor bates a jot of heart or hope, but still bears up, and steers right onward, supported by Truth and Conscience. O doubtful labour, but O glorious pain! And whether we blame or laud the cause for which he toiled and pleaded and suffered, we must feel that all human life has been made grander by his grand self-sacrifice. Yes, while earth disputes, if the strife be righteous, the martyr, Truth's martyr, soars beyond it to the skies. Whatever our state-creed may be, we must all venerate in Milton his heroic purpose; his majestical disdain of self; the soul in which we see conviction welding duty, the iron mainspring of his mind; and man's strong heart-throb beating for mankind and for England's weal. These must move our homage.

Once more the scene changes.

An old man is seated at the door of his humble dwelling. Through the narrow opening you might see uncertain footprints on the sanded floor, which tell of blindness—on the table the untasted meal, the scattered volumes, and that pillowed elbow-chair, in which the poor wanderer, worn out with toil and travel, found repose at last. And while he sate—a timorous trembling step drew near—'twas that of his long-lost Italian love. Year on year she had pined to gaze on that brow, last seen when she was young: —AND NOW!

Thus as she stood and gazed, and noiseless wept, two young slight forms, Mary and Deborah, crossed the threshold, and kissed the hand of the blind grey man; and the old, familiar, sweet, yet stately smile strayed over his lips, and they led him in. The widowed bride stayed without, and wept aloud as she heard slow sonorous deep organ-tones.

* * * * * * * *

Then comes the burial of the Martyr Poet;—and when the rest were gone, an aged woman is seen,

z

veiled and arrayed in sable widowed weeds, kneeling upon the stone. The notes of her low prayer were sweet with the strange music of a foreign tongue. Thrice to that spot Mary and Deborah came with garlands, and decked that grave with flowers. On the fourth day some hand had cast away in scorn the flowers that breathed of priest-craft; but the poor stranger came not with the morn—her heart was broken!

THE END.

LONDON : PRINTED BY MACDONALD AND TUGWELL, BLENHEIM HOUSE.

www.ingramcontent.com/pod-product-compliance
Lightning Source LLC
Chambersburg PA
CBHW021757110726
47902CB00006B/1551